Nobody's Coming

by
HJ Seifert

Dedication

To Everyone...

Prologue
1992

I was millions of miles from my own world, but I sensed feelings of warmth and welcome as if I were in my own dining room filled with family and friends as we sat down for Christmas dinner.

I had asked to visit a planet that was similar to Earth in its age and social evolution. I wanted to see how a civilization like ours could figure out a possible path to survival and to the end of hatred and suffering.

I stood watching with my companions, as we had watched dozens of other planets, but this time was different.

We stood, invisible as always, in a large conference room that accommodated the meeting of the 12 countries on this planet. As it turned out, these countries were in fact the 12 different continents of this world. The continents had come together. Now it was time to see if their world could come together.

The leaders put on their headsets, as if they were at the United Nations. Once everyone was seated, an ebony-skinned woman with beautiful black hair stood and gently tapped a ceremonial gavel three times to bring the meeting to order. She looked around the room with a smile so infectious that everyone relaxed back into their chairs to await this historic moment.

As the participants settled in, I got so excited that I felt goosebumps. I had finally asked my teachers the right question. They had taken me to dozens of worlds that had failed, dozens of worlds that had succeeded, and dozens of worlds where the jury was still out.

Now I was in a world much like my own, one that was trying to stay on the right track, and that gave me hope. Hope for my children and grandchildren and everyone's children and grandchildren, that there could be a beautiful future for all.

1. If you can't be with the one you love...

"Hey man," said my roommate Jacob. "You know she digs you."

"Can't blame her," I answered, as was customary in our apartment of six junior men when these subjects came up.

It is Springtime in 1977. I'm working hard to finish my junior year at Iowa State University.

"Oh bullshit, Miles. I'm sick and tired of you acting like it's no big deal," he said. "We all see the way you guys hang out together. I can't believe you're dating Rebecca back home, and at the same time, the hottest girl in this apartment complex is all over you too."

I didn't let him rattle me. I really didn't let anything rattle me.

"Who doesn't dig me? That would be a shorter list of beautiful women," I said.

As I walked out of the room, smoke came out of Jacob's ears.

I really wasn't a ladies' man. I was six feet three, with long black hair and an athletic build. As an English major, I could play the creative type or just be quiet and become the brooding bad boy. I wasn't the type of guy who would play the field. When I felt something special for a girl, I told her about it. I know I was in love with all my past girlfriends. I was never interested in one-night stands. They didn't make any sense to me. Why would you want to make love to someone you didn't love, or who didn't love you back?

When I met Rebecca, she literally swept me off my feet. There was something about the art of flirtation she had mastered that I had never seen from another woman in my life. What made me uneasy was she didn't need to sweep me or anyone else off their feet. She was beautiful. Her blue eyes, her turned-up nose and her smile were perfect for her long blonde hair. She walked, sat and moved with utter grace. She was the captain of the cheerleaders at her high school and the only woman I ever dated whom I could describe with the word "vivacious."

Even though I would describe our relationship as mostly fire, it had been vacillating between fire and ice a lot the past few months. When we were together and on the same page, it was terrific. Then there were times that arguing had also become part of our relationship. That was the ice part.

Then who was Jacob talking about on that beautiful late spring day?

Alison. Alison. Alison.

Alison had turned my brain into scrambled eggs. She was one of the six female roommates who lived in the apartment right next-door to us. Our two groups had grown extremely friendly and it was kind of an informal fraternity-sorority arrangement. On weekends or snow days, we would get together and drink beer, get high, just talk and have fun. There was a hilarious indiscretion between one of my roommates and one of the girls, who got drunk and decided they would sneak off into the basement and make out. We accidentally caught them so they just had to take it and own the moment. After a while we let it go, because we weren't really jerks. Well, maybe a little....

When I met Alison for the first time, we really hit it off. We both had great relationships with our significant others back in our hometowns, and so there was no pressure for us to be lovers, because we were both spoken for. The ease in which we fell into our relationship was incredibly surprising to me. At that time in my life, whenever a guy said a girl was just a friend, it meant that he had tried to sleep with her, and that she said no. Not so with Alison...we had become fast friends. So, over the course of the school year, we had sought each other out many weekends and evenings just to hang out, tell stories, or go downtown and drink beer with the other coeds.

On the day that Jacob had challenged me it was pretty clear in my mind that I was having a lot more fun hanging out with Alison than I ever did hanging out with Rebecca.

Alison was the opposite of vivacious Rebecca. She was cool and smooth and thoughtful, and her responses were always measured and genuine. She was really smart with a great sense of humor. Alison had beautiful long brown hair parted down the middle, deep brown eyes, full lips and a perfect complexion. When we were together it was remarkably easy for both of us just to be ourselves.

It's amazing how much easier it is to fall in love with a girl, when you're already in love with another girl. It probably helped, that whenever we were together in my room, I played James Taylor records. When "Don't Let Me Be Lonely Tonight" came on my stereo, I knew in the back of our minds that we weren't lonely, because we had each other in that moment — but that there was that next level that we were both curious about.

However, I was in love with Rebecca. We had been dating for a while and our relationship was good. I had no idea what to do. The semester was coming to an end and I knew I might never see Alison again, even though we had one more year until we graduated. The landlord had doubled the rent on the apartments, so neither one of our groups renewed for the next year and we were looking for cheaper housing.

On that day, I knew as surely as Jacob did, that Alison was into me at some level, but that I would never talk seriously to any of my roommates about it. Just as I was standing there and laughing at Jacob, I knew that I was madly in love with Alison.

I was facing the first huge moral dilemma of my life. I loved two women at the same time. I knew this was a great problem to have. My life couldn't have been better. I was getting good grades, I had a lot of friends, and two wonderful women in my life.

There were about three weeks left in the school year. The 12 of us had planned a Saturday cookout, with plenty of beer, alcohol, and weed for those who liked to get high. I didn't know how the night would go, but I knew that I had to get Alison alone. It was like getting a Christmas present from a Secret Santa. Once I got her alone, I had no idea what was going to come out of that wrapped present.

As the afternoon started to turn to twilight, I went up to my room and grabbed a hooded sweatshirt, and quickly came back out looking for Alison. She was standing talking to her friend Robin, and I walked over to join the two of them. Robin went to get another beer and left us alone.

The stereo was playing Crosby Stills Nash and Young "Love the One You're With." I had no doubt it was karma, so I turned and said, "Hey Alison, I was thinking, do you want to get out of here and go for a walk on the nature path?" Without hesitation, she answered, "Sure Miles, I was just thinking the same thing."

4

We finished our beers and then took off, knowing that we didn't want any trouble from campus security about drinking in public places. As we were walking away, we both knew that people were watching us and had been waiting for this moment for a long time—just as we had.

We walked and talked and laughed and she giggled in that way that told me she didn't think I was necessarily funny, but that I was adorable, at least to her. She loved asking me questions about my sophomore year in California. Her sister Dana had just moved there with her husband Billy, so she really enjoyed my descriptions of the beautiful coastline and the paradise that was Southern California.

We were walking very slowly and I said to her, "You know Alison, once we go home for the summer, I'm really gonna miss our talks and our time together." Suddenly she stopped. She nodded in agreement without speaking, and kept her head bent looking down at the ground. Alison seemed for the first time genuinely uncomfortable being there alone with me.

Maybe for the first time, she felt that just being alone with me was a betrayal of her longtime boyfriend back home. We were both reading from the same script, but I was a little bit further ahead. I think she was fighting back tears. I stayed quiet. A few moments passed and I said, "Hey, let's keep walking down to the park." She looked up and nodded in agreement, as if she really did want to continue our walk, and it helped her get over the emotions of that moment.

We got to the park near the Iowa State campus and there wasn't anyone there but us. At that point, I looked up in the sky and it was a perfectly cloudless Midwestern night, with what else, a beautiful bright full moon.

"Alison, look, there's a full moon tonight."

"Yeah" she replied. "And it's aglow with everyone's dreams of the future." She giggled that cute giggle of hers. "Sorry, I didn't mean to get all English Lit on you."

The moment had arrived...

I turned to her. "Alison, getting to know you this year has made me enjoy college life like I never have before. Having you as a friend, well, it has meant the world to me."

She looked straight up and I could see that she was happy. There was no longer an inner remorse battling her in her girl-soul. She had finally slipped into the moment and joined me.

"Miles, I've never really met anyone like you. I have had so much fun hanging out with you and talking about whatever it is we talk about."

Neither one of us were making any references to our significant others back in our hometowns. I knew that my moral dilemma was going to work its way out, one way or another. With no forethought in the least, I grabbed down with my right hand to hold her left hand, but I turned and pointed up at the sky and said, "For the rest of my life, whenever I look up and see a full moon in the evening sky, I will think about you and me on this night forever."

Okay, I had put it out there. If Alison wanted me as much as I needed her, neither one of us would ever be able to return to our hometowns and face the music from our families, our friends, and most of all... our significant others. This would be so out of character for both of us... to be this impulsive, but if she loved me the way I loved her... then there was nothing impulsive about it.

She squeezed my hand tighter, but I just couldn't turn and face her. I knew inside that if I did, I would kiss her. I had gone as far as I could go...it was her play.

Suddenly, I felt her right hand grab my sweatshirt at the left shoulder and pull me to face her. Her five-foot, six-inch frame was standing on her tiptoes so that we were only inches apart.

"Miles, for the rest of our lives, I will never let you forget about tonight, about this moment, because I don't intend to ever let you go."

I felt a rush go through my body like nothing I had ever experienced before. We were gazing into each other's eyes as our lips drew closer together, but just before my eyes closed, I saw what looked like the reflection of the stars in Alison's eyes. Our arms wrapped around each other, and we started to sway ever so gently, back and forth, as we shared our first kiss. The rush going through me refused to end. In fact, it increased in its intensity. This kiss, this embrace, was like nothing I had ever experienced with another woman. There was something marvelous and magical about Alison, and as our kiss continued, I looked forward to learning more about that magic.

2. *Going to California*

When we got back to the party and a couple of "Where were the two of you?" comments were made, I really wanted to sarcastically respond something along the lines of "Somewhere you've never been!" However, I was in too good a mood to go at them. Alison and I had decided that we would go back to the party for a while, then go up to my room to listen to albums where we wouldn't be disturbed, since I knew my roommate and his girlfriend would be heading to her apartment for the night.

A half an hour later we made our exit from the party and I'm sure there were some eyes rolling, but it didn't matter to us. I closed the door to my room and immediately went over to my stereo and I put on our new favorite album, Songs in the Key of Life by Stevie Wonder.

Alison was sitting on my bed, so I went over and joined her. She looked right into my eyes and whispered "So what's our move, Miles?"

I grabbed both of her hands and said, "I've been ready for this moment for weeks Alison... You want to go to California? I know that your sister Dana and Billy are up in wine country, and my friend Michael, from UC Irvine, is living a couple blocks from the ocean in Huntington Beach. What do you think?"

Alison smiled at me as if she was proud of me for having plotted our escape for all this time.

"Well, I've been dying to meet your friend Michael. Plus, everyone will be looking for us at Dana and Billy's. They won't even know we're in California if we stay with Michael for a while."

"Okay, then that's the plan."

The next song on the album was about to start. All of a sudden, Alison kicked off her shoes, got up, turned up the volume on the stereo and then pulled off my tennis shoes. She grabbed my two hands and pulled me off the bed and said, "I feel like dancing." Stevie's next song was called Ngiculela, which is a Zulu word.

Alison and I had never danced together before. I was an okay dancer at the crowded clubs, but Alison had me spinning her around and twirling and shuffling like nothing I had ever done before. As we moved around the room in childlike joy, Alison sang along with all the words of Stevie's beautiful rhythmic song, which combined Zulu, Spanish and English lyrics, ending up on "Let's start singing of love from our hearts."

When it was finally done, we were sweating and laughing so hard, that I picked her up and threw us both on the bed. We had to wait a few moments before we could talk.

Once we both started to settle down, I said, "I can't believe what a great dancer you are... that was the most fun I ever had dancing when I had no idea what I was doing. Thanks for teaching me all those cool moves."

"Miles, I love to dance, so you better get used to it. You're pretty good... but we'll practice a lot more and you'll be great."

I replied, "I was also impressed that you knew all the words to the song, since it was written in three languages, Zulu, Spanish, and English. How long did it take you to memorize the Zulu and the Spanish?" I said.

Alison rolled her eyes at me and said, "You know I speak Spanish, but you didn't know that I also speak Zulu."

"Yeah, right," I said as sarcastically as I could.

"Just face it Miles, I'm smarter than you! I know you always think you're the smartest person in the room, so this must really bother you. Well, learn to live with it," Alison snapped back at me.

We playfully embraced and kissed for a few minutes. On our way back from the park we both agreed that even though we wanted to be together tonight, that we wanted to hold off on that until it could be special. Running back to my dorm room and making love while everybody stood outside our door listening wasn't our idea of a special moment.

Then we talked about our plan. Being college students, by definition, it meant that we could travel light. We were only going to confide our plan to our roommates on the day we were going to take off and we were not going to tell anyone where we were going, but we would reach out to them once we had settled in. It was Saturday night, so we decided to pack up clandestinely on Sunday night and take off early Monday morning. I had an old beat up Toyota sedan and $1,100 to my name. Alison had about $500 in her checking account. We agreed that should last us the rest of our lives.

We got up at 5 a.m. on Monday and quickly packed my car with the help of our roommates, who were in total disbelief about what we were going to do. We hugged both of them and told them that it would not be the last time we ever saw each other.

Off we went on the road to California, except neither one of us knew how to drive to Huntington Beach. We stopped to fill up and bought an atlas. Alison turned to me and chuckled "well there goes the money for our first kid's college education."

We were on a mission. I had called Michael on Sunday and he knew we were coming. We were going to drive straight through and keep changing drivers to get there as soon as we could.

The trip just flew by. The weather all the way there was fantastic. We both felt like we were experiencing what Kerouac did when he crisscrossed America on a lark and ended up writing On the Road. We had the tunes cranked and kept the mood lighthearted.

However, when we hit the California state line, our mood shifted and we turned back into the runaway college kids that we were. We couldn't wait to get to Michael's apartment, because it would be the first place that we would call home as a couple.

At our last gas fill-up, Alison and I decided that we needed to call our parents and let them know we were okay and that we would stay in touch. Both of us being 21 years old, we could pretty much do whatever we wanted. It wasn't like I was kidnapping an underage girl, but we both loved our parents and all of our family and we didn't want them to worry. Our calls went well and I think my mom was really excited for us, even though she had never met Alison. For some reason, she trusted my judgment.

So, it was next stop, Huntington Beach.

We were lucky to get street parking just a few buildings from Michael's apartment. We locked the car and hand-in-hand walked down the sidewalk that was lined with palm trees and had the scent of the ocean breeze filling the air. Of course, who was standing in front of his apartment building, talking to three beautiful California girls? Michael. He had played football in high school and was a surfer his whole life, so Michael was in great shape. I sometimes think

I initially wanted to be friends with him because of all the girls that were attracted to him. He was a ladies' man.

He saw me coming and abruptly but politely asked the girls to hold on, then started jogging towards Alison and me. As he got close, I put my arms out, but in typical Michael fashion, he grabbed Alison and spun her around in the air. Alison was laughing but I could see the apprehension in her eyes that Michael was going too fast and might lose his grip on her. Then he put her down and he hugged me so hard it was quite a shock.

"So, you finally grew a pair Miles! Alison, whatever this guy told you about his time in California, it isn't true. He was so shy around girls that it took them forever to get to know him like I did. Thank God you cracked the code!"

Michael went back to the girls and convinced them to help us move our stuff into his apartment. That's just how charming he was. To their surprise, he asked the girls to leave as soon as we were done, because he had to catch up with us. They were bummed, but who could say no to Michael?

Luckily, Michael had been looking for a roommate for quite a while. His family was very wealthy, so he was being very picky. He had a second bedroom for us to stay in for as long as we wanted. It was very lucky for us indeed, because I really didn't want the two of us to sleep on the floor or on a couch if we didn't have to.

We all had something to eat and caught up on our lives and at about 10 o'clock Michael brought the evening to an abrupt close. He told us that he had bought three tickets to the Long Beach ferry to Catalina Island, which was 22 miles off the coast of California, and that the three of us were going to celebrate for the next two days on the island. We looked at each other and looked back at Michael and told him that we were all in.

Everyone said good night and we went to our room. We stood there looking at each other and all of a sudden, we both started laughing. At first, I didn't know what we were laughing at. Was it Michael, was it the situation, or was it the absurdity of the moment? Then, we both looked at each other, at the same time and said "not tonight." We were so tired and we really needed some rest. Both of us just kicked off our shoes and we slept with our clothes on.

I hadn't slept that well in a long time.

Michael came in to our room the next morning as I slept spooning with Alison. He wanted to make sure we were up bright and early, so that we could catch the 9 o'clock ferry. We got to the ferry landing with time to spare. I told Alison that I really thought it was time for us to call our old significant others because they deserved that. We both made our calls and when we were done, we decided to share our conversations.

"So, what did you tell Jack?" I asked.

"I basically told Jack that I still loved him and that I would love him for the rest of my life," Alison said.

"You said what?"

"Then I told him that I also loved you, but that you were the one. You are the one that I was going to spend the rest of my life with, having a family and growing old together. I told him that I was sorry if I hurt him," Alison said, in the most genuine, gentle tone of voice I had ever heard.

"So, what did you tell Rebecca?" Alison asked.

"Well, I guess I'm just not as eloquent as you in breaking up with someone. I told her that I didn't love her the way that I should, or the way that I loved you. There was a lot of crying, a lot, but after things settled down, I told her that she would find someone better suited for her than I was and that I wished her nothing but the best. I really could have used your help. Next time I break up with someone, I'll check with you first. You're much better at it than I am."

Alison forced a smile as she shook her head at me and said, "I would laugh if it wasn't so serious Miles. She's hurting, but at least that's over."

The ferry trip was beautiful and as we approached the harbor at Avalon, the island appeared to be straight out of a dream. However, being with Michael for the day was like trying to hold hands with a tornado. He knew all the great bars and he knew where all the great music was going to be played. He had picked these dates because there was going to be jazz that night at the Avalon ballroom, which sat on a peninsula that jutted out into the bay.

After we left the ballroom and started cruising some bars, it started to get late. I asked Michael where we were going to stay, because the last ferry to the mainland had left. He told us that he had not quite picked out the girl he was going to stay with tonight, but that the two of us were welcome to stay wherever we wanted. We looked at each other, I laughed, and Alison folded her arms in front of her and gave Michael a glare of disappointment. Like I shouldn't have expected this? Michael was off to see the wizard and left the two of us standing on the beach.

There were large padded chaise lounge chairs on the beach for the high rollers, but the people who ran that resort didn't care who used them at night. Alison and I snuggled up on one so that we could talk about where we could stay.

"Miles, I want to ask you a question. What was the first moment that you started to fall in love with me?"

"That's easy. It was the night we were sitting outside and we all had to say what our philosophy of life was. When you said that your philosophy of life was, 'I love everyone. And I understand that everyone doesn't love me, and that's okay.' After you said it, you looked right at me. From that moment, I knew how special you were."

"So, when did you first start falling in love with me?" I threw at her in return.

"Well, it was the night of the Super Bowl party at your apartment with all of your roommates. I was there with Robin because the other girls didn't care for football or how obnoxious your roommates were when they got drunk. All six of you were talking about sports and somebody had asked what was the greatest event in human history, implying sports. Everyone was arguing back and forth between football, basketball, baseball, hockey, Olympics, etc. You weren't saying anything, but then Eric posed the question to you. Without blinking an eye, you said, 'the greatest moment in human history was when Jesus Christ asked his Father to forgive the very men that were crucifying him, while they were crucifying him.' I knew you said it to mess with them, but I also knew that you meant it. Then everybody started booing and yelling and throwing popcorn and potato chips at you, because you spoiled the mood. You really do love to mess with people's heads, don't you?"

"That's when you started to fall in love with me? Really?"

"That's when I knew I was in love with you. It was because I had already known that you believed in love, because you shared with me how you were in love with Rebecca. Guys rarely show their vulnerable side to anyone, except maybe their girlfriend. But you showed it to me. After that night, I knew that you believed in forgiveness. With those two things, you can achieve perfection," Alison said.

There was a long silence. I was amazed at Alison's wisdom.

We sat there quietly for 15 minutes. Then, we both looked around and saw that the city of Avalon had closed its doors for the night. We were alone on the beach on a very warm California evening. We both knew that this was the special moment we had been waiting for, so we made love as the waves rolled gently upon the shore.

And I'll never forget every moment. I'll never forget. Every. Single. Moment.

3. A Fish Story

The morning light peeked above the eastern horizon and the city of Avalon began to wake up. I opened my eyes and I saw that Alison was still asleep. I also noticed that we were covered by a blanket that had the words Warren Hotel written across it. That was the name of the hotel above the beach where we had slept. Obviously, I had questions about how we got that blanket, but I was trying to stay still and let Alison sleep for a few more minutes. About 10 minutes later Alison started to wiggle and wake up.

"Hey, how did you sleep little girl?" I whispered.

"I slept just fine, Miles," Alison said as she stretched out her arms above her head. "Thanks for keeping me warm all night."

"Can I ask you a question? How did we get this blanket? I don't remember having it before we fell asleep."

Alison explained, "Well, you were pretty zonked out when one of the porters from the hotel was making his regular rounds on the beach. He was about our age and he whispered to me that it was cool that we stayed here for the night. I thanked him, but before he left, he told me that on his next round he would drop off a blanket for us. He said that you can bring it back in the morning and that we should walk into the hotel like we owned it, right up to the hospitality breakfast buffet."

"Well, I hope we run into him up there so I can thank him; should we tip him or something? I'm not familiar with the gratuity rules at swanky ocean-front resorts like this."

"Miles, he didn't do any of that for us because he wanted a tip. He did it out of the goodness of his heart, without expecting anything in return. To offer him a tip would just undo his gesture of kindness. Don't you know that to serve, and to be served, are folds of the same garment?" she said with a gotcha look on her face.

"Yeah I know that. I taught you that. I'm the resident Buddhist expert here," I replied calmly.

We both laughed, because Alison knew that I was a Jack Kerouac wannabe mad Buddhist monk.

"Yes, Miles, I know you taught me that saying, but obviously you never learned its meaning."

She was right.

"All jerks please raise their hand."

I grudgingly raised mine.

We made our way up to the hotel and did as our nighttime visitor advised us to do. We walked right up to the breakfast buffet like we were staying in the penthouse and loaded up our plates with eggs, bacon, hash browns, biscuits and gravy— we were starving. When the waitresses came by, we ordered coffee and juice and kept up our pretense of belonging there. Alison finished breakfast before me and headed to the ladies' room.

Just then, a busboy came over to me at the table and said, "Hey dude, how did you sleep last night?"

"Was it you that gave us the blanket and invited us up for breakfast? My name is Miles and I just want to thank you for your kindness," I said.

"Nice to meet you Miles, I'm Dan. Can I talk to you for a minute before your girlfriend comes back?"

"Sure. And by the way her name is Alison," I said.

With that, Dan sat down across from me and started to speak in hushed tones.

"I want to tell you about something that happened last night on the beach. I noticed the two of you on my first round and your girlfriend saw me and I whispered to her that it was okay to stay there. I was trying not to wake you up. She mouthed the words 'thank you' to me. I told her I'd bring back a blanket on my next round and I went on my way. About an hour later I grabbed a blanket and went back down to the ocean to drop it off. Here's where it gets weird. As I got closer to your chair, I saw what I thought were the stars in your girlfriend's long brown hair, and I don't mean barrettes and things like that. I mean stars that blended in with the stars of the evening sky. I kind of shook my head because some of us porters had split a joint about three hours before, but my head was pretty clear by then. When I got closer, your girlfriend opened her eyes and the stars in her hair disappeared. I opened the blanket and covered the both of you and I can tell you, I was a little bit shook, but the way she, I mean Alison, smiled back at me, I knew everything was okay. She thanked me, but when she winked at me, I could see the same night stars that had been in her hair were now in her eyes! She closed them and went right back to sleep. When I turned around to walk away, well, I just have to tell you what I saw..."

"What did you see?"

Dan said "There were seven dolphins in a crescent moon formation in the shallows of the waves. It was almost like they were watching over the two of you. I wasn't afraid at all. They just looked at me and I looked back at them for about 30 seconds. I turned and walked away, shook my head, and said to myself, whatever was in that joint, I have to get some more. Now tell me, can you explain any of that to me?"

I looked away from Dan and out the window at the morning ocean waves. I took a deep breath and then sighed. The wheels in my brain were spinning at 1,000 miles an hour.

I slowly turned back to face Dan and said, "Alison put you up to this, right? She knows how I like to get in other people's heads and she's just trying to get into mine. Right?"

Dan sat there, just looking at me, wanting an explanation that never came. We were both speechless. I didn't know if this was a put-on or what. If it was a put-on, he wasn't cracking.

Just then Alison came back to the table and Dan stood up. Before she sat, she pulled Dan into her for a hug and said "Hi, I'm Alison. Thanks so much for everything that you've done for us." Then she sat down to finish her coffee.

Dan looked at me, and then he looked at Alison, and then he did a weird half bow to us as he backed away and said: "It's nice to meet you Alison and it's nice to meet you, Miles. Maybe I'll see you around the island tonight. My shift's over, so I've got to take off and get some sleep."

And with that he was gone, leaving only his fish story behind.

4. Return of the Wizard

Since I took pride in my mastery of the practical joke, I decided not to mention my conversation with Dan—at least not for a while. I wanted to see if Alison would crack. I thought Dan was just hallucinating or something, especially about the dolphins. However, because I had seen the same dark sky and stars in Alison's eyes, I tended to believe he might have seen something along the lines of non-ordinary reality.

We got up from the table and headed hand-in-hand towards the small city of Avalon. We both knew that it was unlikely that Michael would be up and around this early, so we decided to take a walking tour of the surroundings and just take in the newfound freedom of our relationship and the moment.

After walking past shops, restaurants, and bars, we decided to head down to the ocean and check out the scuba diving lessons. We were both Midwesterners and knew nothing about scuba diving. We got to the beach and were standing behind the railing watching the instructors with their students, telling them what they were going to do for the next hour. After about 10 minutes, to our surprise, we heard a voice in the distance yelling "Hey! guys!" We turned around and it was Michael running towards us.

I said "So, Michael, are you gonna show us your scuba diving skills today? Don't even try to talk me into joining you because you know I'm a lousy swimmer. Alison if you want to go that's fine, I'll just stay here and people watch."

At that point, I noticed Michael was a little out of breath. "Are you okay Michael?" Alison asked, putting her hand on his shoulder.

"Well, yeah, I'm okay, I guess," he said sheepishly.

"See that house up there on the cliff?" he said, pointing to a magnificent home built on the side of a cliff, overlooking the Pacific Ocean. "Well, after I left you guys last night, I went to Sullivan's bar and I was hanging out with some locals. Anyway, long story short, I really connected with this woman named Amy, if that's her real name. She was gorgeous but in her mid- to late-40s. I had never been with an older woman, so, when she told me she owned the house on the cliff and asked if I wanted a private tour of her home, I agreed. We had a great night, but about 45 minutes ago her husband came home. She had told me she was a widow and that her husband had died in a scuba diving accident. Anyway, as she was trying to explain to him what was going on, I grabbed my stuff and ran out of there as fast as I could. I saw the two of you as I ran down the road along the cliff and here I am. I'm alive for now, but I think we need to cut our stay short and hit the next ferry back to the mainland before hubby decides to come looking for me." Alison just smiled and shook her head.

"Michael, I've told you so many times that you need to stop whoring around. One day it's going to catch up to you and today might still be that day," I said.

"Don't get all righteous with me because I love women Miles," he snapped back at me.

Alison started to laugh out loud.

Michael looked at her. "Just because women want me to make love to them, you can't hold that against me," Michael explained as if trying to convince himself.

Alison's laughing had become contagious and even though I wanted to say something back to Michael, I just started laughing along with her. Michael stood there with his mouth open wanting to say something but not knowing how to handle our utter disregard for his argument—that he was indeed a man of character and integrity, fulfilling his purpose in life, i.e. making love to as many women as possible.

Just as he was about to speak, I quickly pointed behind Michael and said "Hey, there's some big guy coming down the street right at us and he looks pretty pissed. Is that her husband?" Michael turned around and became pale as a ghost.

There was nobody there, but I just wanted to make him own the moment.

"Fuck you Miles. If these roles were switched, I would have your back."

"Michael, these roles would never be switched and you know it, so fuck you."

Alison interceded, saying "Come on guys, you know you are friends and by the way, stop using profanity in public or in front of me because I really don't appreciate it."

"Sorry Alison," I said. "Michael, Alison doesn't swear and I've been trying to give it up as well since two of my favorite people, Alison and John Wooden, both gave up swearing by the time they were 17 years old. Maybe you should get on the wagon with me."

Michael started to snicker and shake his head back and forth. I think he was really relieved that he wasn't about to get his ass kicked. Then he started to laugh and said, "Fuck the both of you and okay I'll get on the wagon with you, but I'd give you 500 to 1 odds that I can't not swear for the rest of the day."

There was a ferry in about 25 minutes, so we worked our way over to the boarding dock and eventually made it back to Long Beach and Michael's apartment. On the return trip we all shared our plans for the future and Alison heard for the first time that Michael was a business major and was planning to run his father's successful company one day. It was one of the biggest defense contractors in the world. It provided the United States armed forces, and many other countries, with a lot of the technology used for radar, sonar and weapons systems.

When we got back to the apartment, we kind of all just flopped down on the furniture to take a minute. Michael asked, "So Miles, Alison, why don't you guys just stay here with me and finish school here? You know you'll have a great time and I can show Alison California the same way I showed it to you Miles."

Since Michael was my friend, I had to deal with it.

"We haven't talked about it too much Michael, but that's a very generous offer and I think I speak for Alison when I say we'll definitely consider it. If you don't mind, we'd like to get our feet under us for about a week and then make up our minds on what we're going to do next."

"A week! Think of all the fun we can have in a week, even if you guys do decide to go somewhere else."

With that, Michael got up and made a phone call. Then, he informed us he had an appointment to keep that evening, but that his apartment was full of food and drinks and we were welcome to all of it. After a shower, a shave and a change of clothes he was gone.

"So, is Michael coming back tonight?" Alison queried.

I replied, "You've only known him for a day and you already have Michael figured out. That's a good question. I'm so impressed with you."

Over the next week we got to play house at Michael's apartment and spend time at the beach. We talked things through and Alison talked to her sister Dana, who was living with her husband, Billy, in the small town of West Haven, just outside Walnut Creek, California. Billy was running the Hendrix Winery and because it had been sold to a corporation, Dana and Billy were allowed to live rent free in the founding owner's home at the winery. They already had two small children, but there was plenty of room in the big farmhouse for us, at least until we got our feet under us and got a place of our own. They were pretty close to the University of California at Berkeley. We did some research and found out that Alison could finish her Advanced Special Education degree and I could finish my English teaching degree and hopefully volunteer time with one of the local high school basketball programs. I planned to become a head boys basketball coach and English teacher at a high school when I graduated.

One night Michael didn't come home, so we just relaxed, listened to music, and got in a lot of sleep to make up for all our travels. The next morning, we were grabbing cereal and milk for breakfast when Alison picked up a piece of paper that was left on Michael's desk.

"Wow, I wouldn't guess that Michael would write poetry," Alison said as she looked at the paper.

"Oh, he's quite the poet. Just ask him. He lets his poetry lay around so people can accidentally read it. So, go ahead."

I had already read many of his works, and having known him personally, I could honestly say he was one of the most complicated or tortured souls I had ever encountered.

"Are you sure it's okay if I read this?"

"Absolutely, and he will be ready to discuss it when he gets home."

This is what Alison read on the sheet of paper:

Point of View

Blazes of suffering streak forth
Bent upon exclamation of the evidence
Hostage shut up, feeble thumb sucker
Reruns exist, your Mistresses replacement
will graduate soon
Peace, an unknown and therefore unwanted item
Justice, maybe, revenge, probably, humanity, certainly!
Missing for ages – where are you – what are you?
Feeble infants lunge in the darkness for your nourishment
Seat of propaganda, you powers – different methods
Same objective, belittle us more,
we will hold the mirror higher
The button doesn't frighten the suffering, so we fight,
Fight us, we die, only to live again, outside of hell.

When Alison finished, she looked at me and didn't say a word.

"I got you on that one, didn't I? Be honest, you never saw that coming did you?"

"Miles, can you explain this to me? He's a 'love them and leave them' surfer beach-bum that's living off his father's millions and plans to take over the very company that provides hardware and software to the military... and he writes this?"

I looked Alison in the eyes and said, "The explanation is easy. He's an undercover anarchist. That's what we came up with after a long night of smoking dope and talking it through. He wants to be the greatest undercover anarchist of all time. And I'm asking you to please **not** ask him about this poem or he'll go off on how once he's in control of the company, he's going to change things. He'll tell you, that living off the profits of the company, and hypocritically banging every hot girl on the Sunset strip, is okay for now. As long as in the end, he turns the tables on **the man**."

"Wow. Okay. I won't say a word, for now. You know I love him as much as you do, but he will find his way one day, I hope. He might just need a little help," Alison said with a tone of kindness.

"Thanks," I said. "One day we can talk about this poem with him, but just not now."

And that was the last we talked about it.

By the end of the week, we let Michael know our plans. Even though he was disappointed, I think he was secretly happy to get his "stabbin' cabin" back. That's what he called all of his dorm rooms and apartments.

Sunday night we packed up, got a good night's sleep, and the next morning the three of us had a big breakfast and said our goodbyes.

I hugged Michael and told him to stay out of trouble, especially with married women's husbands! Alison hugged Michael for what seemed to be a long time without saying a word. Then she pulled away and looked him right in the eyes and said "Michael, Miles and I love you and you're going to be okay."

There was this awkward moment of silence.

First, I know Michael didn't expect that kind of a long embracing hug from Alison right in front of me. Neither did I. He was still recovering from the hug while he was trying to process that he would be okay.

"Ummm, what do you mean I'm going to be okay? Is there something wrong with me?" Michael asked.

Alison started to laugh, and I joined her, but I was on Michael's side with this question about what was wrong with Michael. Plus, I didn't really know how to react to that loving embrace that I just watched.

Alison said "Wow, that's only the second thing I've ever heard you worry about, besides being killed by that woman's husband. Don't worry about it. We'll see you soon."

Michael promised to visit as often as he could. I know he really meant that, but I also know it probably would not be that often.

With that we were off.

Halfway through our drive to West Haven the weather turned foggy and rainy, depriving us of a lot of the scenic view along Highway 1. As we got closer, Alison kept telling me the roads to turn on, since she was holding the atlas. What was interesting was that as I drove down these dirt roads, I couldn't believe that they were even on the map, and I knew Alison had never been to Dana's house before.

I questioned her on it.

"Oh, no Miles, not all of these roads are on the map, but Dana let me know about these turns when I talked to her."

I was perplexed again and I asked her, "We've been together almost this whole time. When did you talk to Dana about directions?"

"Oh, we communicated. I think you were in the shower."

"Must've been a short call."

"Well you know, her two little ones keep her busy so she had to run."

And with genuine excitement Alison chirped, "Here it is Miles. Take a left turn right here and just follow this road up to the house."

The rain and the fog had gotten worse, and I was just happy to be at the end of this journey. As I drove slowly up the winding road to the house, Alison grabbed my right hand and squeezed it and looked at me and smiled in the way that only she could smile at me. We had come a long way from a small little park at a university in Iowa. I smiled back, letting her know that she had become my world.

I pulled in next to the two cars and the truck near the house and turned off the engine. We looked at each other and I said, for the first time, an expression that I would say to my players for years to come when coaching basketball. "Here we go."

5. *You Can Never Have Too Much Wine*

Just as Alison and I slammed the car doors and walked to the house, we found ourselves victims of a cloudburst of rain, so we began to run. During that short run, we were completely drenched. We stood on the porch that wrapped around the beautiful old farmhouse where Dana, Billy and their kids lived. As I was trying to wipe some of the beaded water from my face, I knocked a few times on the front screen door to let them know we were here. Because of the heavy rain, we couldn't hear anything in the house, but in less than 10 seconds the inside door flew open.

It was Dana.

She pushed open the screen door and grabbed her sister. They hugged, like only two sisters who really loved each other do. When they finally parted, they continued to hold hands, and they were both smiling from ear to ear, telling each other how much they had missed spending time together.

That lasted for only a few moments and then Dana turned to me and grabbed my two hands and looking right at me said, "So, Miles, here you are in the flesh, the only person that's really ever made my sister this happy."

I couldn't help but smile sheepishly at her kind words. As she stood there, I noticed that she was in her bare feet, which was just so California. Dana had blonde hair with a natural wave and blue eyes. She was a little shorter than Alison but their resemblance was remarkable.

I eventually gathered myself and said, "Geez Dana, thank you so much for those kind words. You have put me a little off my game right now. I wasn't really ready for that. Thank you for letting us stay here until we can figure out where we are going to go and what we are going to do."

"Blah Blah Blah," Dana blurted to me. "Are you going to start telling your whole life story to me before I get a hug and kiss?" With that she grabbed me and hugged me tight and then reached up and grabbed my face with two hands and kissed me on the lips for about three seconds. I had to admit that these sisters were quite a pair when it came to making everyone around them feel comfortable.

"You're right Dana... sometimes I just let my mouth get the best of me. There's so much more to talk about. Oh, dammit, I forgot to lock the car," I said immediately putting my hand over my mouth, because I had promised Alison that every time I swore, I'd put a dollar in the cuss jar. Alison and Dana looked at each other and then just turned and laughed at me.

"Miles, you're in the middle of Nowhere, California, in a driving rainstorm. Who do you think is going to steal all of your crummy stuff out of that old car? Leave your car and both of you come in and get out of this rain," Dana replied.

Once we were inside the door, Billy was walking up to the small foyer, wiping his hands from dinner. Alison hugged and kissed Billy, who shook my hand and said, "It's nice to meet you, Miles. Alison has told us a lot about you."

Billy was about five foot ten with black hair and was still sporting his academic beard. His body was still in transformation from being a pencil pusher and scientist into a winemaker who worked with his hands every day.

Dana wanted us to see the kids right away. She took us into the kitchen where two-year-old Renée was sitting strapped in her highchair and four-year-old Billy Junior, who everyone called Willy, was finishing up his fish sticks, which happened to be his favorite meal. Apparently, there was no getting him away from the table at that moment. Alison wouldn't take no for an answer, so she immediately picked up Renée and hugged and kissed her and then just handed her over to me, not knowing that I was a neophyte when it came to holding babies or young children. Renée held onto me and was very comfortable with the fact that I was a rookie. Alison then talked Willy into putting his fork down for a minute and so she picked him up and hugged him and spun him around the room. She put him down standing on his chair where he had been sitting eating and said to him, "See, you're getting almost as big as me." He smiled and looked at her and said, "Noooo" in the way a four-year-old does when he knows his aunt is just playing silly games.

Dana handed us a couple bath towels and we cleaned up quite nicely. She had prepared plenty of food, anticipating our arrival at dinnertime. We sat and enjoyed dinner like we hadn't eaten for a week.

While we ate, Dana and Billy put Renée and Willie to bed and by the time that had been accomplished, Alison and I had cleaned up the dishes after supper. It made us feel good to do some work, as if we were paying our way through life. When Dana and Billy came back down they were pleasantly surprised and we retired to their living room to sit and visit.

I learned that Dana and Billy had met about four years earlier while they were both physics students at MIT. Dana was younger, so she was finishing her bachelor's degree, but Billy had completed his masters and had been working on his PhD dissertation in astrophysics. Their spur of the moment romance sounded eerily similar to ours. Although

Dana had finished her bachelor's degree, Billy never did finish his PhD. Billy had decided to be a winemaker, so he convinced Dana into moving to California. His scientific background and interview skills landed him this terrific job of running the Hendrix Winery, which had recently been sold from the original owner to a corporation.

Then came my turn for show and tell.

Dana asked, "So Miles, tell us about your family. Alison's already filled us in on your college background, but we would love to hear about your family back in Iowa. By the way, Miles, Alison never told us your last name."

I replied, "It's Christian. Miles Christian."

"So, does that mean your family comes from a long line of theologians, Miles?" Billy asked with a playful smile.

"No, no," I laughed. "My dad was a soldier in World War II when he met my mom, who was 19 years old and a German refugee living in Frankfurt. So, my dad is American and my mom is German. My dad tells people that our last name was passed down to us because we are direct descendants of Fletcher Christian, of the Mutiny on the Bounty fame."

"Is that true?" asked Alison?

"Well, he tells everyone it is, so I just go along with it. Maybe that's where I get my practical joker nature, from my dad's side. Who knows if it is true? I just know that's my last name."

We visited for about an hour and a half. Billy was big into Steely Dan and Donald Fagen albums that night. He was playing their music in the background. We all had at least three glasses of wine. The wine was wonderful.

The rain, the fog, the farmhouse, the music, and having Alison with me with her loving sister and her husband made for an A+ evening.

All of a sudden someone started to cry upstairs and Billy jumped up and told us he would check on the situation and that we should all three stay and relax.

It was at that point, after Billy went upstairs, that Dana made an interesting request to me.

"Miles, if you don't mind, I would appreciate it if you would not bring up the subject to Billy of why he never finished his PhD in astrophysics. If he brings it up that's okay."

I told her I didn't mind at all and that I would be very careful to stay away from the subject. Dana thanked me and smiled. Her eyes glistened just like Alison's would when she looked right at me. She turned and looked at Alison and said, "I can already tell, Alison, you are right; he is the one for you."

With that, Billy came sheepishly down the steps and turned to Dana and said, "I think Renée ate too many grapes and I made quite a mess upstairs trying to change her and spilled over into her crib. Can you give me a hand?"

Alison jumped up and said, "Dana come on, lets you and I get the kids back to bed and let these guys spend some time together."

The two sisters flew upstairs, Alison with her great anticipation of spending time with her niece and nephew again. Billy just flopped down on the sofa. He had put on Donald Fagan's Kamakiriad album and the song Tomorrow's Girls had just started to play.

We enjoyed the music for a few moments. We had gotten to know each other just fine over the last few hours and I knew this was going to be an easy steppingstone to whatever came next for Alison and me. However, I also sensed that he had the same magic going between himself and Dana as I did with Alison. Neither one of us really understood it completely. All we knew was that we were incredibly happy to be their significant others.

Coincidently, we both took in a deep breath and exhaled simultaneously. We looked at each other and laughed at the incredible timing. Then he turned to me, lifted a wine glass for a toast, and wryly said, "I know they're not Tomorrow's Girls, a reference to the song playing in the background, but they're something. We just have to figure out what."

6. I Can Beat That

The next day, Alison and I slept in because we were tired from the long trip and the late evening and the wine. When we finally stumbled out of bed and headed downstairs to the kitchen, it was already late morning. We passed the den where we saw Willie and Renée and Dana in the middle of their homeschooling for the day. Even though Willie and Renée were very young, they were remarkably focused on everything Dana said. After a few moments, Dana saw us out of the corner of her eye, turned and smiled and said, "I forgot what it was like to be in college and sleep in every day you lazy bums." We smiled and went into the den to say hello to the kids and apologized for disturbing their learning.

"I heard the two of you rumbling upstairs and I knew you'd be down soon, so I made a pot of coffee. I'm going to make you the biggest farm house breakfast you'll ever eat." I was about to object and say that we could make our own breakfast, but as if Alison was reading my mind, she put her left hand over my mouth and turned to me and whispered "Just let her do it. It would be a waste of time to try and talk her out of it." Alison knew her sister, and when Dana had her mind set, there was no changing it.

We had a huge meal of thick cut bacon, scrambled eggs, and hash browns, and for dessert, some delicious blueberry pancakes. The aroma of Dana's cooking was almost as good as actually eating it.

"You know Dana, we really appreciate you cooking us such a fabulous meal, but even though it all tasted great, it's probably not the healthiest breakfast diet to live on," I said as I leaned back in my chair and rubbed my belly.

"Yeah, yeah, yeah Miles, like you're going to live forever. You should probably worry much less about what the famous 'they' say about nutrition, and enjoy your life and what's put in front of you," Dana retorted.

It was all funny and good-natured, but I was sure that if I ate a breakfast like that every day, I would fall over dead from a heart attack before I was 50, so I just let it go.

"Miles, Billy wanted you to know that he'll be back around lunch time to grab a sandwich and that he wanted to take you out to the vineyards this afternoon, if you're interested," Dana said.

"Absolutely, that's a great idea. I've never really been in a vineyard. My mom grew up in a German settlement town in Hungary, called Mucsi. She used to tell me stories of their small wine operation, along with the rest of her tales about farming in central Europe in the 1930s and 1940s."

Just then, Billy came in the back door and said his hellos, while taking off his stylish hat that he hung on the peg on the wall. I told him I was excited about spending the afternoon with him and he told me to go upstairs and get a long sleeve shirt, long pants, and if I had a hat, to bring it.

Billy said "We all have to respect the sun's rays." About 25 minutes later, we were ready to go. I climbed into the passenger seat of his old pickup truck and we headed to the vineyards.

It was a gorgeous California day. There were just a few clouds playing peekaboo with the sun, but it was a warm afternoon, probably about 80 degrees, with a nice cool breeze that kept the cab of the old pickup truck tolerable, since it didn't have air-conditioning. Seeing the rolling hills and the rows of grapevines all around me took me back to the stories my mom would tell about her old hometown. I thought about what it was like to live off the land back then. She always told me that they wanted for nothing and that everyone in town was incredibly happy living the simple agrarian life style.

Billy was a terrific tour guide. It was almost as if he had been a docent for a living. When I told him that, he said that the corporation had sent many visitors out here and that he had gotten good at giving tours to potential bigwig investors who had so much money that they found it adventurous and romantic to be part-owner of a winery in California.

Three hours later we headed to the warehouse, which was built up against the hill. Billy parked the truck and we both jumped out. All the time Billy was explaining that the final product was made and stored here.

It was at that point that he strayed from the narrative of the afternoon. He turned to me as he entered the building, which was about 20 degrees cooler inside than outside. He took off his hat and said, "Miles, you seem like a decent guy. I want you to know that I love Alison like she was my real sister."

I thought, here it comes, he's going to give me some sort of warning about how I better not mistreat Alison or how I better not break Alison's heart or something along the lines of what a big brother might say, or threaten, but what Billy said to me next was right out of left field.

"Miles, I know the two of you have only been together for a short time, but, there's no easy way to put this: have you ever experienced something with Alison that your senses really just can't explain? I mean, I'm trying not to sound like a nut here, just something unusual that you may have thought you saw or experienced and then thought it was a dream or the light was playing tricks with your eyes etcetera? I have my reason for asking and I'll let you know what it is if you would be kind enough to answer my question."

I had to gather my wits for a moment.

"That really wasn't what I thought you were going to say Billy, not even close. Though, in the back of my mind, yes, there was a possibility that you were going to ask me that question, just not today."

"My answer Billy is yes. Let me tell you about it."

I proceeded to tell him that sometimes I thought I saw stars, like the stars in the cosmos, in Alison's eyes. Then I told him the story of Dan the porter and our experience at the Warren Hotel on Catalina Island. I told him that I was sure Alison had put Dan up to telling that story as a practical joke, so I never brought it up to her, thinking that she would eventually crack before I would...but she's never said a word, and I have yet to confront her about it.

The metamorphosis I saw in Billy over the next few seconds was remarkable. It was almost as if someone had told him that Santa Claus was real and had proof. We stood there quiet for a few moments.

"Thanks for sharing that, Miles. I know we haven't known each other a long time, but I sensed that you and Alison have the same deep connection that Dana and I have. I can't tell you the amount of times in the last seven years that I thought I saw stars in Dana's eyes or in her hair. But each time it happened, it was either in the half-light of the evening or early morning when I didn't know what was a dream and what was real. A couple of times I told Dana right when it happened, that I saw stars in her eyes, and her comeback was always that 'I see stars in your eyes too'."

Billy told me he had a few other stories that he could share with me, but today he wanted to share the one that happened about a year ago.

"There was a meeting that night of the City Council in downtown West Haven. I was attending because there was going to be some discussion regarding the taxes on wholesale wine and all of the vineyards would be represented in the gallery. I got cleaned up from the fields and put on some city clothes and jumped into our car to drive downtown. I left at dusk and I had plenty of time to get there, but about 10 minutes out, I realized that I had forgotten my wallet. So, I turned around and headed back to the farmhouse. From a long distance away, I could see the farmhouse, just as twilight was turning into nighttime. What I thought I saw was Dana holding Willie and Renée on the front lawn. It looked as if the three of them were glowing, like a lantern in the distance. But in the blink of an eye they were gone. I went into the house and grabbed my wallet. They were nowhere to be found. Well, I needed to make that meeting. My brain told me that what I thought I saw couldn't possibly have happened and that they had probably walked up to the top of the hill behind the house to do stargazing. I just didn't have time to go up there and find them. So, long story short, when I got home that night, everybody was asleep in bed. I crawled under the covers and waited till morning to talk to Dana about what I thought I saw. When I shared it with her, she said, 'that's interesting. So, you say that I was holding Willie and Renée and we disappeared into nothingness? Is that the story you want to go with?' I told her I was pretty far away; it might've just been the light playing tricks with my eyes and that you guys were probably up on the top of the hill behind the house gazing at stars. She laughed and said that I should probably stop drinking so much of my wine during the day, because it was giving me hallucinations. Anyway, like many other times before, I just dropped the issue."

"When I got home from work at dinner time, I took Willie out back where I was teaching him how to play soccer. After a while we both got tired, came into the kitchen, and sat to drink some cold water. I said to Willie, 'So did you miss daddy last night, because he had to go to meeting?' Willie said to me, 'No daddy, I went with mommy to her hometown. It was really nice. All the people wanted to play with me and they wanted to hold Renée. It was fun.' So, I told Willie that mommy said they had watched the stars on the top of the hill last night. Then Willie says to me, 'Oh yeah, that's what we did. What I told you was just a dream. Anyway, that's what mommy told me to tell you. She told me that I only dreamed that we went to her hometown'."

At that point, Billy stopped talking and was looking for some sort of response from me. I asked him, "Well, how old was Willie when that happened, like three and a half? You know the imaginations of young kids. So, what happened?"

"Miles, I know you haven't been with Alison for as long as I have been with Dana, but I'm telling you that these things keep happening and I can't explain them. I'm telling you they have started happening with Alison, they will continue to happen, and you won't be able to explain them either."

I was standing there with my hands on my hips, looking down at the ground, mulling over everything that Billy had just told me.

He continued, "Well, maybe now that there's two of us, we can get a second source corroboration if something happens in the presence of both of us. It's one thing if one person has a hallucination, but I don't think it's a hallucination when two people see the same thing. Keep your eyes open and let's see what happens."

I looked up at him and replied "Okay, that makes sense. We'll stay diligent. Hopefully, sooner than later, we will get to the bottom of this."

With that he turned on the master switch for the warehouse, which included a sound system that Billy had put in to make work more enjoyable. The first song that played on the system was the Beatles' Magical Mystery Tour. As they sang "roll up, roll up for the mystery tour," we looked at each other and smiled. He slapped me on the back and returned to being my tour guide.

"So, what kind of wine do you like with your Beatles, white or red?"

7. Paradise Found...Lost...Then Found Again

We didn't have the money to finish school right away, so we both got jobs and started looking for an apartment between West Haven and Berkeley, home of the main campus of the University of California. We discovered that if we worked in California for a year, that would establish our residency, and the cost of college would drop dramatically. I had some experience during the summers helping build new homes, and California was having a housing boom. I was able to hook up with a union carpenter crew and make some pretty good money. Alison worked at a daycare center, where of course she was terrific with both the kids and the parents. The owners of the center adored her and were ruing the day that she would leave to go back to school.

Being a traditionalist, once I got a few dollars in my pocket, I went off on my own and bought Alison a beautiful engagement ring, one that fit my budget.

One night, Alison and I went up to the top of the hill to look at the stars. Before we sat down on the grass I said, "Hey, do you think that's the same full moon we saw in Iowa? We **are** pretty far from there."

With that, Alison looked at the moon. I told her to close her eyes for just a second. While she did, I got down on one knee and grabbed her hand.

"Now open them."

I had the engagement ring in my right hand and she looked down at it and gave me a big smile.

"Alison, I know I'm just a young guy without a lifetime of experience, but I seriously doubt if there's any woman out there that could ever make me as happy as you have. In the short time that we've known each other, I can't imagine my life without you in it. So, Alison, will you marry me?"

I had tried to rehearse what I was going to say to her, but every time I did, it all sounded so clichéd. So, I just stopped trying and I hoped that she knew I was speaking from my heart, even though I probably did sound clichéd.

"Yes. Yes, Miles, I love you."

I stayed on my knee and said "Alison, I know your dad died in that car accident six years ago or I would've asked him for permission to marry you. Since he wasn't around, I asked Dana and she said that your dad would definitely have given me his blessing. Anyway, by proxy, Dana gave me his approval. Wow. That might be the most unromantic thing anyone ever said during a proposal. I hope you can forgive me."

"Well, I'll have to see that proxy." She was just rubbing it in, and I loved her for it.

I stood up and put the ring on her finger, and we embraced, with our lips coming together ever so slowly. A few moments later we heard applause—whooping and hollering—from Dana and Billy and the kids down at the bottom of the hill. They were shining a flashlight on us—we were in the spotlight!

We waved back and I yelled "She said yes!" They eventually turned off the flashlight and went back in the house, leaving us to enjoy the starry night from the hilltop.

We both agreed we wanted a simple wedding here in California with whoever could make the trip. We knew those who couldn't would be here in spirit. We had been going to church with Dana on Sundays at this beautiful little mission-style church. It had to be 100 years old, with dark walnut pews and beautiful stained-glass windows that depicted the stations of the cross. When we attended Mass on Sundays, you could feel the history, the smell of the old clay beneath the floorboards, and you appreciated the craftsmanship of the altar with the handcrafted wooden statues around it. We had volunteered there on Sundays and had gotten to know the pastor, Father Mendez, and we liked him a lot. We decided to ask Dana and Billy if it would be okay to have a small outdoor reception behind the farmhouse and just pray for beautiful weather.

Once we talked through the details, Alison grabbed both my hands and looked right at me and said, "There is one thing Miles, that I wanted to talk to you about: kids. I know we've talked in a general way that we want to have a family, but I don't want this to come from left field. My sisters Dana, Jessica, and I all promised my mom and dad that we would try to have a big family if possible, because they convinced us that the best thing we had in our lives was our family and our friends. I really hope you're okay with that Miles."

"So, define big."

"Like at least three or more?"

"Or more?"

"How does four sound as a compromise? Deal?"

"Deal."

"I'd love to have a big family, if things fall in place. When my younger brother, Thomas, passed away after being with us for only a week, I was still pretty young, so I got over it much quicker than my parents did. Once their grieving was over, life for me went back to pretty much the same as it was before. But as I got older and I hung around with my friends who had big families, I really regretted being an only child. The doctors told my mom that she needed a hysterectomy at an early age, because of some tumors that they found. She couldn't have another kid because of that. I know my mom and dad will be crazy good with us having a lot of kids, and more importantly, so will I. Especially the little girls that will look just like you."

Eventually, we went back down the hill to the farmhouse and let everyone know our plans. It came together pretty quickly. A wedding date was set about six weeks later. Alison's mom, Hope, and her sister Jessica, along with my parents, Steve and Nadine, would be coming from the East. Most of our friends really wanted to come, but being poor college kids, most of them couldn't really afford it. They all promised to visit soon and they sent their best wishes.

Given that set of circumstances, I asked Michael to be my best man, even though I had a couple closer friends from the Midwest that couldn't make it. Of course, Michael was excited, since no one had ever asked him to be the best man at a wedding before. I'm sure he thought that the wedding was about him, especially about him being the **best** man.

The next six weeks flew by and our wedding day was quickly upon us. Dana had been married in her grandmother's wedding dress and Alison wanted the same. I was glad that I had taken the advice of the salesman in my hometown and bought a black suit for job interviews. He had told me that a black suit goes with everything and all occasions and that just changing the shirt and tie would make me look different every day.

Dana and Billy's house had so many bedrooms and bathrooms, that it easily accommodated our immediate family and Michael. We had gotten to be friends with a lot of Dana and Billy's friends around town, and many of them were able to attend. So, there were 40 to 50 people at Santa Anna Catholic Church at 3 o'clock on September 16 when the *I do's* were said.

First, Billy walked Hope down the aisle, followed by my parents, Steve and Nadine. Then came beautiful Dana, Alison's matron of honor, arm-in-arm with Michael, the best man. Finally came adorable Rene and handsome Willy as flower girl and ring bearer. They were remarkably poised and full of restrained childhood wonderment of the occasion.

Then, I saw Alison for the first time that day, standing in the back of the church. She was wearing a modest but beautiful white wedding dress. It had a small train and the top of the dress was covered with ornate lovely lace. There was no veil and I was glad, because Alison was so beautiful. The dress had long sleeves and Alison was holding a gorgeous bouquet of white and red roses. White baby's breath had been interwoven into her lustrous beautiful brown hair by her sister Jessica.

Alison had told me that her father had dreamed his whole life about walking down the aisle with her and her sisters. She was sure that even though he was gone, he would be walking next to her down that aisle. Even though it looked to everyone else that she was walking alone, Alison and I knew that she was walking arm-in-arm with her father.

The ceremony was short and sweet. We had both agreed not to drag it out and put pressure on each other to write our own vows. Someone had once told me that a wedding day was all about the bride and I wanted to make sure it was. All I wanted was for Father Mendez to say the words, "you may kiss the bride." I think we set a record for length of kiss as everyone politely applauded. We turned around and waved and briskly walked down the aisle. We all gathered together outside as the celebratory rice was being thrown and then we got into my car and drove to the farmhouse.

It was pretty much a tradition in the West Haven area for neighbors to help each other out with the important parties and our party was no exception. Dana and Billy's friends were doing a pig roast and there was plenty of food to go around. The backyard was set up with outdoor lighting using Christmas lights. As evening arrived, the party continued, lit only by these lights and the stars above. Our wedding had gone smoothly and the reception was beginning to take off.

I could tell that my dad and especially my mom really loved Alison. I was happy, because of the impetuous way we had run off; I was afraid they thought I had lost my mind. But now they saw in Alison the things that I saw in her, and that put me at ease. I made sure to dance with Alison's mom, Hope, a couple times. It was easy to see where Alison and Dana and Jessica had gotten their temperament and their love of life, as I talked to her and got to know her better. By the end of the night, I was calling her mom, and every time I did, her smile got bigger and bigger.

Hope and Jessica had arrived two days before the wedding, so I got to spend an hour getting to know Jessica, the third and youngest sister of the Smith family. Jessica had a remarkable resemblance to both Alison and Dana. When they were all close together and smiling it was hard to tell them apart, except by the color of their hair—Jessica's being a shade between Dana's blonde curly locks and my Alison's medium straight brown. Jessica's hair was also curly but in a long wavy way. She had green eyes and she was taller than her sisters, maybe five foot eight or nine. When she walked, it was with grace and control, and it made every man in the room turn their head. As I have been known to say to my friends, "when a tall, beautiful girl enters the room, it has a magical effect on all men's eyes, because she represents the extra-large version of what every man wants." Back at the university one night when I said that out loud at a campus bar, Alison was the only girl at our table who laughed. She immediately pulled me aside and said that **she** thought it was funny, but speaking for women in general, she thought I should probably keep that comment as an inside joke with my guy friends. So, I did just that.

It didn't change the fact that Jessica was young, beautiful, smart and available, and I was glad she was able to attend our wedding.

Until the moment arrived when the music from the DJ started.

What happened?

Michael happened.

I watched it from a distance. He started walking across the yard with that look in his eye. That look that he had found the woman of his dreams, at least for that night. And who was he walking towards? Jessica of course. Alison had her arm around my arm and was in the middle of talking to some of our California friends who had just arrived, so I couldn't run out there and tackle Michael. All I could do was watch from a distance.

I knew Jessica and Michael had met earlier in the day at the church, but Michael was in the middle of performing his best man duties, and I had to tell him in his own vernacular, that if he fucked this up today, that I was going to kill him, so he was on his best behavior at the church.

Now, he had a couple drinks in him, and there was a bull's-eye on the vivacious Jessica.

Michael and Jessica stayed on the dance floor for three dances. The first song was September by Earth, Wind and Fire, followed by the second up-tempo number, Brick House by the Commodores. The third song was Color My World, by Chicago, and I grabbed Alison and in the firmest tone I had ever used with her, I said, "Let's dance." I dragged her out to the center of the dance floor, as close to Michael and Jessica as possible, in order to keep Michael—and especially his hands—in their appropriate places.

What happened next is what always happens with Michael. His patented move was about halfway through a slow song; he moved one of his hands lower and lower, until he knew whether or not she was the one for the evening. I had seen girls allow it more times than not, and they became his girlfriend for the night. A lot of girls would just grab his arm and pull it back up to their waist level. Depending on how drunk Michael was, he might have or might not have tried to let it slip down for a second time. I did see one girl pull away and try to smack him, but he was too quick and she whiffed. Michael always had a quick come back, so I heard him say that night, "Jeez, if you didn't like that song, you could've just told me."

Anyway, I was praying to God that he wasn't going to try that with Jessica. However, about halfway through the song, his right hand slowly started to drop, but before he could get into the danger zone, Jessica took her hands from around his neck and began to straighten his tie, which caught him unawares, and he stopped moving his hand altogether. Then I heard her say "Michael, I'm sorry, I need to find my mom. I promised I would do something with her for Alison later tonight and we have to get ready." With that, Jessica was gone and the albatross fell from my neck. When the song was over, I told Alison what had happened and that she had missed it all playing out right next to her. She giggled as I said "I'm going to talk to Michael right now," but as I pulled away, she said, "Miles, Jessica's a big girl and she can handle herself, but if you want to talk to Michael, that's your call."

"Hey dickhead! Did you see me dancing next to you? Did you see me watching you as you tried to drop your hands all over my new sister-in-law's keister? You just got lucky that she had to go. Can you please just be a civilized human being for one night? This is my new family and I love them and I picked you as my best man and I expect you to behave accordingly," I said to Michael. I think being dressed in a suit kept me from taking a swing at him.

"Calm down Miles and stop yelling at me. People can hear, you jerk. How am I supposed to know if she digs me unless I take her on the dance floor?" Michael replied sheepishly. I could tell by looking at him that he knew he had messed up, but I wasn't letting him off the hook.

"This is why you've never had a real relationship, Michael. You think you're going to get to know someone if you take her on the dance floor and put your hands on her ass? You just summarized your pathetic love life in one sentence. You need to get to know Jessica by talking to her! I've only known her for a short time, but you would be the luckiest man in the world if any girl like Jessica would ever fall in love with you. But it's never going to happen by grabbing her ass in front of 50 people. Her having to leave you at that moment will probably go down as the luckiest thing that ever happened to you."

"If you really want to get to know her, if you really want to start changing your life for the better, if you really want to know what love is about for **real** people, this is your chance. When she comes back out here, ask her if she wants something to drink and sit down with her and relax. Then, talk to her like a human being. God gave you two ears and one mouth, so if you start listening, twice as much as you do talking, you might actually get to know someone. If you try any of your other dumb moves on her, I swear to God I'll smack that smile off your face all the way into the Pacific Ocean! Do you understand me?"

There was a long silence between us. Michael put his hands on his hips and stood there like a schoolboy who just got scolded by a coach. I had never seen him like that. I didn't know what to think.

"Mile, I'm really sorry. You're right. I had a lot of time to think on my way up here for the wedding. The time I spent with you and Alison at my place, and now here during the wedding, well, I can honestly tell you that I'm kind of jealous of what the two of you have. Maybe it is time for me to grow up. Thanks. But you're still a jerk."

And with that, Michael became a gentleman for the rest of the evening.

We partied until about two in the morning and everyone finally made it home or to bed safely. I was exhausted and had no plans of getting up early. However, we all have that body clock that seems to want to wake us up at the same time every day. So, I got up about 6:30 and Alison was not in bed with me. I figured she was either in the bathroom down the hall, or that she had decided to get up and let me sleep. In any case, I was thirsty, so I headed towards the kitchen fully intending to get a drink of water and go back upstairs to sleep. As I came down the steps, I heard my mother talking. My mother was an amazing person with languages. Even though she only went to formal school until she was 14, because of the war, she could read and write in German, Hungarian, and English. After about 10 seconds, since I spoke English and German, I knew she was speaking in Hungarian. I stayed back and out of sight, because I didn't know who she could be talking to, other than my father, who knew very little Hungarian. Then I heard Alison's voice speaking Hungarian back to my mother in lengthy, emotional sentences. This went back and forth for about two minutes, but who knows how long they had been there before that.

Suddenly, my mother began to weep uncontrollably and I peeked around the corner and saw the two of them sitting on the bench side of the kitchen table next to each other. Alison put her arms around my mother. They were both crying now, but my mother was much more upset. Alison began to stroke my mother's hair and whisper in assuring tines in Hungarian, all unfamiliar to me. Quickly, my mom started to calm down. Alison grabbed for two napkins on the kitchen table, but she wiped the tears away from my mother's face first and then from her own face. She said a few more things to my mom and my mom smiled and grabbed her face with her two hands and kissed her on the forehead and in English said, "Alison, my new daughter, thank you."

Alison got up and said, "Mom, I'll get us some coffee. What do you want with it, cream or sugar?"

I didn't hear anything after that. I was just stunned. I stayed in the other room out of their site. I knew that when I walked into the kitchen, I wouldn't want to refer to anything I had just heard, but I knew I was going to ask Alison about it as soon as possible. So, I went into the kitchen, pretending not to have seen or heard anything. I hugged and kissed my mom and had coffee with the two of them for about 15 minutes.

Then I said, "Alison, can you come upstairs with me for a minute? Someone gave us a gift and the tag fell off. Maybe if you look at it, you'll remember who it's from, so I can thank them personally before they leave."

Alison said, "Sure. Mom, we'll be back in a few minutes and we'll have some breakfast." My mom said, "Don't rush, I'm not a big breakfast eater," so we scampered up the steps to our room. It crossed my mind that Alison thought I had amorous intentions this morning because I could tell she didn't believe my ruse for a second.

Once we were both in the bedroom, I closed the door behind me. I spilled my guts on what I had heard and I asked Alison to explain what was going on.

"Miles, I've never lied to you and I'll never lie to you for as long as we live. I'll always answer all of your questions. Yes, I do speak Hungarian. You know I'm really good at languages and I picked it up on a senior class trip to Europe to Budapest and the surrounding countryside. I asked your mom about her hometown of Mucsi and she painted me a beautiful picture of this agrarian village where she grew up for 14 wonderful years. Bottom-line Miles, because I know she's told you this many times, World War II destroyed her hometown, her home, and almost her family too. Fathers and sisters and sons and daughters were being dragged off by the Russians or by the Germans into slave labor or onto the front lines. The town is still barely there, with many of the homes no longer standing, but there is a huge monument near the cemetery with the names of those who never came back. She told me about the knock on her door at midnight, with Russian soldiers telling them they had one hour to grab whatever they could carry and they had to return to Germany because she was an ethnic German and now that the war was over, only Hungarians were allowed to stay. Their family had lived in that farmhouse since 1729. Did you know that? She told me about her older sisters being taken away to work as slave labor in the coal mines. She told me that only she and her mom made that journey to the Allied- occupied part of Germany, what became West Germany. She told me that had it not been for the intervention of one moral Russian captain, the two of them would've been raped and probably killed one night. Then your mom was quiet for a long time. I let her gather herself and then I asked her if she was okay. She said that she dreamt many times that she was a young girl back in her beautiful hometown and on those mornings when she would wake up from that dream, she would always start the day with tears of sadness in her eyes. That's when she and I began to cry together."

I took a deep breath and asked Alison, "What was it you told her to calm her down?"

"I said to her that I had seen the monument in Mucsi on my senior class trip, and that it had brought a somber mood to all of us that day. I told her that the next time she dreamt about her hometown, that she should hold those memories joyfully in her heart. It was okay to wake up to tears, but they needed to change to tears of joy, because those 14 years of wonderful memories could never be stolen from her."

In my mind I thought, this is one of those moments that Billy and I had talked about. How is it that Alison had been to this small town that barely existed anymore? How is it that she's so fluent in Hungarian? How is it that she's wiser than any clergyman I had ever heard speak, consoling my mother?

I wanted to get into it with her right there and then and demand a better explanation for all of these so-called coincidences, but before I broke my silence Alison spoke again.

"Miles, I know your mom has said this to you many, many times, but hearing it from her and her first-hand account moved me to tears, which you know isn't easy to do."

"Your mom said to me, 'There is nothing good about war...nothing.'"

"When your mom said that to me, it seemed to transfer all of her suffering on to me, and it was just too much for me to hold in. The world out of control, with madmen killing what, 60 million people? And for what? Land, money, fame. It's sickening."

"You're right," I said in a hushed tone.

I was relieved that Alison was there for my mom. I realized that whatever coincidences had put Alison in my life, there was some higher intelligence moving around the chess pieces on this board.

"Alison, thanks for being there for my mom." I hugged her as tight as I could and when I was done I looked her right in the eyes and said "I love you, and I'm so incredibly lucky to have found you. Thanks for helping mom with her memories of her hometown. I know that's always been very hard for her to deal with."

"Miles, me being in your life has nothing to do with luck."

We both took a deep breath and then went downstairs and joined my mom, and eventually others, for a big farmhouse post-wedding breakfast.

8. The Sisters

Over the next couple of days, the out-of-town wedding crowd began to leave for home. There were many goodbye scenes. Having my mom and dad meet Alison for the first time was one of the highlights of our wedding weekend. My parents seemed genuinely happy for the two of us. Before they left, my mom did tell Alison again that she had always wanted a daughter, and that now she had one.

It turned out that Michael took my advice and did get to know Jessica a little bit at the wedding, and a little bit more the next day before he left for Long Beach. He told me that they were going to stay in touch. He was really happy with himself that he now actually had a friend who was a girl. By his old definition, that meant a girl he had hit on who wouldn't sleep with him but still liked him enough to talk to him. Now he had a real friend that just so happened to be a girl.

The last two visitors remaining were Jessica and Hope. They had decided to stay for a couple days, because the sisters loved to hang out together and it was great having their mom with them.

That gave me a chance to get to know my new mother-in-law better. Hope was delightful, but still held the heavy burden of losing her beloved husband six years ago in a car crash. She was in her mid-60s now and yes, over the years she had been approached by men to go out on dates, but she had declined them all. Alison told me that her dad, Jack, was the love of her mom's life. She said many times that the years they had spent together could never be matched. In that way, she was content to be alone and happy, which is a powerful human attribute. I had learned a long time ago, that even though I love my family and friends, when I did have time alone, I cherished it and loved it. It's not the way I would choose to live my entire life, but sometimes having the world stop and become quiet was a marvelous feeling.

Soon it was the day before Jessica and Hope were going to leave. We finished lunch and Dana was going to put the kids down for a nap. Billy had a meeting with the corporate guys from the Hendrix Winery in Berkeley, so he was gone until early evening.

Hope told us, "I really feel great. It's been a terrific trip, and with a full stomach and a tired body, I want to take a nap on the couch over there. If you young people want to do something, go ahead. I'll keep my eyes, or should I say ears, on the kids, and deal with them when they wake up, Dana."

"Hey Miles," Jessica said, "Alison told me that Billy had given you a tour of the winery. Do you think you could take us around and show us a few things?"

"Sure," I replied. "I remember a lot of the layout of the place. The problem is the pickup truck is not really conducive to seating four people."

Dana chimed in, "Miles, didn't Billy tell you that we have this fabulous four seat golf cart that he uses for his corporate tours? It's under a tarp in the big barn behind the house. It's really cool. It's electric, so we just charge it for about an hour, and then we can drive it around for about four hours. It's so quiet, being an electric motor, that it really lets you travel around the grounds and appreciate, not only the sights, but the sounds of the California hillsides."

"What do you say Alison, are you in?" I asked.

"Well, I have seen the winery, but I would be glad to go along, even if it's just to critique your docent abilities, Miles," Alison replied.

"Okay, then it's on. Everybody get ready," I said as if I were the captain of the golf cart.

Dana and I went out and uncovered the magnificent golf cart, one that actually held six people, not just four. We plugged it in to the 220-volt charger and went back into the house to change.

An hour later we all assembled at the cart wearing hats, short-sleeved shirts and shorts, with walking shoes. The cart had a roof to shield us from the sun.

Dana said, "Miles you drive. The path starts over there by that pecan tree. That's the route that Billy uses, and we can just follow it around. It should make driving a pretty easy chore. That should leave your mind available for a stimulating and entertaining description of the winery."

They all laughed at me, but I didn't take it personally. I knew they really didn't expect much out of me other than to keep us on the path that Dana had just described-- and not flip the cart over.

"Everybody in?" I asked. No objections were forthcoming, so I said, "Here we go."

Dana had told Hope that we would be gone about an hour and that the kids would probably be waking up shortly before we got back. Hope had plenty of time to get some rest before having to do hand-to-hand combat with the kids. Alison said "Jessica, I saw you were spending an inordinate amount of time talking and dancing with Michael the other night. What was that all about?"

I sensed this could be good, so I kept my mouth shut and listened.

"Yeah, it was an interesting evening, spending time with Michael," Jessica began. "At first, he came over and asked me to dance. He seemed a bit drunk, but because he was the best man at your wedding, I felt obligated to accommodate him. We danced a couple up-tempo numbers that were followed by Color My World, which by the way, I still can't believe they're using that at weddings. Isn't that song from the 60s?"

Dana chirped "Actually it's from 1970 and don't ask me how I know that, but go on."

Jessica continued, "Anyway, I could tell he couldn't really slow dance, so I put my arms around his neck and he put his arms around my waist and we rocked back and forth. The smell of Jack Daniels on his breath was pretty apparent. When we first started to rock back and forth, I thought he was going to tip over, but he steadied up about halfway through."

Alison said "So what did you guys talk about while you were dancing?"

Jessica replied "We didn't talk about anything while we were dancing. About halfway through the song, I noticed that he had this half-crazed look in his eyes, so I politely excused myself, because I didn't want to give Michael a chance to say or do anything that he was going to regret later."

It was interesting that Jessica had sensed that he was indeed, Michael the Masher, and that she had saved him from himself. I couldn't let that go without giving Jessica an atta girl.

"Jessica, I want to thank you for doing that for my friend. He did have a bit too much to drink early on. He is quite the ladies' man, so your intuitions were probably right."

I thought to myself that I was really getting to know the sisters better by being their chauffeur and letting them talk amongst themselves.

Alison added "Just so you know, yes, Michael is a ladies' man, but he is a beautiful person with a great love and passion for life. Miles and I love him like a brother. He's got a way to go on his journey and we hope he completes it and grows up, but this is a tough time for him."

Dana said, "Interesting, I haven't had much of a chance to talk to Michael, but from the little I have talked to him, he seems extremely articulate. It's also hard to ignore that he is 6 foot 3, handsome, with long blonde hair and that classic California surfer look that women love."

Alison couldn't keep herself from chiming in as she looked right at me, "Yeah, I guess he's the extra-large version of what every woman wants!"

They all started laughing. Dana and Jessica were laughing because they hadn't heard that colloquialism before, and I was looking at Alison, because she had just turned the tables on me and had gotten me good.

I said, "That's very funny Alison, maybe you should do 10 minutes of standup at one of the comedy clubs down in Newport Beach some night."

Alison looked at me and smiled. Then she took the middle finger and thumb from her right hand and flicked her middle finger across the tip of my nose. I must say, it hurt. A lot. "Gotcha!" Alison replied. I just wanted it to die there, because I didn't want to be embarrassed by explaining that I used that joke all the time when talking about tall beautiful women.

In trying to move on quickly, I said "So Jessica, how did the rest of the night with Michael go?"

"You know, it's funny. I came back out about 20 minutes later, and we sat down and drank ice water to cool off from the dancing. We spent about 45 minutes talking. It was almost like he had a multiple personality disorder. He was a totally different person that I was talking to than the one that I had danced with earlier in the evening. The vibe he was giving off was just way different—almost human."

I said "Well, I will share this with you ladies. Michael did enjoy meeting all of you and did say how much fun he had dancing and talking with you, Jessica. The three of you are just so in tune with each other. It's hard to sometimes tell you apart. Ya'll seem to have a sense of people's needs, and you give them what they need, at the time they need it." I said that in my best fake Southern accent, as I was trying to be funny. "Why is that, ladies?"

Dana answered, "It's something our father taught us, Miles."

Then all three replied in one robotic, Stepford wives voice "We love everybody. And we understand that everybody might not love us. And that's okay."

I took my foot off the accelerator and came to a slow rolling stop. No one was laughing like people normally do when they accidentally say the same thing at the same time. I turned around so that I could look at all three of them and they were all smiling in the most angelic way.

With a single eyebrow raised and looking right at me, Dana said in her best Southern accent, "Cat got your tongue, Miles?" I think we weirded him out ladies. Sorry, we just love pulling that prank on people whenever we get a chance."

Then they all started laughing at me.

I sensed there was something greater lying beneath Dana's explanation. Of course, I didn't know what it was. Neither Billy nor I could explain any of this stuff that could be dismissed as coincidence or the twilight of the sun rising or setting. Being in the presence of the three of them by myself for the first time, it was as if Alison, Dana and Jessica were special in an inexplicable way.

I joined in the fun and said, "Cat just let go of my tongue. Let's continue with the tour. Please keep all arms and legs inside of the vehicle, ladies, for your safety."

They all laughed and we moved on past the moment. They started to talk about the things that sisters talk about and I kind of just kept my mouth shut and tried to learn as much as I could about Alison's two sisters.

I couldn't stop thinking about what they had all said in unison. I was trying to put them in some sort of category. I was really searching my mind so that I could move on. Then, the craziest memory came back to me.

One night a couple years earlier, when we were sitting around smoking some choice hashish, we started playing one of those head games where everybody had to take a turn at whatever the game required. That night's challenge was to try and come up with an original way of defining how this particular high made us feel like nothing before. Thankfully, I got to go last, so I had some time to think about it. When it was my turn, I said "Close your eyes everybody, and pretend that everything in this room, including all of us, are hovering just a fraction of an inch above the ground, and we never knew it until just now!" A couple of my stoner buddies yelled out "Whoa, that's heavy. I can actually feel it."

I won the contest.

But in thinking about that, it was the only thing that I could come up with that was close to defining these sisters.

All three of them, were so special, they seemed to be hovering just a fraction of an inch above the earth, above me, and above everything and everyone else.

9. What Love Is Not

Three weeks later, Alison and I sat at the kitchen table after cleaning up the dinner dishes. We had insisted that Dana and Billy spend time with their kids.

"So, you're the financial guy in this marriage, Miles. Have you figured out how we are going to finish our college degrees yet?"

"Well, I'm glad you asked me that, because I've been playing with some numbers and I come to the same conclusion every time. We really need to just work for a year. It will create residency for us as California citizens, and that drops our tuitions dramatically and at the same time, increases our savings. That way we don't have to go to school forever or have two million dollars in student loans. I also have some apartment ads that I found in the newspaper, and I want us to look at a couple of them this weekend. I already set up times with the landlords."

It wasn't the greatest news that I could've told Alison.

"Miles, you have a look on your face like you're letting me down. Don't you think I knew that this was going to be a longer journey than we first planned after what happened that night at the park back at Iowa State? That all sounds great! Don't feel like you're letting me down in any way."

Dana and Billy walked into the kitchen, having just put the kids to bed.

"Sorry guys, we didn't mean to eavesdrop on your conversation, but we probably heard the last minute or so because we were cleaning up toys in the living room. We just want to let you know that whatever you decide we're 100 percent behind your decision," Dana said.

Billy chimed in, "Dana and I have been talking about getting to know the two of you over the last few weeks, and we wanted to add another option to your plans. Dana and I are completely happy to have you guys live with us while you're trying to save up money for college and before you move closer to Berkeley. If you guys can just chip in for groceries, this house is big enough for all of us. You don't have to pay to live here, because the corporation wants me on site, so we live here rent- and utility-free."

Dana added, "however, we do understand that you are newlyweds and may want to have your own place. You won't hurt our feelings if you decide to go ahead and take an apartment. Anything you want is fine with us."

Alison and I looked at each other and I'm sure we both had a look of gratitude on our faces for the generous offer that Dana and Billy had made.

I said to them, "That's really terrific. We are so grateful to have that as an option. Alison, why don't we take a look at the apartments this weekend, throw the option of staying here into the mix, and then come up with a decision? What do you think?"

Alison stood up, went over to Billy, gave him a big hug and a kiss on the cheek and said "Thank you for looking out for us." She then embraced Dana and said "Thanks Sis, you are the best."

I got up to follow Alison's lead and shook Billy's hand, thanking him, and then gave Dana a big hug.

That weekend we looked at the apartments that I had scheduled and after we were done, we stopped at a local diner to share a slice of fresh baked peach pie, ice cream, and a cup of coffee. The smell of fresh baking pies in the diner made it a relaxing setting to talk things through.

"So, what do you think, Alison?"

"Well, I think I know what I want to do, but how about this idea?" She reached into her purse and pulled out a notebook and she tore off some paper and handed me a pen.

"Let's both write down our decisions and then exchange them to see if we're thinking the same thing."

I thought that was a great idea, so I nodded and we started writing.

"Okay, let's exchange," I said. We exchanged papers and I told Alison to go first. She opened my paper and read aloud, "Let's stay with Billy and Dana. Your turn," she said. I opened up her paper and I read aloud "Let's go to the parking lot and make love in the back seat of the car, then take the Billy and Dana option." I was smiling so hard and trying not to laugh out loud as I looked up at her. Our eyes met and she was bewitching me. She had taken off her right shoe, and was rubbing her foot up under my pant leg.

"Stop" I whispered, not really meaning it. I saw the waitress catch a glimpse of Alison's foot massage and she just smiled and turned away.

"Okay, okay. You need to get serious," I said to Alison.

We were in agreement. Knowing that, even though we wouldn't have our own place for 6 to 9 months, it would make life a lot easier for us going forward.

Alison then said, "But I do have one more thing I would like to do before we put our noses to the grindstone. Miles, I know everything that's happened over the past few months has been kind of a world-wind romance and marriage. I know we're kind of broke, but I really think we should take a long weekend somewhere close and inexpensive and have a real honeymoon that we can remember, one we can tell our kids about when we tell them about our lives."

I quickly smiled and said "After dealing with all this, Alison, a honeymoon weekend is just the thing we need to clear our heads before we hear the starting gun."

We did some brainstorming and decided to drive up to San Francisco and walk the streets and see the museums, the wharf, the night clubs, the bay, the Golden Gate Bridge, and all the sights.

We ate and then paid our check. As we got to the car, I turned back to look at the diner and could see three waitresses looking out the window. One of them must have overheard me read Alison's note, or read it as she cleaned up our table. They were hoping to see a free show in the backseat of the car. I was sorry to disappoint them.

We went back to the farmhouse and let Dana and Billy know our plans. Dana made a joke that they were really hoping that we stayed. That way, they could have built-in babysitters, knowing that we were broke and they could go out to the movies or dinner whenever they wanted to and leave the kids with us.

The city of San Francisco was incredible and the time spent alone was the same. We both loved walking the streets and discovering the nightlife of a big city. We loved the smell of the nearby ocean. We loved the semi-seedy jazz and blues clubs that were filled with all types of people just enjoying life and each other's company. There were some incredibly talented musicians gigging in these small clubs. All in all, our honeymoon weekend was just what the doctor ordered. We were both very calm and happy as we drove home to West Haven on Monday afternoon.

Over the next couple months, Alison and I, Dana, Billy, and the kids all went about the business of running our lives with a purpose. I went to the local high school and asked to volunteer my time with the basketball program, knowing that it would help my resume down the road. The head coach there was happy to have my help, mostly because he knew I was knowledgeable in the game, but also because he lacked experienced coaches. He had lots of offers from parents to fill those coaching positions, but my presence got him out of that predicament. He taught me my first basketball lesson on being a head coach, and that is to never have parents on the coaching staff unless you absolutely have no choice and there is absolutely no one else to do it. He brought me right up to the varsity, even though he had an assistant. I was younger, therefore I was perfect for that gofer position, since I had all the energy in the world. I was glad to scout games for him. I was glad to break down film for him. I was glad to jump into practice and demonstrate for things that he could no longer demonstrate, because of his age.

As time went by, every once in a while, Billy and I would ask each other the question "Anything?" That meant have you noticed anything about either of the sisters that you can't explain? Neither one of us had witnessed any phenomena of an astounding nature lately.

However, there was one behavioral characteristic of the sisters that neither one of us had ever witnessed before.

There were many times in the evening after dinner, or on a slow Sunday afternoon, when I was sitting on the living room sofa, and Alison and Dana would both come and cuddle up under my arms, pulling their feet up under their body, and saying something like "we're cold, warm us up," or "snuggle with us."

Dana and Alison must've done it a dozen times with me, and I walked in many times to find Alison and Dana snuggling with Billy. It wasn't sexual in any way... it was just them showing genuine affection to us. Sometimes, if the kids were still up, I would find Dana on one side of me and the two kids on the other side of me, curling up on the sofa.

Then, they started to cuddle up to each other's husbands. If Dana was cold, and I was on the sofa, she was up under my arm and pulling her feet up under herself and just relaxing. Remarkably, it made my own level of relaxation increase.

One day, Billy and I did talk about it and we were in agreement that it was okay with both of us, even though it seemed unusual. When we asked Alison and Dana about it, they said that this is how they were brought up in a household of three sisters, a mom and a dad. Everybody wanted to sit next to dad and have him put his big arm around them. So, it became common practice as they grew up. Now Dana and Alison wanted it to continue, because it was a great example for the children as well as being an expression of love. We did love each other's wives as sisters and agreed that we should just accept it as something that made them who they were.

I finally heard from Michael. He was coming to visit for the weekend. He would be coming in late Wednesday night and would be leaving early Sunday to go back to Long Beach. He had some good traffic on Wednesday and rolled in just after dinner. We made sure that he was fed and we drank wine till about 11 when all the working stiffs had to go to bed. He was doing fine and both of us were looking forward to spending the weekend together.

We all had a blast Thursday night and were looking forward to staying up late on the weekend with Michael, as he was such a ball of energy. Unfortunately, I had to go scout a game on Friday night about an hour's drive away. I told Michael that he had driven far enough to visit us and that I didn't want him to feel obligated to come with me to scout the game. If he wanted to just stay with Alison and Billy and Dana, that was cool with me. I told everyone that I should be back before midnight.

On Friday afternoon I left about 4:30 to drive to my scouting assignment. We were going to play one of the top teams in the area and they were facing a formidable opponent that night. When you scout games, you sometimes hope for a blowout so you can leave early, because the outcome of the game has been decided. However, this game went into two overtimes and then I had to drop off my notes at the gym so that Coach would have them first thing in the morning. I didn't get home until 12:45. The house was still and I made myself a quick sandwich and headed upstairs to climb into bed with Alison and rest up for the weekend.

Morning light came and I stayed in bed an extra hour. When I woke up, I got dressed and went down to the kitchen for breakfast. The kids were playing outside and Dana was working in her herb garden, keeping an eye on them. Billy was at the warehouse where they kept the wine, because he liked to perform his acidity checks on the product on Saturday morning when no one was around to harass him.

I kissed Alison good morning and grabbed some coffee and some freshly baked blueberry muffins whose wonderful aroma filled the kitchen. As I came to my full senses, I turned to Alison and said, "Michael still sleeping in? Boy, what did you do, make him run hundred-yard dashes? I went to bed later than everyone else and I'm up."

With that, Alison sat down across from me and said "Michael left last night."

I was astonished and the first thought that came to my mind was that he had gotten a call from home with some family emergency, so I asked Alison if that's what happened.

"No Miles, don't worry about Michael's family, they are all fine. I need to tell you what happened last night. "

"Okay."

"Well, Billy was tired, so he told Dana and Michael and I that he would put the kids to bed, because he wanted to go to bed right afterwards. He said we should go to a movie or something. So, we went and saw a movie at the Arcadia 10 and we got home about 10. Michael turned on the television to check out the sports news of the day and the three of us split a bottle of wine in the living room. Well, it was a bit chilly and Dana and I were cold...and you know us...we like to snuggle."

I felt frozen in place and fully expected to hear how the night imploded.

I said "Go on..."

"Well, Michael obliged us and put his arms around us and he watched television as Dana and I just relaxed. About 30 minutes later, Dana heard Willie upstairs, so she left the couch and went upstairs to take care of Willie before he could wake up Billy.

"About a minute after they left, Michael turned to me and said, 'Alison, you know you are just so beautiful.' I said 'Thank you' and continued to just sit there with him watching television. He leaned over and kissed me on the lips for about three seconds. Then he said, 'You know Alison, I love you.'"

"I told him that we all loved him too and went back to watching television. About a minute later, his hands started to move into places where they shouldn't. I grabbed both of his wrists and leaned backwards and said to him, 'What are you doing Michael?'"

He said, 'I thought you wanted me to do that, I mean you're so soft and warm and beautiful and close...you know.'"

"I took his two wrists as I pulled away from him and placed them on his knees. I looked him right in the eye and said, 'Just because Billy and Dana and Miles and I love you, it doesn't mean we want to have sex with you.'"

By this point I was furious. But I really didn't know who to be furious at. I mean, Michael is Michael. That's who he is and that's what he does. He's a man-whore, although some would say that's redundant. Was it Alison and Dana's fault for snuggling up to him and showing him that they loved him? Was it Billy and my fault for letting this behavior become standard operating procedure in our home?

I sternly said "Go on..."

"Well, Michael said to me, 'That's what love is. When you really love someone, you make love to them. You make love with them. You know what I mean.' So, I told him, 'Michael your ideas about love and what love really is, are about 180 degrees apart. You can love someone, you can love everyone, and it means that you would do anything to protect them, including lay down your own life for them, if need be. Just because Dana and I snuggle up to you, it doesn't mean we want to have your baby. You have a long way to go until you understand unconditional love.'"

"He didn't say anything for about a minute and then he got up and excused himself and went upstairs to his room. I went into the kitchen to make myself some tea before going to bed when I heard his car start. I ran to the front porch. He was backing out of his parking spot. I ran over to his car and told him that everything was okay and that he didn't have to leave.

"He said to me, 'Alison, now I fucked up the only genuine friendships that I ever had, and I really can't face Miles when he gets home.' With that, he put his car into drive and started to pull away. As he turned from the driveway onto the road, I yelled at him, 'Maybe you should start by getting a dog!'"

"I repeated, 'Maybe you should start by getting a dog!'"

I stayed silent and thought about the absurdity of that statement, when in fact, it was probably the exact thing that Michael needed to do. I have grown up with dogs, and Billy and Dana had dogs, and quite frankly, that's probably where we all learned about unconditional love. Because when you come home, no matter how bad you feel, your dog loves you, unconditionally. I shook my head and started to chuckle.

Alison said, "Miles, you know I love you and there was no way I was coming on to him. You know I love Michael, but Dana and I talked about it and we purposely did that for his own growth. He needed to go through that. I'm asking as your wife, please forgive him, because you know that all three of us knew how he would react to that situation. Just give him a couple days and then reach out to him. You'll be calmer by then."

She got up from the table and sat right next to me, put her arm around me, and told me "I'm really sorry if any of this has hurt you, but please know that we had to do this to change the trajectory of Michael's life. If you love him, you'll forgive him."

In my mind, I thought that even though this wasn't some sort of crazy unexplained magic, that it was the damnedest thing I had ever heard.

At that point, Dana came in the kitchen from outside and said, "So, did you tell him?"

"Yeah, I just got done telling him Dana," Alison said.

Dana said "You have to forgive Michael. We did this on purpose for his own good. You have to realize Miles, that the world is what's around you. Those are the people that we can help."

I still sat there saying nothing. Then, it just settled in to me that these sisters were trying to change the world one person at a time if they had to.

I finally looked up at them and said "So, what kind of dog do you think Michael should get?"

10. The Game

All day Saturday I was plagued by the drama from the night before. I loved Alison like I had never loved anyone before, so I couldn't get the picture of her cuddling with Michael on the sofa out of my mind.

Three times Alison came over and said that she could sense it was bothering me. She assured me that she and Dana had planned this scenario for Michael's own good. Each time, she insisted that there was nothing going on between them.

After dinner I was sitting alone on the front porch when Dana sat down on the rocking chair next to mine.

"How's it going?" she asked me.

"It's going," I replied.

"Miles, I know it's been impossible for you to let this go. It's going to take time for you to accept that what Alison and I did was in your friend's best interest. Maybe it helps if I tell you that it was Alison that was supposed to excuse herself, to leave me alone with Michael. But when Willie started crying upstairs, we had to play the hand we were dealt. Give it a couple days. Your friend is going to be much better because of what he went through. And you'll be much better if you can find it in your heart to forgive him and forgive Alison and me."

I was looking down while Dana was talking. Finally, I sat up, clenched my hands behind my head, took a deep breath, and exhaled. I got up from my chair, walked to the porch railing and looked out on the darkening landscape.

Dana got up, walked over to me and put her arm around my waist. I naturally put my arm around her shoulder and pulled her in close. Through all of this I was learning more and more about myself and more and more about what love really was. I hugged Dana. We started swaying back and forth.

"This doesn't mean that I want you to have my baby," I said to Dana jokingly.

We both laughed. When we broke our embrace, Dana grabbed my hand and said, "Let's go back in the house and find everybody else."

So that's what we did.

From that moment on, I forgave Michael and I understood what Dana and Alison had done for him.

I called Michael on Sunday night and was glad he was home to answer the phone. I just let him talk. I knew he needed to get it off his chest and that I just needed to be a good listener. He apologized profusely for misinterpreting Alison's tenderness towards him. He said that on the ride home he had taken stock of his love life and saw what an incredible sham it had been. He said he was immensely jealous of what Billy and I had, but he realized he wasn't anywhere near ready for a real relationship. He knew he had some growing up to do.

When he was done talking, there was silence for a bit.

"I forgive you for what happened Michael. I can't tell you how happy I am for you that you've come to some serious realizations about how you're living your life. Don't worry, we are still friends exactly as we were before. Nothing has changed. Alison and Dana are very affectionate people, and sometimes others misunderstand their affection. Even I am still getting used to it Michael. Take whatever time you need to get your feet back on the ground. I'll be waiting for your call when you're ready to come back up here for a long weekend. and I can't wait for that to happen. In the meantime, if you find a special someone that you want to bring along, please feel free to invite her," I said.

And with that we both agreed we were good.

Monday arrived and everyone had to get back to the real world. With each day that passed, things became more and more normal. By Friday I had accepted everything that happened as being for the best.

A few weeks later, I got a call from Michael. He wanted to come up the weekend after my basketball season was finished.

As the weekend approached, Michael called and said, that while he was dating a new girl, it was too early in their relationship for a getaway weekend. I told him there was plenty of room for them to sleep in separate rooms, but he didn't want to bring a total stranger into the mix. He wanted to use the weekend to get everything back to normal, so that was our plan.

Michael arrived on a Friday, he and was already hanging out with Dana, Billy and the kids by the time Alison and I came home from work. There were hugs all around and no mention of what happened the last time he was here. Everyone seemed to have made a pact to leave that night behind.

Friday night we all told stories, catching up on what was going on in our lives. We made plans for a cookout Saturday night and everybody went to bed a little early after a long week.

Saturday night came upon us quickly enough. Michael and I handled the grill and cooked up hamburgers, brats, and Italian sausages, corn on the cob and portobello mushrooms. The ladies made a big batch of their mom's signature potato salad, and baked a decadent chocolate cake for dessert, to be served with vanilla ice cream. Billy was feeling guilty that all he provided was the wine, but Dana told him that it was his job to clean up afterwards and not to try to sneak out and leave it until tomorrow.

Billy had mounted outdoor speakers on the back of the house and was spinning quite the eclectic mix of music, from Frank Sinatra to the Beatles to Steely Dan to Stevie Wonder to the Doobie Brothers. The back yard had an enormous fire pit and could accommodate 15 to 20 people, and Billy had built a big pile of firewood, logs that were now just waiting to be lit.

When dinner was over, we let Billy think he had to clean up by himself. Then, about 10 minutes later, we all pitched in. When it was done, Billy lit the fire and the kids roasted marshmallows for an hour before they went to bed. We sat around the fire pit with our favorite wines, though some of us had already moved on to water. We were just talking, letting the conversation go wherever it took us.

Then Michael said "Hey Miles, why don't we play your game? That's always a lot of fun."

I knew just what he meant. It was an intellectual game that I liked to challenge people with, but I didn't know if I wanted to play it that night, because it sometimes made the conversation get a bit heavy.

"I've heard about this game," Alison said. "I know you played it with the guys in your apartment, but never when any of us ladies were around. Tell me again, what are the rules?"

"You're sure you want to do this?" I asked.

Both Alison and Michael nodded yes.

"Okay, here's the rules. We take turns going around the circle. When it's your turn, you state a fact that each of us has to accept with absolute certitude. It can't be questioned. It must be accepted and digested. Then we go around the circle, and each one of us has to say whether or not this new fact would change the way they live their lives, and if so, in what way."

"Yikes," said Billy. "Where did you come up with this game? I may have already had too much wine."

Dana said, "Yes, absolutely, let's play. Does anybody need anything before we start?"

No one said a word and they all looked at me.

"Okay, here we go," I said. "Michael, because you played this game before, you go first."

Michael looked down at the ground and played with a stick, drawing pictures in the dirt like a little kid. Evidently it helped him think.

"Okay, how about this? Dolphins are smarter than human beings."

A moment of silence followed.

I asked "So does anyone here think their life would change if dolphins are smarter than humans? To make this go faster, raise your hand if your life would not change. If you don't raise your hand, then state how your life would change."

Dana, Alison, and I raised our hands.

Alison said, "Geez Michael, you know we've met enough knuckleheads to know that's probably already true for a lot of humans."

We all laughed.

Billy, being the scientist, had the floor. "If dolphins were smarter than humans, then we should be reaching out to them to establish a system of communication, a language to bridge the communication barrier. We can learn so much from them and further enhance both human and aquatic life on the planet. Clearly, we would need to make sure that these crazy fishermen, who are accidentally or purposely killing dolphins, need to be stopped at all cost. I don't think I could sleep at night if I didn't work on that cause."

"I just love idealists. Great answer Billy," Michael said. "Okay Miles, you're next."

I went right to one of my go-to questions.

"There is a heaven and there is a hell. Discuss."

Alison, Dana, and I raised our hands indicating that our lives wouldn't change in any way. I called on Michael to explain his thoughts.

"Well, I'm never been much of a spiritual person. I know I can't undo the things that I've done, especially when it comes to hurting people's feelings and taking advantage of them. I definitely would start to fly a straighter path from here forward."

Then Michael started to choke up. He stopped speaking. I never thought this silly game could upset him. Besides, Michael had heard this one before. He was clearly a changing man.

Alison said "Michael, all those people that you think you've hurt, I am speaking for them now, they forgive you."

Then Dana said "Michael, you just need to forgive yourself and move on, and don't make the same mistakes again."

The tension seemed to make the fire brighter and hotter. Michael started shaking his head nodding it in a yes, yes, yes, manner and he looked up at them and said "Thanks ladies, thanks for helping me through that."

Again, there was silence.

Michael said "OK Billy, you didn't raise your hand. What have you got to say?"

"I'm changing my answer and I wouldn't change anything about my life," Billy said.

"Come on you agnostic," said Dana. "You're just trying to dodge the bullet now."

I jumped in and said "as Commissioner of this game, I rule that people are allowed to change their votes. However, people who change their votes must go next in their statements. So, Billy what's your statement?"

Billy had wiggled out of that one, with my help.

"Does everybody see the brightest star over that third hill on the right?" Billy asked. We all indicated that we did. Billy said "There are intelligent aliens living on a planet around that star."

Once again Alison and Dana raised their hands, but Michael and I did not. I went first.

"Well it would seem to me that we need to make every effort possible to contact them or travel to their planet. We need to let them know that we are here. It also toys with the concepts of creation here on earth, being alone in the universe etc. etc. I don't know Michael, what about you?"

"Yeah, that would freak me out a little, knowing that it was fact that there were aliens living on a planet going around that star. It would make the earth seem a lot smaller to me right away, because I just haven't thought that much about these kinds of things. I guess I've always lived my life as if the earth was the center of the universe, which I know isn't true."

Dana chimed in "Well, about 500 years ago, all of the great scientists on earth were in agreement that the earth was the center of the universe, along with it being flat. Isn't that right, Billy?"

"Is she allowed to speak, Miles?" Billy asked. "After all, she raised her hand."

I could see there was some tension growing between Dana and Billy and so I said, "As Commissioner, yes, she can speak, but she has to keep this civil."

I said to Dana "Why did you raise your hand that it wouldn't make any difference in your life knowing for certain there are aliens living on a planet around that star?"

"Because that star and the planets around it are so far away, that no one from there, and no one from here, could ever communicate or visit each other. They have their world to worry about and we have ours."

It was a blockbuster of a statement and I knew that this game, which was supposed to be fun, had gotten way too serious.

I looked at Billy and I could see steam coming out of his ears. There was an uncomfortable silence around the fire.

Billy broke the silence when he said, "I think I'll check on the kids. Does anyone want something from the house?"

Michael, being unaware of the tension, said "Yeah Billy, bring me a slice of that cake with some ice cream. That would be great."

With that, Billy walked away.

"Well, I guess the game is over," Michael said.

I looked at Alison and our eyes met as if to say I feel really bad about whatever is going on between Dana and Billy.

After a minute of everyone silently staring into the fire, Michael, asked "Dana, didn't you major in physics?"

Dana said "yes, I have a master's degree in physics. But astrophysics is part of my degree."

Michael continued "So how far away is that star?"

"About 500 to 1,000 light years away," Dana replied.

Alison and I just sat back and listened.

"So, how long would it take to get there?"

"Since no one's invented anything that can travel at the speed of light, I can only use the fastest object that we have built, which is a satellite. It would take that satellite over 800 million years to get there."

Dana abruptly got up and said she was going into the house to find Billy. It finally hit me that whatever Dana and Billy were going to talk about was tied to Dana's request that we never bring up why Billy walked away from finishing his PhD in astrophysics. I knew that the discussion tonight had hit on that nerve in their relationship. Knowing Dana, I expected that she would smooth things over and be back shortly with chocolate cake and ice cream.

Michael looked up at Alison and me and said "Wow, that's a long time. Do those satellites have first-class sections?" He was playing the fool on purpose to cut the tension. He loved doing that and it did make people feel at ease in these situations.

Dana and Billy did return with ice cream and cake for Michael and we sat around for another half hour just talking about music and books and movies and sports. The night then wound up and we all headed back to the house and to our bedrooms.

Alison was already in bed, sitting against the headboard, waiting for me to join her. As my head popped through the Chicago Bulls t-shirt that I often slept in, I realized that the view right outside of our window was of Billy with a garden hose, putting out the bonfire.

A few seconds later I saw Dana walk out to join Billy.

I turned off the light switch in our bedroom and walked slowly across the room as the starlight came through our window. I came to a stop and stood by the window for a few more minutes, even though I could not hear what was being said between Dana and Billy.

As I spied, Dana reached her hands gently around Billy's face and Billy grabbed Dana around the waist and started to kiss her. And then it happened. The stars in the night were in Dana's hair. The kiss continued, and now the stars were also in Billy's hair. As the kiss continued, their silhouettes disappeared into the night sky. They became totally engulfed in the starry backdrop.

I was in awe. I was completely mute, unable to talk. I rubbed my eyes with my hands and as I did, I saw the two shadowy figures return to the earthly realm, beside the bonfire, which was now almost completely out.

I looked over at Alison and saw that she had lay down facing away from the window and was already asleep. What did I just see? Did Billy see it? Did Billy feel it? It was very late and I watched as Dana and Billy walked to the house. I knew that tonight was not the time to grab Billy, after what they had been through for the last hour. I had a hard time falling asleep, as I was anticipating my talk with him tomorrow.

But when the morning came, and he and I had that talk, Billy had no idea what I had seen. All he could tell me was that sometimes he and Dana had intense moments like the one around the bonfire. They always talked it through and it ended in moments of wonderful romance. He told me that being with Dana was a truly magical experience to him, like nothing he had ever experienced with any other woman. He sounded just like me talking about Alison.

But now — I had seen the magic.

11. *Mozart and the Monkey*

Afterwards, Billy did talk to Dana about what I had seen from my window. But in typical Dana fashion, she told Billy "It was dark, there were no lights on, you were dousing that huge bonfire with water and embers were floating up into the sky. So, what do you think is more likely, that we vanished and came back, or that Miles just lost sight of us for a few moments?"

Game, set and match to Dana. There was just enough ambiguity to make Billy drop his inquiry.

Life went back to normal for the next six weeks or so. One night around the dinner table Billy told us that his friend Zach, who was working towards his PhD at Berkeley, had invited him and Dana to a Saturday night dinner and Mozart concert, which involved rubbing elbows with other PhDs.

Dana was really excited, because she had vocal training in classical music and was our resident expert on that subject. Billy asked Alison and me if we would mind babysitting and of course, we agreed.

The morning of the concert, Billy got an early morning call from Zach saying his wife and one of his kids had the flu. Zach knew how much Dana and Billy were looking forward to the evening, so he insisted that they attend and that they should invite Alison and me to come along to fill their spot.

Alison said "Of course we want to come, but we need to find a babysitter." Dana made a few quick calls and booked a babysitter for the evening and the night was set.

Hors d'oeuvres were at 5:30, followed by dinner at 6 and music at 7:30. Thankfully, it wasn't black-tie, so there was no reason to rent any tuxedoes. But it was coat and tie and dresses.

Alison and Dana looked devastating in their dresses. They had taken turns putting each other's hair up. This was an entirely different look for them and I told them both they were gorgeous from head to toe.

We made it to our table on time and Billy introduced us to Zach's boss and mentor, Dr. Norman Carson, and he introduced us to his wife, Jane. Then he introduced us to his colleague, Dr. James Hurt, and his wife, Mary, along with his PhD intern Jeff and his fiancé, Zoe.

Thankfully, the remarks that began the evening were short, lasting less than ten minutes, as the night was designed to enjoy the company and the music. The chemistry at our table seemed fine, but I did notice that Dr. Carson and Dr. Hurt seemed to be conversationally isolated from the rest of us until Dana interrupted them.

"Dr. Hurt, I couldn't help but overhear you talking to Dr. Carson about Darwin. I just love the story of his life and what a thrill it must have been for him to spend time on the Galapagos Islands back in his day."

As if slightly annoyed by her comment, Dr. Hurt replied "It's Dana, right?"

"Yes, it is Doc," Dana said, giving it right back to him, as if they were in a Bugs Bunny cartoon.

"Well, I was just filling Dr. Carson in on what our master's degree students were up to this semester."

"This is really a chance of a lifetime for me, to talk a couple of PhDs in biology. I've always wanted to know what you say to people when they ask you if humans came from monkeys," Dana said.

Dr. Hurt and Dr. Carson both chuckled.

Dr. Carson chimed in, "Yes I would expect that to be the standard question of the uneducated, isn't it Dr. Hurt?"

Dana jumped in again, saying "I'm sorry, I must not have asked my question clearly. I did not mean to be derogatory or to generalize about a group of people as being uneducated."

Dr. Hurt and Dr. Carson were still smiling and gently laughing, but Dana had created the tension that only she could, when dealing with the ill-mannered.

Dana continued "Should I take your good humor to mean that you tell these people that we are descendants of apes and monkeys? And I'll bet you that the next question you usually get from people is, if we descended from monkeys, then why are there still monkeys?"

Now Alison jumped in and I finally got the sense that the two of them were up to something mischievous.

"Yes, why is that? It seems to be the reasonable next question," Alison asked, playing the fool.

I folded my arms across my chest because of the tension that was rising at our table. I didn't know where this would go next.

Dana said "You know Alison, it's not entirely true that we are direct descendants of apes and monkeys." Dana had changed her speech pattern from asking a question to teaching a lesson.

Dana continued "If I remember my Darwin and his friends correctly, we did not in fact come directly from apes. What's generally accepted is that both ape and man come from a common ancestor, an extinct ancestor. In fact, while there is worldwide agreement in the scientific community that my statement is true, we have no evidence of this extinct ancestor, which some refer to as the Missing Link. Am I correct?"

The laughing had stopped and Dr. Carson and Dr. Hurt looked at each other for a moment. The uneasiness at our table was like being at a family dinner where one of the kids just talked back to their father and we were awaiting his response.

Dr. Carson said "Where did you find this one Billy? She certainly is a keeper. Dana, I think you've managed to do something that I've never been able to do, and that is render my colleague Dr. Hurt speechless."

We all chuckled to break the tension.

"If I didn't know better," said Dr. Hurt, "I would swear you two sisters have practiced this in advance. But I know that by sharing dinner with you tonight, you were not raised to be this treacherous, were you?"

Dana and Alison looked at each other and Dana winked, and just like the silly Stepford wives they love to imitate, they replied in unison, "No, we would not be treacherous." And the chuckles at our table grew to genuine laughter.

Dana took the floor again, saying "After all, with the amount of genetic tinkering over the millennia that it would take to change an ape into a human, it's just as likely that you could make a human out of dirt," driving the final nail in her argument.

"Yes, yes. My smart and lovely Dana," Dr. Carson said. "But that's enough shop talk for the night. You are testing all the agnostics and atheists' convictions at this table, and tonight was meant for merriment and Mozart."

Dana laughed and said, "Of course you're right. I apologize if my discussion made anyone uncomfortable."

Dana continued, saying "I read the program for tonight and I am familiar with almost all the Mozart pieces that will be performed. I would leave everyone with this thought. I find Mozart's music to be divine in nature, and to quote the so-called uneducated, I don't think any of you will think that Mozart came from a monkey, once we hear his music performed."

Everyone seemed to sigh in relief and Alison got up and said "Ladies, I'm going to freshen up, if anyone would like to join me."

With that, dinner was over and we found our seats in the beautiful auditorium and sat back to listen to the two-hour program.

I wasn't much of a classical music buff, but Alison knew quite a bit because she had paid careful attention to what Dana had learned in her training.

The program opened with the overture from the *Marriage of Figaro*. I was pleasantly surprised that I recognized many of the melodies and even more appreciative of hearing it played so beautifully by a full orchestra. It was a special treat for me. The evening rolled along and the last piece before the intermission was Mozart's *String Quartet in C*. I was swept away by the intricacy and the simplicity that went on simultaneously and I remembered Dana's statement that this music was as close to the divine as music could be.

After the applause, a 15-minute intermission was announced, and we made our way into the lobby to stretch our legs, and for some of us, to have one more drink.

Our group of ten stayed together, talking leisurely as the intermission went on. Dr. Carson made his way over to Dana and Billy and said loud enough so that the rest of us could hear it, "It was beautiful music Dana, just as you promised, but I do find it funny that you compared it to something divine. And yes, I am an atheist, but I'm not an evangelical atheist, so don't be afraid, I won't try to convert you."

Dana replied "No offense taken, my atheist doctor friend. But please, let me have one more chance to convince you about the divinity of Mozart's music. In the next half, there will be a soprano solo from Mozart's Mass in C minor, called *Et Incarnatus Est*. It is an extremely beautiful and extremely difficult piece to perform. That it's even on this program tells me they have a virtuoso soprano who wants to take this on. I would ask that, during this piece, everyone think about the person they love the most. Then we'll talk after the performance.

"And as for your lesson in what's funny, Dr. Carson, I'm glad to help you with that as well," Dana said as she snuggled up and put her left arm around him. Then all of a sudden Dana had a pair of scissors in her right hand, which was now in front of Dr. Carson, and she cut his tie off just below the knot. We all started to laugh, unencumbered by the suits, ties and dresses all around us. I'm sure we made quite the spectacle.

Dr. Carson stood there red-faced as Dana picked up his tie from the floor and handed it to him.

His wife and Dana put their arms around his neck, and Dana poked her finger into his sizable gut, until even he started to laugh.

"I'm sorry, Dr. Carson, but my father made us huge Marx Brothers fans and Harpo was my favorite. I always keep a pair of scissors with me when hijinks are required. Besides, that tie you were wearing was pretty ugly and had seen a better day, wouldn't you say, Jane?"

"Dana, I've been trying to get him to throw that tie away for years. Not only is that the funniest thing I've seen in a long time, but it's the most practical. You should be thanking this young lady, Professor!"

As outrageous and fun as that moment was, we all knew that it couldn't last, and we gathered up our things and went back into the auditorium.

When the lovely young soprano sang *Et Incarnatus Est*, I did what Dana had asked, and I thought about Alison. As the song went on, I understood what Dana was talking about. The song was mainly the soprano's voice, with flutes and clarinets interwoven like a tapestry. I leaned over to Alison and was about to tell her how right Dana had been, when out of the corner of my eye I saw Dr. Carson fighting off tears. I kept my mouth shut, just to watch. Now Jane had noticed, and she grabbed into her purse and handed him a tissue. She put her hand on his forearm and squeezed. He looked at her, and maybe for the first time in a long time, their eyes met, and then something wonderful happened. They sat hand-in-hand for the rest of the performance. Every once in a while, I would spy at him. He looked like an entirely different person. He was much more at ease and very much enjoying the closeness he felt with his wife.

That performance received a standing ovation. Shortly after the program ended, we all made our way out of the auditorium and our group got together to say our goodbyes. I saw Dana say goodbye to everyone else first and leave Dr. Carson for last.

In her way, Dana grabbed the big fella and gave him a hug and a kiss on the cheek and pulled away still holding his arms and said to him, "It was so nice to meet you Dr. Carson. I really love you and your delightful wife Jane, and I hope we have made some new friends tonight."

He hugged her again, rubbing her back, as if she were his daughter.

On the way home, Billy and I both recognized there was a giant elephant in the car with us.

I broke the silence.

"So, ladies, the evening was a blast and your shenanigans just added to the entertainment. However, I have to ask you a question. Was the point of all that to get Dr. Carson to believe in God?"

Dana turned around from the front passenger seat so that she and Alison were both looking at me. Then Alison said "No Miles, we just wanted Dr. Carson, and everyone there, to believe in love."

Dana chimed in "Yeah, once a person believes in real love, believing in something that's greater than yourself comes easy."

And the magic of these sisters took its curtain call for the evening.

Part Two

1. Tommy

I snapped up into a sitting position in my bed and my heart was pounding out of my chest. I had only been asleep for about an hour.

Alison turned to me, put her hand on my shoulder and said, "Miles, are you okay? Was it that same dream again?"

It was a dream, but this wasn't a nightmare.

I had once described it to Alison as an overwhelming feeling of dread. In my dreams I get this feeling that I knew about someone who died, and that no one else knew about. It was like a secret I couldn't remember. A secret that something horrible had happened once, and that I alone knew about it, but I can never remember what it was.

Only once did the dream include one of my friends, John. That night when I was awoken by the dream, I was sure that he knew about it. So, in the middle of the night, I called and told him the story. All he could do was laugh at me and tell me I was insane, that it was just a nightmare. He said we did not know about something horrible or some dead body that no one else knew about. Then he accused me of pulling a practical joke on him, like I used to do back in high school and college days. He ended the call by saying, "Miles, you're an idiot, go back to bed, I'm not going to fall for this." And so I was sure that it was just coincidental that John had been in my dream that night.

This time, I rubbed my face, turned to Alison and said "Yeah, it was that awful feeling of dread again. I'm so sorry I woke you up. Go back to sleep. I'm going to get a drink of water and I'll be back in a couple minutes." Alison and I had been married 15 years and I had this dream probably once or twice a year, although I never did a count on it.

We were living in Woodstock, Illinois, a distant northwestern suburb of Chicago. I had been teaching English and coaching boys basketball for seven years at Abraham Lincoln High School, the last four as head coach after three years as a varsity assistant. Alison was working part-time in special education at Woodstock Middle School, and together we were raising our three daughters, Jennifer, Maggie, and Laura.

We had a three-bedroom home in a modest subdivision on the edge of town. Downtown Woodstock was very old and was centered around a traditional Town Square with a good-sized park, one that featured a huge gazebo where you could put a blanket on the lush green grass on a summer night and listen to musicians filling the Midwestern evening with beautiful sounds.

I went back to bed and Alison cuddled up next to me and held me and said, "It's okay, Miles. It's okay. I'm here. Just go to sleep and put that feeling out of your mind."

That was all I needed to hear, and in just a few minutes, I calmed down and fell asleep.

It was Christmas break and school was closed, but we were playing in a terrific Christmas basketball tournament in Vienna. It was a small town, but the gym could hold 2,000 people and I swear everyone in town came to at least one of the games, because it was always packed. The tournament featured small and medium-sized schools, and the competition was very good for a school our size. We couldn't really compete with the larger schools closer to Chicago, though I made sure we played a handful of them every year so our kids understood the level of play that high school players could achieve.

We had a late afternoon game after qualifying for the quarterfinals. We were going to play a team that I considered to be a 10-point underdog to us, but we always had problems with teams, like them, that played zone defense. In high school, you can never take anything for granted. Once the game got underway, the gym was about two thirds full, which was pretty good for a late afternoon game, as the basketball-savvy fans from Vienna came to cheer for everyone who played hard.

I had a young team and the only senior starter was Tommy Kramer. Tommy was almost 6'6" but there was nothing on the basketball court he couldn't do. I made him my point guard, captain, and leader of a team of mostly sophomores and juniors. Tommy was one of the few African American kids in Woodstock and came from a family of four—Tommy, his brother, Danny, and their parents. He was incredibly well-read and articulate and struck me as a Renaissance man because he could converse knowledgeably with adults on a wide variety of topics. I trusted his opinions as much as I trusted my own or those of my assistant coaches. I knew that he and his family were devout Christians and when my spiritual batteries were low, I could call on him to lead our team prayer. His prayers were humble and giving, a trait not found so easily in the teenagers of our time. By the middle of the game's third quarter I saw that we just couldn't shake our opponent. The lead we held wobbled between four and eight points and we should have had a more comfortable margin by then, but we just couldn't crack their zone defense. It was very rare for me to be angry with my team during a game, because I believed that a team takes on the personality of its coach. If I were calm and confident during games, especially close games, my team would play accordingly.

Normally, practice was the time when I might show anger, but during this game, I felt angry.

It was standard procedure that when I called a timeout, the coaches would stand out on the floor and talk first, and then I would address the players, who were sitting on the bench, drinking water, and relaxing. My assistant and I went out on the court and I took my anger out with him there, because I didn't want the players to hear our emotional explosion.

"Did we not go over dribble penetration into the gaps?"

"Did we not go over screening the zone and hitting the skip pass?"

"Did we not go over moving the ball from side to side at least twice and making their defense move?"

"Did we not go over the post player positioning of short corner and mid-post?"

"Do we not go over the post players catching and facing the basket?"

"What the heck is wrong with these guys?"

I could see my assistant, Gary, absolutely knew that I was not mad at him, but that I was just venting. Then, I was surprised to see Tommy standing on my other side. He put his hand on my shoulder and said, "Coach, we went over all those things, and I get it because I've been with you for three years. But these young guys really don't get it completely. You need to figure out a way to explain it to them better—to simplify it."

Then he turned and walked to the bench, sat down and got a drink of water.

I looked at Gary and I asked him, "Gary, you agree with Tommy?"

Gary said, "Yeah, but I don't have the words to give you to make this clearer and simpler. So good luck coach, you know I'm with you —win or tie."

"Very funny," I said.

I slowly walked to the bench where the five players that were in the game were sitting, not knowing what I was going to say, but confident that I could come up with something by the time I went to one knee. As my knee hit the floor, I started by looking at the players sitting in front of me. Then, I turned up the volume on my voice and said, "Everyone give me your eyes and ears right now!"

I had gotten their attention. And with that I gave one of my greatest timeout talks of my career.

"We should be up by 15 by now, but give them credit, they've been playing hard. We really haven't been doing a great job with our zone offense. At the suggestion of your captain, Tommy, I'm going to try and make our zone offense simple for you."

"Just go where they aren't. Got it?"

It took a few moments, but I saw the light bulbs going off over kid's heads. I didn't say anything more. I stood up to break the huddle with everyone's hands touching in the center of the team circle. However, instead of usual, "one, two, three, Lincoln," I maintained eye contact with as many players as possible and said in my calmest voice, "here we go."

I don't know if it was my coaching, or if the other team had just gone as far as their talent would take them, but we took the game over from that point and won by 17. The locker room was a joyful one and I could tell the kids were happy, because they finally understood the fundamentals we had gone over in practice and used them during a game.

As usual, Coach Gary and I stayed to scout the next game, because we would be playing the winners in the semifinals. However, both Gary and I knew that undefeated Charleston Benedictine, with their five senior starters, would probably blow their opponent out of the gym. I considered them to be about 10 points better than us. Just as we thought, they had a 20-point lead by halftime and Gary and I left early, because we knew what our game plan had to be: to slow the game down and keep the score in the 40s. We both wanted to get home because we had young families and wives who could use our help. Alison and I got the girls to bed pretty early. I was tired and went to bed before Alison. Some time after I fell asleep the phone rang and I heard Alison pick it up. I was still in a half-dream state when she came in to the bedroom and handed me the phone and said "Miles, it's Coach Gary."

I didn't even sit up. I just grabbed the phone and in a groggy voice said, "What's up coach? You caught me going to bed early."

"Miles, my brother Jim—you know he's a sheriff's deputy—just called me. Evidently Tommy's brother, Danny had just dropped Tommy off at his girlfriend's house, and a drunk driver ran the red light at Richmond Boulevard and slammed full speed into Danny's car."

I sat up in the bed. "How is he? Is he hospitalized? What hospital did they take him to?"

"Coach I don't know how to say this other than...Danny was killed in the accident. He was probably killed almost instantly. It was that bad of a wreck. "

I went silent and began tearing up, about to start sobbing. I sniffled once and wiped the tears from my eyes with the back of my hand.

This nightmare was real.

Gary said, "What do you think we should do?"

"Let me call Tommy's dad and get updated on the situation and I'll call you right back." I called Mr. Kramer and he thanked me for the call and told me that the family was gathering at their home as we spoke, and that both Coach Gary and I were welcome. Alison had been standing in the doorway and made her way over to me as I stood up. We held each other and cried.

After a few moments passed, I stepped back and told her, "Gary and I are going over to the Kramer's now. I'll give them your condolences."

I called Gary back and we both hustled over to Tommy's house.

The next couple hours were disbelief, mourning, tears, and a lot of prayers. Tommy was holding himself together. We both hugged him when we got there and he was remarkably composed under the circumstances. Before we left, at about two o'clock, I told him that he did not need to be at our practice or the game tomorrow. I told him he needed to be here for his family. He thanked us and told us to be safe driving home.

The next day came and I made a number of phone calls to coaches, looking for someone that had experience with this kind of situation, but I was coming up dry. Alison gave me the name and number of a counselor that her school used in these situations. I called and she gave me tips on how to talk to my teenaged team about the unexpected death of a young person. At practice we never even took the basketballs out. We found a classroom and sat in a circle and I asked everyone to talk about how they were feeling. After about two hours, I can honestly say that most of us came to terms with this disaster and the pain that came with it, but that didn't stop the mourning.

That night I showed up at Vienna High School about 90 minutes before game time. To my utter surprise, as I stepped inside the gym doors, there stood Tommy. He was greeting every single player, coach, fan, mom, dad, sister, brother that had anything to do with our team as they came. He made sure that they all knew that he was okay and that they should be okay. It was truly an amazing feat of composure and maturity. He had put every single person in his world ahead of himself. I had never seen anything like it.

We had gotten a babysitter, so Alison was at my side as we came in the gym. Tommy hugged Alison and then hugged me. I said, "Tommy, I told you not to worry about tonight and to be with your family. I'm so proud of you and the young man that your parents made you. It's truly my honor to have you on our team, but I want you to finish here and go home and be with your mom and dad."

As calm as could be, Tommy looked at me and said, "Coach, I know that Danny would want me to be here and play. So, I'm going to play."

I sensed he was using this as a distraction from his emotional pain and I asked him, "How many hours of sleep did you get last night?"

"About two and a half hours," he replied.

"And you think you're rested enough to play these monsters tonight?" I asked, my voice rising. "Please Tommy, go home and be with your mom and dad, they need you tonight."

"Coach, my family is home with mom and dad right now and I'll be home soon enough. So, if it's all the same to you coach, with your permission, I'm going to dress and play tonight."

I looked over at Alison and she nodded in affirmation. I turned back to Tommy and said "Okay Captain, go get dressed."

The whole town and all the teams in the tournament knew what had happened to Danny. No one knew how to behave when we took the floor for warm-ups. When the teams walked out for the opening tip, there was an uneasiness among the players as they shook hands and loosened up. Right after we came into the gym, the Charleston Benedictine coach gave me a card of condolence to Tommy that had been signed by every one of their players and coaches. They were a class act, as well as being undefeated.

This first semifinal game, in all likelihood, was for the championship. We were the two best teams left in the tournament, but the circumstances surrounding the moment were almost unbelievable to everyone in the gym.

No one knew what to expect, including me.

The game started and it was as if no one wanted to be there except Tommy. He was clearly struggling from lack of sleep, but he was the best player on the floor all night. When the Charleston Benedictine team saw that Tommy didn't want them feeling sorry for him, they started playing hard.

With about three minutes left in the game, they were up by 14 and Tommy got his fifth foul. He left the game to a standing ovation from the packed gymnasium. When the final horn sounded, we had lost by 18, which was understandable for our young team against their veteran squad. We all shook hands and walked to the locker room.

Tommy was first in line to go through the doors. The coaches always came in last and when I came to the door, I could hear that Tommy was in a different aisle from the rest of the team and was crying.

I turned to Gary and said, "Coach, go talk to the team and I'll stay with Tommy. You can handle it." Gary nodded and went over to our team for a short post-game breakdown. I went into the aisle with Tommy. He was standing there as if he were waiting for me. I grabbed him and he held me tight and he buried his face in my shoulder and cried uncontrollably for 2 to 3 minutes, trying to release the pain. All I kept saying was, "It's okay Tommy, let it out, I'm here for you, we're all here for you." When the post-game talk was over, the rest of the players came over to join Tommy and console him. Gary and I left the locker room and Alison was waiting outside.

"Miles, I would like to talk to Tommy, if it's okay with you. And when I say I want to talk to him, I mean I want to talk to him alone. Can you please let him know?" Alison knew all my kids, but this was an interesting request she had given me. After a minute, I thought "who would I rather have talk to Tommy than my Alison?" As usual, Tommy was the last person to get dressed, but before he left the locker room, I had Alison go in with him, and they talked for about 15 minutes before they came out. He turned to me as he walked by and said, "Coach, thank you for letting me talk to Mrs. Christian. I'll see you tomorrow." Alison was only a couple steps behind Tommy as she came out of the locker room and she and I just walked to our car. I didn't care at all about the next game we would play, the one for third place. I wasn't going to stay and scout, and we would live with the consequences.

Once we got to the car and started driving home, I turned to Alison and asked her, "What did you and Tommy talk about?"

"For the most part I tried to get Tommy to talk. I kept asking questions about how he felt, if he missed his brother, if his family was okay, and things like that. Then I gave him some advice about dealing with his grief. I told him that even though Danny was physically gone, he was still here with us and that with each day, he would get to understand that better."

I was glad that Alison talked to him.

I was so tired I couldn't talk. The rest of the ride was nearly silent, with only the sounds of the turn signals punctuating the quiet winter night.

The next day came and our third-place game was at 6 p.m. As soon as I got into the locker room, Tommy pulled me aside into the corner to talk privately. He said, "Coach, you see this small trophy? Well, Danny asked me to play in a two-on-two tournament with him years ago, and as you probably know, because you've seen him play, he kind of sucked. I agreed to play with him and we got lucky and won the tournament. I told him to keep that trophy, because I knew that I would be playing varsity basketball and have other trophies. If it's okay with you, I'd like to reserve a place on the bench to put this trophy on during our game so he can be with us."

I looked at him and rubbed my chin with my right hand and I said, "Tommy, I don't see why not. In fact, it's a great idea. I will let the team know and I'm sure they'll be pleased to know that Danny's sitting next to them all night."

As expected, Tommy and our team got a standing ovation when we were introduced before the third-place game, which took place before the tournament championship game. It didn't matter who the other team was—that night our boys gave a man's effort, diving all over the floor for loose balls and getting every rebound, and we won by 17.

They awarded us the third-place trophy right after the game, and Tommy, our captain, went to center court to receive it to thunderous applause. He had the big trophy in one hand and in the other hand had Danny's little trophy.

There was a great sigh of relief in the locker room and the kids all dressed and stayed to watch the first-place game. Charleston Benedictine proved to be as dominant as expected, by winning and staying undefeated for the season.

After the game, the tournament committee called for all the players that had been named to the all-tournament team to gather on the court. Of course, that included Tommy, who ran out to receive his medal.

Then it was time for Charleston Benedictine to receive the first-place trophy. Before it happened, their captain walked over to Tommy and put his arm around him, and as I later found out, said to him, "Tommy, you are our team captain tonight. We all want you to accept this trophy for us."

From the crucible of high school basketball emerged the lesson that all good coaches try to teach their teams—that there are more important things than winning and losing.

In two nights, I had witnessed two of the most selfless acts I had ever seen. There wasn't a dry eye in the gym when Tommy accepted the first-place trophy.

And with that drama, the tournament came to a close.

Again, Alison had come with me that night to make sure Tommy was okay. I got to talking with some of the other head coaches and newspaper reporters, which was typical. When I was done, I had to go look for Alison. I couldn't find her. I decided to go back to our locker room and grab my stuff and look for her again or look at our car.

When I went in to the locker room, I saw Alison and Tommy holding hands, facing each other with their eyes closed. No talking, just silence. They sensed my presence and they both turned to me as Alison said "Hi Coach, great job tonight."

I said "Thanks, are you guys okay?"

Tommy said "Yes Coach, I'm more than okay."

Alison said "I'll go out and warm up the car. It's kind of cold outside. I'll meet you there."

In an instant, she was gone.

I couldn't let this go. I went over to Tommy and said "Captain, what in the world was all that with Mrs. Christian?"

He looked right into my eyes and he said "Coach, Mrs. Christian said that I should not say anything to you earlier, but that now, I should tell you everything that happened last night and tonight."

That stunned me a bit, but I gathered my wits and said "Okay..."

"Last night when Mrs. Christian came in and consoled me, she asked me a lot of questions. Then she said that she knew Danny had a request for me. I asked her how she could know that and what was the request? She said that Danny told her to tell me that he wanted me to bring that little trophy with me that we won in the two-on-two tournament and put it on the chair for the game. At that point, I thought that I had probably told her that story, since I can never stop talking about anything; my mouth seems to have a mind of its own."

I smiled and chuckled inside, because that was true.

"But then Mrs. Christian said, if you doubt what I'm saying Magic, then just read the bottom of the trophy when you get home. We hugged and she left. I thought about how Danny was always bragging to his friends about how good I was and he would call me Magic. When I got home, I found the trophy and looked at the bottom, which I had never done before, and on it was written 'Magic won this trophy and gave it to me. Love you forever.' She had told me, word for word, what was written on the bottom of that small trophy and so I knew she wasn't making it up about the request from Danny.

"Just before you came into the locker room, she had grabbed both my hands and told me to close my eyes and to trust her. So, I did what she asked. After a few moments, I heard my brother's voice saying 'love you forever, Magic,' and then he was gone. She told me to keep this between the three of us, and that it was my enormous love for my brother that allowed all of this to happen."

There was dead silence. I stood there motionless. Tommy had just taken my mind somewhere it had never been before.

I hugged Tommy and said "I love you too. Now go home and be with your parents and leave all of this between the three of us, like Mrs. Christian said."

As he walked towards the locker room door, he turned and looked back one more time, and said, "It's Mrs. Christian that's Magic Coach, not me."

2. A Train Car Named Amazement

By the time I got to our car, I could not remember the walk from the locker room to the parking lot, because my mind was racing with what Tommy had told me. Alison was already sitting in the driver's seat, so I opened the back door, threw my stuff on the back seat, and climbed into the front passenger seat. Alison was looking straight forward and said "Ready to go?"

"No, no, no. Alison, look at me."

She kept her hands on the wheel of our old Chevy but turned and looked at me. There was a long silence between us. I was not going to talk. I was like a baseball pitcher who had the bases loaded and two outs, and was staring in at home plate, only I knew I was not going to throw the ball, but instead was going to stand there until the batter called timeout.

So, I waited. Alison finally spoke.

"I guess Tommy told you the whole story, Coach."

"Yes."

I waited again.

"I know the time has come to talk to you about everything, but this is not the place. However, the place is just down the road at the Train Car Café. Okay?" Alison asked.

There was silence again. Alison put the car into drive and started the trip to the café, which really was an old converted train car in the middle of Vienna.

As Alison kept driving, I asked "So, all of what Tommy told me is true, right?"

"What did he tell you?"

I repeated to her almost word for word what Tommy had said, because I'll never forget that story. When I was done, I asked "Did I get it right?"

Alison had kept her eyes on the road until then, but now she glanced at me and said "Yeah, that's pretty much what happened."

I started to lose my patience with Alison. Billy and I had been witnessing all of these small, inexplicable oddities over the years, but this was an entirely different story. I didn't know what to do or say but I needed her to know that some lame excuse or theory of what happened would not rationalize tonight's events away.

"Alison," I said in my sternest coaching voice, "That's enough! You need to tell me what's going on with you. You need to tell me what's going on with you and your sisters. You think Billy and I don't talk all the time? I'm not going to let you explain this away with some crazy story that you once helped Mrs. Harper clean her house and you read what was on the bottom of that trophy, because I know that never happened!"

Alison was pulling into the parking lot of the restaurant, so she didn't talk until she parked the car and turned off the ignition.

"Miles, I love you and I want you to know that what I did for Tommy needed to be done. And that I knew that after talking to Tommy I had to start telling you the things about me that I never told you before."

She grabbed my left hand with both of hers, looked me in the eye and said, "But not out here in the cold. Let's go grab a booth in the diner and order a cheeseburger because I know you're starving and so am I. We'll talk in there."

I looked at her, she smiled, and my anger dissipated. I sighed and said "Okay."

We got out of the car and went into the Train Car Café and I saw that the last booth was empty. Whenever we went there, we sat in the last booth, because we liked the nostalgia and the privacy.

As we walked down the narrow aisle to get to it, one of patrons reached out and grabbed my arm. He said, "Coach, I just wanted to let you know that I'll never ever forget this tournament. I've lived in this town my whole life and I've seen all of the 49 tournaments that came before this one."

I relaxed, went into my coaching mode and said, "Thank you sir, that means a lot to me, and I'll pass it along to my team."

The patron said, "I know it was a horrible tragedy, but out of it we witnessed an amazing story of perseverance and selflessness. Maybe the world's not going to hell in a hand basket after all."

He smiled and I patted him on the back and said, "Maybe. Thanks again and have a great New Year."

We made it to the last booth and sat down. The train car had seen a better day. The seats were starting to get small tears and the Formica table was chipped on the edges. It was a place that had served comfort food forever. It wasn't the first time that Alison and I, or my coaches and I, had taken in its smells and ambiance.

The waitress came right away because it was getting late. We gave our standard order—a cheeseburger, fries, and a chocolate malt to share. The waitress left and the moment had arrived.

"Alison, you really did communicate with Danny, didn't you?"

"Yes Miles, I did."

"Are you going to make me play 20 questions?"

"No Miles, if you just relax, I have some things to tell you about me."

"The floor is yours" I said as I leaned back in the booth. I was in a state of both wonder and fear. I was about to find out something about the love of my life, something that I knew would change our relationship forever.

"Miles, I was born into this world by my mother and father the same way that you were born into this world by your mom and dad. My parents raised my sisters and me like any American family living in Iowa. We played as children, went to school, did the same things teenagers do, and then grew up into adults. I was lucky enough to find you in my life. I have loved you as my partner ever since that night in the park at Iowa State and I will love you for the rest of my life. I can see the worry on your face and I want to make sure that you know, first and foremost, that the things that I tell you will not change who we are and how our lives will move forward."

"Simply put, I am just a lot older than you. A lot older than you might ever guess."

The waitress came with our food and so Alison waited until we were all set up with our meal. The waitress asked, "Is there anything else I can get for you?" We both turned and said no, and then I said, "Thank you, it looks great." With that, she was gone. My fears begin to melt away. I was dying to ask questions, but I also knew I needed to just let her talk, so I said "Go ahead, Alison, I'm listening."

"Miles, what I'm going to tell you now, I was going to tell you in the next couple days anyway. You know Dana and Billy and Jessica are coming for our annual belated Christmas visit tomorrow. The three sisters had planned on talking to you and Billy about all of this because it's time. However, with what happened to Danny, I had to step in and help Tommy. My helping him brought about what happened tonight, which I'm going to disclose to you."

I took a bite out of the cheeseburger because I was really hungry, but my eyes never left Alison's face.

"Miles, I am 2,219 Earth years old."

I stopped chewing. My mind was processing that statement in so many ways that I was almost getting dizzy. How dare she make fun of this? Is she serious? Am I delusional and hearing things?

"Keep chewing your burger, Miles. I know what you're probably thinking, but I promise you I'm going to explain what I just said."

"You see, there are only two worlds in this universe of ours. The physical universe that you and I exist in while eating our cheeseburger is one of the worlds. That world also includes the entire expanse of the physical universe, which is much larger than any scientists on earth have ever imagined. The second world can be referred to as many things: realm, dimension, heaven, infinity, you get the idea. In that world, we exist as, again using our language, a being, an essence, a spirit, an individual, or a soul. Most accurately, you and I are infinite beings living temporary physical lives. Long ago, 2,219 Earth years ago, I was conceived into the physical universe and my infinite being was put into my body and I lived a wonderful life. When my physical body passed away, I was 77 earth years old. Then, my infinite being passed into the infinite universe."

"Alison, why are you saying Earth years ago? I guess I'm kind of taking this as you saying that reincarnation really exists? Again, what do you mean by Earth years?"

"What I mean by Earth years Miles, is 2,219 Earth years ago, I was born on a planet that is about 80 million light years from Earth."

I was starting to get angry. I wanted to believe Alison, but this seemed too preposterous of a story, so I said to her, "Are you serious?"

She didn't flinch, and she continued to look right at me, but now it was as if her eyes were looking right through me. She stopped talking. She was waiting for me to become calm. Since I had her attention, I took the moment to ask my first question.

"Okay, so you're from another planet and you're 2,219 Earth years old. I assume your sisters are from that same planet. How old are they?" I said in a sharp tone, one that conveyed doubt.

"No, Dana and Jessica are not from my planet; we are from three different planets. As for their ages, Dana is 8,747 Earth years old and Jessica is, well, 879,989 Earth years old."

I stopped eating altogether. I looked around the diner. Then I pinched myself to make sure I wasn't in a dream. "879,989 years old! Alison, what you're telling me is ridiculous!"

In her calm voice, Alison continued, "Miles, please let me finish. Let me paint the big picture of the universe. There are millions of planets where humans exist, just like here on Earth. People are conceived with a body and an infinite essence, and they live their physical lives and then their essence passes into the infinite world, just like I did and just like my sisters did. We just move from one plane of existence to the other. If you want to call my Second Life on Earth reincarnation, that's fine, because that's not important. It was our choice to live another physical life with a higher purpose here on Earth. You see Miles, this civilization, this world, is capable of creating such wonderful joy, but at the same time it is committing such horrible atrocities, purposefully or out of neglect.

"Our civilization is at the point where there's a fork in the road. Our civilization is in the process of choosing which path it is going to travel. I chose to come here to find someone like you, and to have a family that I can pass this wisdom on to, so that their lives and their children's lives can continue to push this world toward the right path. While I'm here with you, I'm going to do as much good as I can for the people around me. I know you've heard me say this many times, the world is what's around you. The world is not what's on television or in Washington, D.C. or at the United Nations. Our world tonight was that basketball tournament and this train car. In Africa, where people are only living into their 40s, their world is one of hunger and pain and disease and hope that someone will help them. If this change is going to happen, it's going to take generations to accomplish, but only if we pick the correct path. If we don't pick the correct path, it's possible and probable that our civilization will destroy itself, either by its own hand or by its neglect of the world that was given to us to care for and cherish."

Alison stopped for a few moments and just stared at me with a look of love.

Then she said "This is really only the tip of the iceberg. I have so much more to tell you, and my sisters have so much more to say these next few days. I hope you can be patient with me and with us. I know that you and Billy have seen a number of unexplained phenomena over the last decade or so. Most of it was an accident by us, not staying within our physical forms. However, some of it was on purpose. The night we first kissed, the night on the beach on Catalina Island, when you saw Dana and Billy disappear by the bonfire, the night we conceived our first child, those were moments when I didn't want to hold back my joy. You did see the stars in the sky in my eyes and in my hair as you always described it to me."

"You see Miles, my sisters and I exist in both worlds at the same time. We can also understand and speak in any language in the universe because of our infinite nature. I know that's a hard concept for you to wrap your mind around, but it's not important, other than that you know it. That's why I was able to talk to your mother in her native Hungarian. I know Billy will be driving Dana crazy, asking her to prove all of this stuff within the scientific method, but that's just a waste of time."

Needless to say, neither one of us had eaten much of our meal and the waitress came down to remind us that the restaurant was closing in 15 minutes. Alison thanked her for being patient with us.

"Miles, I'm hungry and I know you are too. Let's finish this food and we can talk a little bit more about it as we eat and as we drive home. I know I've given you a lot to think about."

So, we proceeded to make a serious effort at eating. When I finished my hamburger and fries, and took my first sip of that chocolate malt, I had that rush of joy that chocolate malts always gave me. I related it immediately to what Alison had told me about joy in our world. I thought to myself, who wouldn't want to choose that path.

As we got up from the table, I took my wife's face in both my hands and gave her a kiss. She put her arms around my waist and I took my hands and pushed her beautiful brown hair behind her ears. She gave me a big smile.

"Thanks so much for helping Tommy get through all of this," I said.

"You are helping Tommy get through this, Coach. It was Danny who asked me to tell his brother one more time that he loved him. The joy they got from that three seconds was greater than a thousand fireworks going off at the same time."

With that, we made our way to the register, paid our check and walked into the frosty Midwestern night.

3. Spirits in the Material World

It was about a 30-minute ride to our home in Woodstock.

"Alison, I know I usually drive home, but would you mind driving tonight? I'm exhausted and my mind is spinning and about to come in for a landing when my head finally hits the pillow," I asked.

"No problem Coach, I've got the bridge," Allison replied.

"You're in charge, Captain. I'm just a passenger."

Five minutes into our ride, the car finally warmed up. The winter roads were clear and the sky was cloudless. The 20-degree weather made the country air so crisp that if you took a bite out of it, it would've sounded like crunching into a fresh Macintosh apple. I didn't want to create a distraction for Alison while she was driving, but I couldn't resist, so I said, "Sweetheart, if you're comfortable talking while driving, I do want to ask you one question."

"Depends on the question."

"Danny?"

"Danny. Yes, I can talk a little bit about what happened. Just like Gary's brother reported, the wreck was incredibly violent and fatal and Danny's body passed away almost instantly from his physical injuries. Since my sisters and I exist in both universes at the same time, I was aware of what happened shortly after the accident occurred. However, Danny did not reach out to me the night he died, but he did the next day after the game, when you and Coach Gary were in the locker room with the players and Tommy was breaking down in tears. Danny came to me and asked me if it was possible to get a message to his brother. He told me that as soon as his bedroom door closed the previous night, Tommy had cried himself to sleep. He refused to cry in front of his family or friends, but once he was alone with this nightmare, he was devastated."

I sat there like a young child hearing the Night Before Christmas for the first time.

I asked, "Danny told you about the small trophy, the note written at the bottom, and that he wanted it placed on a chair during the game tonight?"

"Yes. Then after Danny saw our game and the touching ceremony after the championship game, he came to me and asked if there was any way he could tell his brother he loved him just one more time. You see, simply stated, individuals that have just passed from their physical bodies into the infinite universe cannot yet do some things that older individuals living in the infinite universe can do. I asked Danny if Tommy would be able to keep this communication between us a secret and without hesitation Danny said yes, absolutely. Danny told me that because of his brother's faith, and his relationship with me, he had no doubts."

Alison looked over and said, "So I helped Danny make it happen."

Alison had given me too much to think about. I was tired, but I still had a sugar high pulsing through my veins from that chocolate malt. My mind went into a lot of different directions as I mulled over Alison's explanation. After about five minutes, I closed my eyes and concentrated on the rhythm of the road under our wheels. The rhythm calmed me down, but finally my mind circled in on another question and out it came.

"So, Grandpa Christian..."

Before I knew it, Alison was interrupting me.

"Miles, what I'm talking to you about now and what we are going to talk about over the next couple days are not séances or parlor tricks. I knew you were going to ask me about your Grandpa Christian because you were so close to him, and now you want to know if I could put you in touch with him. I shared a lot with you in the diner and now I shared a lot with you about Danny and that's really enough for tonight, Miles."

I was sitting with my arms folded to stay warm and I had reclined the seat for comfort. As Alison glanced over at me, though my head was facing forward, my eyes turned to meet hers in that boyish way that she loved and that she normally couldn't resist.

"All right, I might as well tell you. He was there tonight watching your game like he watches all of your games. Before I went into the locker room with Danny, he told me how proud he was of you. I saw him one more time tonight and he specifically said to me that he was really proud of his little Shooter. Was that his nickname for you, Miles?"

My eyes opened as big as saucers. Alison continued driving with her eyes on the road, thank God. One of us had to be disciplined enough to get us home safely.

I replied, "My Grandpa Christian was a high school basketball coach too, Alison. I think I told you that. When I was little, he worked with me all the time on my basketball fundamentals. I became a pretty good shooter and that was his nickname for me. So, he's there at all of my games, watching?"

"That's what he told me. Most of the time he sits right next to me. Sometimes he goes into the other team's timeout strategy sessions and then comes back and tells me funny stories about the other coaches and their idiosyncrasies and mannerisms, just for the joy of it. Sometimes he sits with his old friends and coaches just to listen to the bullshit. Those are his words not mine, so, don't try to fine me for the cuss jar."

"That is so cool. That is just so cool. So, who else is at my games?"

"Stop! That's enough for tonight."

We were getting close to home, and I needed to deal with the real world again.

"So, Dana and Billy are renting a car and Jessica's flight is coming in at the same time tomorrow, is that right?" I asked.

Alison started to get on one of her super-organized rolls.

She said yeah, it sounds like they should be getting to our house early afternoon. Let's figure out what we want to do for dinner tomorrow night. I think we should just head over to Luigi's Pizza and keep it simple. The kids can play video games and we won't have to clean up after dinner. They'll be tired because it's a travel day and the next day, Saturday, is our belated Christmas Day. The kids will be looking forward to their presents and by the end of the day our house will be a mess. Once the kids are in bed and asleep, we can all head down to the basement and start to talk."

"Sunday we'll get up and go to church and then late afternoon, I have Dora and one of her friends coming to babysit for the rest of the evening. The five of us can go out to dinner at Blackbirds. I reserved a private booth so that we can continue to talk to you and Billy."

I replied "So, does Billy know what I know? Does he know more than I know or less than I know? Is it okay if I talk to him about it?"

"Yes, he knows exactly what you know, because Dana told him exactly what I told you, word for word. I don't think it's a good idea for you guys to talk about any of this until later on when the kids are in bed. Our house is small and there's so many people that there's really no privacy and you don't want the older kids hearing things that they'll ask questions about later. Tomorrow is about Christmas, and you and Billy can open your presents tomorrow night. How does that sound?" Alison summarized.

"Got it Captain. "Alison pulled our car into the driveway and into the garage. She turned off the ignition and closed the garage door with us still inside the car. Dora was inside the house babysitting. We stayed in the car because Allison didn't want Dora to overhear what she had to say.

"Miles, Dana, Jessica and I knew this day would come. It is both a relief and a burden. We want to be honest with you, but we have kept so many things from both of you for so long, we didn't want it to change our lives and our relationships with families and friends. We all have a lot of work ahead of us. It's important that Billy and you, and eventually the kids, know the things that we know, so we can pass them forward from generation to generation. At the end of this journey of revelation you should all come to the same final epiphany on your own and at your own speed. And when you do, we will be there to tell you if you got it right."

Amazing! I constantly scold my players and students for using and over-using that word, letting them know that amazing only applies to a few things in their lives, but it applied to this moment.

I now realized that I was about to get into something that was way over my head. Was I expected to pass some sort of test? It created doubts in my mind as to whether I was up for this incredible challenge. I looked over at Alison and with the back of the fingers of my left hand I tenderly brushed her cheek and said to her, "Thanks for getting us home safely, Captain. I hope I can get to the end of my new journey safely."

"You'll be fine, Miles."

We leaned toward each other for a quick kiss before we went into the house. I paid Dora for babysitting, and then drove her home. Shortly after I got back, we collapsed into our bed to grab some needed rest for the big weekend ahead.

4. Three French Hens... Two Turtledoves

I thank God for our terrific babysitter, Dora. She had worn out Jennifer, Maggie and Laura and they actually overslept, which allowed us to sleep in the next morning, and we badly needed the rest. The kids were in full Christmas enthusiasm mode, and the rest of the crew was due in a couple hours, so there wasn't time to further our discussion from the night before. We were both focused on getting the house ready for our traditional belated-Christmas celebration.

Soon enough, the doorbell rang. The kids ran to the door, followed by Allison, as I stood back. When the door opened, everybody inside and outside was yelling Merry Christmas, and the jumping and hugging began.

After about a minute, I said, "Okay, okay everybody, we need to come inside, it's really cold outside and the furnace is running too fast for my pocketbook." They all hustled in and Renée, Willie and Johnny all came in and hugged their Uncle Miles at the same time. They were great kids, very affectionate and enthusiastic, all taking after their mother, Dana. However, being from California, well, they were freezing!

Renée said, "Uncle Miles, why is it always so cold here when we visit? How can you live here when you can almost never go outside without three jackets on?"

I picked her up and swung her around and said, "Renée, you are definitely your mother's daughter, always giving me a hard time about something. You know the answer to that question just as well as I do. It's not always cold here. We have Winter, Spring, Summer and Fall. Christmas just happens to come in the middle of winter, and that's why someone wrote the song, White Christmas."

And with that, I started one of our traditions, singing "I'm Dreaming of a White Christmas," and by the second line, everyone was singing along, "Just Like the Ones I Used to Know." Right after the final verse, "may all your Christmases be white" there was a big cheer from everyone—Christmas had arrived!

The adults unpacked and got settled into the cramped sleeping quarters in our small house. Once that was done, we knew the kids couldn't wait, so we went ahead, opened presents and played with the kids and their toys for the rest of the afternoon.

As for the adults, we always did a white elephant gift exchange. You had to find something in your house that you hadn't used in over a year, wrap it up, and put a sticker on it with your name. Then we had a random draft of names and everybody picked a present. You ended up with crazy stuff, like old unused bowling balls, ridiculous computer mouse pads, or an odd home decoration, like a painting of dogs playing poker and smoking cigars. It was always a blast.

When it was all said and done, it was late afternoon. We packed up the kids and were off to Luigi's Pizza for games, pizza and beer. The kids had a ball running around while we sat at our table, which was like a big picnic table that had been varnished 10 times.

Billy said, "Well ladies, Miles and I have not talked, but I assume tonight is on as promised—correct?"

"I don't know what you're talking about," said Dana. Then she started to laugh. "Yes, yes, yes, we're headed for the basement tonight, Professor Billy."

"Okay then," I said, "A Merry Belated Christmas toast to everyone." Our beers and our sodas had all been poured into plastic cups from pitchers on the table, so when we touched our cups together for the toast, there was no clinking sound and we all laughed.

We eventually knew it was time to leave—when some of the younger kids started to migrate over to us and put their heads on our laps. We gathered up the crew, made it back to our house and tucked everyone in for a nice long Christmas dream.

I found Billy and told him that my saying sweet dreams to the kids reminded me that I had this great George Benson album with the song "Summer Wishes, Winter Dreams." We decided to go downstairs and listen to it, because the ladies were going to try and clean up the house before they came downstairs.

I said, "Allison, Billy and I are going to head downstairs for a little jazz guitar music. How long do you think you ladies want to straighten up?"

"Probably about 15 or 20 minutes," she replied.

"Okay. We'll see you downstairs." Billy and I grabbed our drinks and headed to the basement.

Billy had done very well for the company that owned the winery. He had been promoted and he was being paid both a salary and stock options, which was great, but he said the stock was not traded on the New York Stock Exchange or the NASDAQ, so he wouldn't know how valuable it was until he tried to sell it. After Billy and Dana's youngest child was old enough for kindergarten, Dana started to teach part-time at the community college. She enjoyed being able to teach in her wheelhouse: physics and astronomy.

Jessica was still living out East. She had become a medical doctor after graduating from Johns Hopkins University.

Then she received her PhD in cancer research from Harvard and was working on a post-doctoral fellowship in biology at Princeton.

Unlike many academics who achieved what she did, Jessica remained very humble. However, she was a rebel in the scientific community. She had just started to give lectures and get articles published. She had firm convictions. She stated in the strongest possible way that universities were being too lenient with inventing majors and giving grant money to projects that were of little or no value to advancing the human condition. Many had challenged her convictions and found her to be too formidable. We were all very proud of her.

The previous owners of our modest home had made a very serviceable rec room out of the basement. They had sprayed the ceiling joists and all the pipes that ran inside of them with black paint, like a restaurant might do with an old commercial space. They had put up drywall just inside the concrete walls and glued down Berber carpeting. The carpeting was a light tan and the walls had been painted a light beige. However, when you dimmed the lights, it could be a very warm romantic getaway for Alison and me, once the kids were in bed and asleep. As always, I had a very nice sound system down there, because we both loved all types of music.

While we were waiting for the ladies, Billy and I compared notes about what we had heard from Alison and Dana, and as expected, we each pretty much knew what the other knew. Being the scientist, Billy did question me about the incident with Tommy and Danny.

"So, did you actually hear Danny's voice in the locker room?" Billy asked me.

I replied, "No, but I saw Allison and Tommy holding hands. Tommy told me that Danny only spoke for two or three seconds and that was right before I came into the locker room."

"That's okay Miles. With all of the stuff that's gone on over the last 10 years, it was a relief to know that I wasn't crazy, even though the story Dana told me was. I guess we're going to get Chapter 2 tonight and we'll see where it takes us."

A few minutes later, Dana, Alison and Jessica came down the stairs holding their drinks. Jessica had a big bowl of popcorn and Alison brought the old baby monitor so we could hear if any of the kids woke up. We each found a place to sit, with Alison next to me. I took a deep breath and relaxed. I felt a sense of anticipation grow, but I knew that I should give the ladies a few minutes after the clean-up they had just done.

I got up from the sofa where Alison had sat next to me and said, "Billy, another George Benson?"

"Yes, I think he's perfect as a musical backdrop for the evening."

"George Benson it is," I said as I put on his "Breezin" album.

I said, "Alison knows this, but the rest of you might not. It's my dream to one day own the same Ibanez hollow body electric guitar that George Benson plays. The problem is, it costs more than our car is worth. I think I need to get a part-time job in the music store, so that I can get a discount. What do you think, Billy?"

"What do I think? I think we've waited long enough ladies, so if you don't start talking right now, Miles and I are going to go out and find that guitar and buy it and bankrupt your budget, Alison!" Billy replied playfully.

"See, I told you Professor Wine had a good sense of humor," Dana said.

Jessica stood up and the room became quiet. She was like a teacher who had let class get out of control and now she was about to reel us in.

She said "It's time to say the things we need to say and begin to go to the places that we need to go."

I had seen Jessica speak on television and also in person before hundreds of people. She was dynamic, but also full of humility. I was surprised that Dana wasn't taking the lead, but at the same time not surprised, because of Jessica's accomplishments and how old she was in her infinite essence. All bets were off on what Billy and I actually knew to be true anymore, and we were just hoping that the sisters could make some sense out of it for us.

"Gentlemen, we all know what happened over the past few days with Tommy, Danny, Miles, and Alison. Things that were revealed during that process don't need to be restated tonight, do they?" Jessica first looked at Billy, who shook his head no. Then she looked at me and I said, "I'm good Jessica, go on."

"Thanks guys."

"The universe is like a beautiful handwoven tapestry. The physical world occupies only the colored patterns. The infinite world occupies the entire tapestry as well as the spaces in between the fabric. However, human beings that have passed and entered the infinite world exist in both worlds at the same time. That is why the three of us can be in two places simultaneously.

All three of us have chosen to live another physical lifetime on Earth, to help this civilization to find the true path. While all three of us have known each other in the infinite world, we came from three different planets in the universe, and all of us were human beings before, just like we are now on earth."

Billy interrupted, "I have a question..."

Jessica cut him off, saying, "Billy I'm sorry, this is a solo act right now."

There was a moment of silence and Billy leaned back in the lounge chair.

"We, meaning infinite beings like us, should not preach to you too much about morality and values and about how human beings should live their lives on earth. It's been proven over the millennia that it doesn't work. What we can do is show you human beings on other worlds that are living lives different from your own. Right now, I know that with every sentence I utter, you have two more questions you want to ask me. Well, asking them and answering them, that's the same as us preaching to you. What I'm asking you to do tonight is just listen to me and accept that this is how the universe works. Then we will show you existing civilizations, different from our own, that are on different paths than we are on here on Earth. Some are on the right road. Some are on the wrong road. Some have not yet chosen the final road they want to travel, much like those who are here."

I was glad that Jessica had dumbed-down her explanation of the universe, but I still sat there trying to process it all.

"Know this: Dana, Alison, and I will do the best we can to be your teachers for however long these earthly bodies allow us. We will do the best we can to direct as many minds as we can to choose the right path. We can't read your thoughts. We can't tell you what happens in the future. We can't bring dead people back to life. We are human beings just like you, only much older and much wiser and with the experience of living in the infinite universe for thousands of years. We are human again, which means that we will die one day, and we don't know when disease or accident or old age will end our physical existence on Earth.

"However, there is one thing that we can do that other human beings cannot. Because we have passed into the infinite universe, we are not bound by physical laws. We can create non-ordinary states of reality. We can travel to the ends of the universe and back in the blink of an eye. As long as one of us is with one of you, our two infinite essences can take the trip together. You need not worry about what is happening here on Earth while you are gone, because the one of us that is with you will be in both places at the same time and will make sure that the two bodies are protected here. When you arrive at your destination, you cannot be seen by the human beings on that planet. You exist only as essence. The sisters can understand all their languages and we also have a previous knowledge of their civilization.

"This is the method that has been used by the infinite universe for millennia to teach civilizations what works and what does not work, everywhere in the cosmos."

There was silence and it appeared that Jessica was awaiting a question. With Billy's background in astrophysics, he had to be dying to ask a million questions.

"Jessica, can I ask you a question now?" he said.

"Yes, Billy, go ahead, but only one question and then it's Miles' turn."

Billy continued, "From all the things that Dana told me to bring me up to speed for tonight, and with the things that you have told us, it seems to me that what you are saying is that throughout the cosmos the only form of intelligent life that human beings will find, are in fact, other human beings. Is that what you're saying? On these billions and billions of planets throughout the cosmos, you are saying that the only other sentient beings that exist are humans, and that they live on earth-like planets?"

"Yes," Jessica said softly, yet emphatically. "Aren't your brothers and sisters in the sciences always looking for earth-like planets? Then what do you think you would expect to find on an earth-like planet? Human beings, animals, and landscapes similar to Earth, right? If I lived in Boston, and drove all the way to Los Angeles, and went to McDonald's, wouldn't I find a Big Mac?"

Dana and Allison started to laugh.

"With all due respect," Billy said, "That seems impossible to believe given the theory of..."

Jessica interrupted, "Billy, are you going to quote me a bunch of theories that earth scientists have come up with that are all hypothetical and unproven by your own scientific method? Because if that's where you're going with this, it's going to be a long night of you listing theories and me saying, well that theory is wrong, and here is why."

"Billy, I promise you, before this night is over, I will put your mind to rest about all of that. I promise. Please be patient," Jessica said, looking at Billy with sincerity.

Billy took a deep breath. Jessica then turned to me.

"Miles?"

I wasn't looking at this drama the same way Billy was because I wasn't an astrophysicist. I was a high school English teacher, a coach, a father and a husband, but I think I know a lot about human nature.

I replied, "I guess the first question that comes to mind ladies, is if we have all of these extraterrestrial brothers and sisters, will we eventually be able to communicate and visit with them? We could learn a great deal from them and they could learn a great deal from us. Is that possible?"

Alison got up from her seat next to me. She turned to us and said, "No Miles. The physical worlds that exist are too far apart for that to ever happen. That was done for a reason. I know for a fact that we all watched Star Trek while we grew up and even now into adulthood. So, let me use an example from the Star Trek universe. Their number one law was what Billy?"

Billy thought for a moment, then said, "That they could not interfere with development of any other civilizations throughout the universe. I think they called it their prime directive. Is that right? I haven't seen a show in a long time."

"That's right," Alison said. "Let me put it to you this way. The universe was created with the prime directive embedded into it. All of the planets that contain human life have been set far enough apart to have their chance to build their own civilizations without interference from other planets. Believe me, even knowing what I know, while I watch those old shows, it is a beautiful concept: mankind reaching out to the stars to try and discover other peoples, other races and civilizations. But we would be lying if we told you it was possible in the physical universe."

Jessica jumped in. "Alison, Dana and Billy can check my math, and I would be glad to show you on a chalkboard just why it would be impossible to travel the distances between stars to contact other civilizations. Do you want me to start by using speed of light computations? That is, 186,000 miles per second? Or would it be more fun to convert that to miles per hour, meaning 670,616,629 miles per hour, Billy?"

Jessica continued, "All these theories that travel is possible at the speed of light do not take into account the fact that space is not a complete void. There are pieces of star stuff, to quote Carl Sagan, one of my heroes, floating all around. If you were able to actually get a starship to fly at the speed of light, which you can't, if it hit an object the size of a fleck of paint, it would rupture the hull and the ship would explode. AND, if you think it would be hard to get a ship to travel the speed of light, just think how hard it would be to brake and slow that ship down."

"So, do you want me to do the math on a chalkboard or not?"

There was dead silence. The obvious answer was no.

"Why do you think I have been fighting so hard against the funding of pseudo-sciences and grants being given for experiments that will never add anything positive to the human condition? Simply stated, we can never travel fast enough or safely enough to get to other star systems. And if you put a gun to any real astrophysicist's head and asked them that question, they would answer the same way. All of this hypothetical mumbo-jumbo, as if we can somehow escape the earth when it's time and re-settle our civilization somewhere else, needs to be put in its proper place. Not Science Fiction. No, Science Fantasy!

"Your turn, Billy," Jessica said.

"Well ladies, if you are not going to let me argue any of the astrophysics theories out there and you're just going to tell me that I am wrong, then I don't have any more questions, but I have one request. I want you to prove to me that we can travel somewhere else in the blink of an eye. Now, right now," Billy said with a rising voice.

Billy turned and looked right at me and said, "Miles, are you with me?"

I looked at him. I was no match for Jessica. Somehow, I was also sure that Allison and Dana were just as smart as her. Yes, there were many other questions in my mind that I wanted to ask. How was the universe created? How did we get here on this planet.? Is there a God, and if so, will we meet her or him or it or whatever? However, knowing the direction the evening was headed, it just settled into my brain that if they could take me to another planet in the blink of an eye, that would be pretty impressive.

"I'm with you Billy. Let's go, ladies."

Dana stood up and took control of the moment. "Billy, if you and Miles would please stand up and hold hands with the rest of us, we'll get started."

It was as if standing up and holding hands was an act of faith, that this was really going to happen. I felt as nervous as a basketball player shooting one free throw in a tie game with one second left on the clock.

Dana continued, "Billy, do you remember about 10 years ago, when you said that you saw the kids and me disappear one night? The next day you questioned Willie and he said I had taken him to my hometown? Remember that night?"

"I'll never forget it."

"That's where we went."

"That's where we are going tonight. It's about 40 million light years away. My planet still has a vibrant population. I'm happy to say that the civilization living there learned the most important lessons of life before it destroyed itself. The people who live there now live in peace and harmony."

My sense of anticipation was at its peak. I was waiting for Dana to start some incantation in a strange language, try to put us into some sort of trance, or light a weird candle.

"Okay," Dana said. "Is everybody ready to run counterclockwise in a circle?"

Billy and I sheepishly said "Yes."

The ladies started laughing at us.

"Good one," Jessica said to Dana. Even Alison couldn't stop snickering at me.

"We're not witches, guys. There will be no incantations or spells. But I do have a good card trick I want to show you later. I'm sorry, but I need to have a little fun with this to keep your stress levels down."

I was embarrassed, but then realized how funny that really was, and I smiled.

Dana took over again. "Seriously, the process is pretty simple. Let's stand in a circle and everyone hold hands. This time I'm going to count backwards from three like this: three, two, one, close, open. When I say close, close your eyes, and when I say open, open your eyes. Any questions? Here we go."

"Three, two, one, close..."

Before I could open my eyes, I felt a stiff warm breeze hit my face and push my hair back.

"Open..." Dana finished.

We opened our eyes.

"Oh my God," Billy and I said at the same time!

We were standing on a path halfway up a mountain. There were mountains across a sprawling valley from us. To the right was darkness, but to the left was a city in the half-light of the sunset. The sun was setting behind us. The path we were standing on looked like it was used by hikers. The plants and rocks looked familiar to me, not alien. I could see a sign ahead on the path, but its alphabet looked like hieroglyphics to me. Where we were standing was safe, but about 10 feet straight ahead was a sheer cliff that dropped at least 1,000 feet. There were no people around, but we could see vehicles moving in the distance on the roads below. It was impossible to make out the design or details of homes, buildings and cars. We stood there quietly, taking in all of what had just happened. The mountains on the far side of the valley were turning from red to pink and then dark as the sun set completely. Then the lights from the buildings, homes and cars began to light up the night. The city sprawl continued to the left, where it ended at a great body of water. As the city lights grew brighter, we saw something astounding towards the water's edge. Though most of the lights were white or light yellow, there were some blue lights in an enormous circle, and blue lights inside the circle formed what looked like a snowflake. Just where were we?

Pointing at that enormous symbol I asked, "What is that? Obviously, it has a purpose doesn't it? Dana, you said this is where you come from, so, do you know what it is?"

Dana responded, "All of the major cities on my planet have an officially adopted symbol, which is lit up at night as a way to give a peaceful greeting to people traveling through the air and to show the pride of the citizens of that particular city. It's not organized by any government. It's completely organized and constructed by the people who live in that area. Let's just leave it at that for now."

Dana changed the subject

"Look up guys," she said, pointing to the sky. We saw not one, but two moons. They were both bigger than our moon, and each moon was in a crescent shape, but facing each other, like giant celestial parentheses.

The ladies were not talking and neither were we. It was enough just to be there and look around and watch the evening unfurl.

We were probably there for 20 or 25 miraculous minutes.

Alison said, "Time to go home, fellas. Let's get in our circle and hold hands."

We did as she instructed. Alison continued, "Three, two, one, close, open." And we were home.

"How was that for a sleigh ride?" Dana asked.

We all laughed.

"Amazing," I said.

5. Blackbird's Singing in the Dead of Night

It took a few moments for Billy and me to regain our bearings.

Then Dana said, "I want to give everyone a chance to talk before we break for the night. Miles, why don't you start us off. Just share with us whatever is on your mind right now."

This time it was on me. Many times, I had asked one of my students or one of my players to talk about something spontaneously, what we were studying in class, or something that happened in practice or during a game. Now I was on the spot.

I said "I just want to thank you Alison, Dana, and Jessica for letting Billy and me be part of your world. I know we are students and we'll do the best we can to learn. Just having this opportunity is an enormous honor. Again, thank you, all three of you."

Billy was speechless. I could hear him taking in heavy breaths and breathing out through his mouth. Billy being an astrophysicist, I knew his world had just been ripped into shreds. Much of what he thought that he knew was now useless.

He finally mustered the composure to speak in a hushed tone. "Yes, Miles, I agree with you wholeheartedly. Thank you, ladies, for letting us be part of this journey."

There was silence. We were all looking at Billy and knew he had something else to say.

"I do have a question."

Dana replied, "sure, go ahead Billy."

"We just went on this miraculous trip. Who are we? Who are you? Who am I? Miles and I were told that our bodies stayed here. You keep referring to a person having an infinite essence. Tell me what that means." Alison replied, "Billy, Miles, your infinite essence...is you. It is the sum of you. It is your mind. It is your heart. It is your soul. It is the totality of all of your experiences. Joy, sorrow, pain, loneliness, love, laughter, tears—all the emotions you have ever felt. It is also the knowledge that you have gained in living this temporary human life on earth. Most importantly, it is that infinite spark that lives inside all of us that will continue on forever. Tell me, have I explained it so that you can understand?"

Billy looked at me. Although it was all new to me, I somehow understood and nodded yes.

Billy replied, "thanks Alison, you gave me enough information, I just have to digest it."

Alison replied, "obviously I speak for all three of us when I say, you're welcome. The two of you are very special individuals. Know that you were chosen by us because we knew you could handle it. We are all grateful that we found you and could share all of this with you."

We broke up for the evening and went to bed, because tomorrow was going to be a full day. It was rare that Alison and I both went to bed at the exact same time. She was a morning person, so she would usually beat me to bed and to sleep. I was a night owl, watching game film and sometimes old movies. Tonight was different. Both our heads hit the pillow at the same time.

We were lying in bed looking at each other and I put my hand on the small of her back and pulled her closer to me. I moved closer to her so that we were face-to-face and staring into each other's eyes. I took my left hand and stroked Alison's beautiful brown hair while I gazed at her, something I didn't do enough of since the kids came along. I remembered how much I loved to caress her and just look at her as she slept. I had never loved anyone like I loved Alison. I was afraid that the days to follow might change that feeling. That part of me wanted to turn around and go back, but I knew it was too late for that.

I said, "Alison, it's been too long since we just lay here like this and I was able to stare into your glimmering eyes and touch your face and smell your hair and tell you how lucky I am to have found you."

She gave me one of her big smiles and began to twist my hair and play with it.

She whispered, "Yeah, we need to do this more often. I miss this. With the kids, and all that we do, we are so tired when we go to bed every night. I think that maybe what we're saying to each other is that we both miss that newlywed lifestyle, don't you think?"

"Yeah, but I know that neither one of us would give up our three girls and what they have brought to our lives. One day they'll be grown up and out of the house and we'll have more alone time together, just the two of us. Won't we?

"That's the plan," Alison said. "I'm looking forward to it."

I was feeling a little insecure about what had happened tonight. I let that insecurity get to me. I didn't want to lose Alison. In my mind, the future now seemed like a train that was about to run out of track.

With that uncomfortable feeling I said, "When the kids are grown up and out of the house, you aren't going to take off on me and go back to your home between the stars are you?"

In a soft, tender voice, Alison said "No Miles. I came here to live out my life with you, for as long as this body will allow me."

We leaned in and kissed. When the kiss was finished, I pulled Alison in close to me, because she liked to fall asleep with her head on my chest. It was bliss...even if only for a moment.

The next morning, Sunday, was filled with breakfast, bathing kids and getting all dressed up for church. We went about our normal business, but remembered what happened the night before and were aware that we would have a chance to talk that night at Blackbird's Restaurant during dinner.

Since Billy was an agnostic, he usually stayed home from Sunday services, but this day was different. This day there was an enthusiasm to him about going to church that I hadn't seen before. Alison and I were members of St. John's parish. We loved attending the 11 o'clock Mass, because it was accompanied by the teen choir plus their guitars, percussion, violins, and whatever else they wanted to throw in. The 11 o'clock Mass was lively and I knew a lot of kids in the choir who had been my students in high school.

That morning's services went pretty much as expected for a Sunday Catholic Mass. However, after communion, Father Williams told the congregation that the choir had prepared a special song for the recessional. Normally we would walk out of church while the music was playing. He told us that he had heard the choir rehearsing and we should sit down and enjoy the music and then we could leave church in silence. So we sat and waited with a heightened sense of anticipation.

Jenny Williams, who had been in my class a year before, stepped to the microphone and said "Thank you, Father

John. The song we prepared for you this morning is called There Is a Reason, written by Ron Block and recorded by Alison Krauss.

Jenny's soprano voice was angelic. The guitars and harmonies blended perfectly with her singing. I had heard the song many times, but I started to feel it was about to set off my tears, which was surprising, because I am not a crier. When I looked around, I saw almost every other man and woman fighting back those same tears. Most of them lost the fight.

When the song ended there were a few moments of silence. We all started applauding.

We stood.

Then, as a congregation, we became one.

The most surprising thing to see was that Billy was crying harder than anyone. He had sat down and covered his face with his hands. Dana sat next to him and rubbed his back, held him close and whispered in his ear. I couldn't hear what she was saying, but it was a moving moment for me to see.

Father Williams asked the group to take a bow, they did. With that, the services were over and we filed out.

The rest of the day was a blur because of the kids' constant activity. However, for Billy and me, dinner time couldn't come fast enough. I left early to pick up Dora and her friend to babysit.

We were all happy to have some adult time that evening, and we drove to Blackbird's Restaurant.

Blackbird's had been there for a long time. There were stories that it was a meeting place for mobsters back in the 20s and 30s. It had real brass railings everywhere and ornate wallpaper. The plush carpeting and curtains were dark red and green and may have dated to the time of John Dillinger and Bonnie and Clyde. I think that's why it remained so popular over the years. You walk through the doors and time-traveled back to those wild days. Alison had requested our favorite booth, which was in a corner, and it had a velvet curtain. That meant that after we were served dinner, we could have the waitress close the curtains for complete privacy. We always speculated that's where the mob bosses met to make their deals.

Once we got settled in and had a round of drinks, the waitress took our orders and left, and then it was time to talk about the night before.

I said "Ladies, I need some answers."

Alison replied, "absolutely, we'll answer all the questions that we can and all of the questions that we are allowed to answer."

She didn't explain why they were not allowed to answer some questions.

I said "We all went to church today. I think we all agree that it was a wonderful service. I've been a person of faith my entire life, but without giving much thought to the vastness of the universe. I know you told Billy and me that there is another world, an infinite world, but you have not been very specific about God and the details of what the infinite world is really like."

"I guess what I'm asking is, after all these years, are the things in my Catholic faith that I've been taught to believe—are they true?"

There was a moment of silence.

Then Alison spoke. "Miles, tell me if you remember this story that you once told me. Your basketball team was playing an away game that I couldn't attend. Before you left for the game that night you told me that you had the better team and you expected to come home with a victory. However, by the end of the third quarter, you were losing by 14 points. You told me that you knew your team had the ability to win that game, but that it wasn't about plays and strategies, it was about your players believing in each other. You told me the speech you gave them about believing and trusting in each other, that they could win if they played unselfishly and as hard as they could for the final eight minutes. You told them you had faith in them and that they should have faith in each other."

"Yes, I remember that game very clearly."

"How would you have felt if I had walked up to you right after that time out, and whispered in your ear, 'you are not going to win?' How would you have felt if I had whispered in your ear, 'you are going to win?'"

Again, there was a moment of silence.

"Well," I said, "If you had done either one of those things, it would not have changed my belief at that moment that we were going to win that game, because I had faith in them and I could feel that my team had faith in each other."

Alison said "It is not for Jessica or Dana or me to question or reaffirm your faith in God. It is not for us to redefine it and shape it. It is your faith and it is a strong one and it's one of the reasons that I knew you were the one for me. You believed in something greater than yourself. I'm sorry if this answer is insufficient for you Miles, but right now, you should be happy with the things that you believe in. Because when you strip it down, away from all the pomp and circumstance, your faith is telling you to love your brother and sister as you would love yourself. That's wonderful. Isn't it?"

Jessica added, "We are not here to go through the details of the Old Testament and New Testament, or Buddhism, or Hinduism, or Islam or the other isms. Don't let anything that's happened change the beliefs that make you a moral and ethical man, Miles."

Dana jumped in "Billy, I know that your being a scientist, and having to wrestle with the scientific method has made you vacillate between being an agnostic and an atheist over the years. You are a good man, a moral and ethical man, and I have seen you stand up for all the right things over the years. Could you use a little more faith in things in your life that you can't actually see? Probably. But who couldn't? You are my husband and I love you with all my heart. I know you love the kids, and I know you love me. Our kids love you as their father and that's easy to see for anyone who's looking. This road that we are going to take you on, you and Miles, will be an eye-opener. However, don't either of you doubt who you are and the simple but important things that you believe in right now. Just keep an open mind and there will come a time when..."

Dana looked at Jessica, then Alison looked at Jessica.

The three of them connected on some different level for a moment.

Then Jessica said, "Yes, there will come a time when we can answer more, if not all of your remaining questions, but not before we have completed our travels through the universe."

Billy and I looked at each other and we both seemed relieved that there were answers forthcoming by the end of this journey.

Jessica said "I promise, if we missed something along the way, you can ask your questions then."

I think that made us both relax.

Dinner arrived. Once everyone was served, Alison turned to our waitress and said, "If you wouldn't mind pulling the curtains, we would love to eat in private. She smiled at Alison. As she started to back out of the booth and pulled the curtains closed, she said "Have a great Christmas dinner everyone. Thanks for coming to Blackbird's."

6. Gimme Shelter

A couple of days later, everyone had reached home and gotten through the holidays in one piece. Jessica was back at Johns Hopkins; Dana and Billy were at the winery, and Alison and I were back to working, teaching, coaching, and raising our family.

I was eagerly awaiting information about the logistics of our future trips, since we lived across three different time zones. Alison explained that our trips would take place during sleeping hours. All five of our bodies would be receiving the rest that sleep provides, even though our infinite essences would be visiting other worlds.

Billy and I were told to keep a journal, to write down what we saw, what we smelled, what we touched, what we heard, and what we felt about each planet that we visited. Most importantly, we needed to write down what we learned about our visits. Alison told me that we probably only travel about two nights a week, so that we would not be overwhelmed and would have time to digest our observations and write in our journals. She told me that we might even visit multiple similar planets on a given night.

Basketball season was coming to a close in the next three to four weeks. One night when I got home after a late practice and a tiring day, Alison turned to me and said, "Miles, tonight we're going on our first trip and I can see by the look in your eyes that you're tired. Don't worry, your body will get the rest it needs."

I was tired and I started to make myself a cup of coffee before I plopped down at the dinner table. Alison said, "No Miles, you don't normally drink coffee after 2 o'clock and you're thinking you need to drink it to stay awake for this, but you don't. Your body needs its rest and doesn't need caffeine or you'll never fall asleep. Just relax and have some dinner and I'll put the kids to bed. Dana will reach out to Jessica and me when her kids are in bed and asleep. Then we will be off."

A few hours later, I lay down in bed and thought about how wonderful our first trip had been. I started to get excited remembering the beautiful sights from Dana's home world, the fresh ocean breezes that had blasted us in the face. It was like Christmas all over again.

Alison came to bed, but she seemed nervous, which was unlike her. I'm not sure that I had ever seen her this twitchy, but I didn't say anything. I just reached down to grab her hand as we lay next to each other in bed. She finally seemed to relax.

About five minutes later she squeezed my hand, we turned to look at each other and she said, "Miles, it's time to go, but I just want to tell you something."

"What is it?"

"Not all of our trips are going to be like the first trip. Remember, don't let yourself have any expectations or..."

She stopped talking.

"Or what Alison?"

"Just keep your mind open to everything and anything that might happen. Don't worry, we won't expose you to anything that you can't handle. Are you ready?"

This discussion briefly disrupted my relaxed state of mind, but I exhaled and said "I'm ready."

"Okay. Three, two, one, close. Open."

When I opened my eyes, I quickly tried to orient myself to my surroundings. There was no beautiful scenery or ocean breezes this time. The five of us were standing behind two rows of five seats, which faced an enormous window. There were people occupying nine of the 10 seats. We were looking directly into outer space. We could see a planet below us, which we appeared to be orbiting. The four women and five men in the seats were talking to each other. You could feel the tension in what they were saying, even though their language was foreign to Billy and me.

Alison had told me we should just refer to our visits as Planet 1, Planet 2, Planet 3, and so on, because on each planet there were multiple languages, and so to make up a name for each planet out of those languages would be meaningless. Billy and I were told that if **we** wanted to name the planets after a visit, that we could, but that we should still maintain the numbering system.

Alison said we were on a space station orbiting the home planet of the nine people in the seats, who were astronauts. Having never been in space, both Billy and I were really excited. To look out and see the darkness that surrounded the beautiful world below, which looked like Earth and had more azure-blue water than land, was spectacular. You could see the weather systems and whiteness that seemed to cover their North Pole but was absent from their South Pole.

Jessica said "Remember, no one can see or hear us, so we can talk to each other openly."

She continued, "Let me give you the background information you need to know about this visit. This planet is slightly more technologically advanced than Earth and most of the countries and continents have reached a stage of being able to provide shelter and food to their populations.

However, there is one continent that is still lagging behind in their ability to feed and nurture their population.

"Unfortunately, these wealthier nations, while they do send cursory aid, are not doing enough for the countries on this poverty-stricken continent. Hence, the level of disease, infection, and the shortness of life span on this continent, are huge problems.

"Also, the countries on this planet have not evolved past the old grudges and bad feelings towards other nations, because of past wars, current wars, or various injustices. So, to say that this planet is at peace just because they've reached 80 percent technical proficiency in providing their populations with food, medicine, education, and order, would not be correct.

"Questions?"

Jessica gave Billy and me plenty of time to think. She was in no rush, and we could see her demeanor had changed from the first night, to being more open and patient with us.

I didn't have any questions, because I was just blown away by where I was and what I was seeing as I walked around. Just like on earth, the astronauts here were of different races.

Billy said "I guess my question is, though I can see we are not orbiting Earth, why are we in a space station orbiting this planet? You could have just taken us up to the International Space Station orbiting Earth."

Jessica replied, "On this planet, there are many more nations that possess nuclear weapons and the means to deliver them than there are on Earth. These missiles have the ability to defeat 95 percent of the defense systems that these nations cling to as false hope against surviving a nuclear holocaust. This world is incredibly similar to Earth in that it is still dependent on fossil fuels. They are also still producing other consumable products that pollute the environment. Therefore, the countries that do have oil wells and coal mines are of the utmost importance to everyone on the world stage."

I said "I've seen simulations of holes in our ozone layer, but I don't see anything like that here. Is there a part of the planet that you want to point out to us? Did you bring us here for a lesson in environmentalism?"

Dana said "No, I wish that was why we were here. Jessica is just giving you the needed background information on Planet 2."

Jessica said "Now, let me set the stage for you about what has happened here in the last 10 days. A terrorist group successfully carried out the largest terrorist attack ever witnessed on this planet. They were able to set off a small nuclear device in a stadium holding 70,000 people, killing all of them. Another 30,000 in the surrounding area also were killed. As you can imagine, many more are now suffering from radiation burns and sickness.

"What's been going on here is that the two most powerful nations have been talking to the leaders of the assaulted nation. They are trying to convince the victim nation, that while the attack was horrific, striking back with a nuclear device would be extremely dangerous to the entire planet, due to the complex nature of the treaties among the nuclear-capable nations.

"However, what none of these nations know, but what we know, is that there is one rogue nuclear power whose eccentric leader, better described as a dictator, is minutes away from deciding whether to launch—or not launch—a nuclear strike against the already-terrorized nation. While the rogue nation doesn't have the capacity to destroy that nation, the nation that was already attacked has defense systems that would probably launch massive nuclear attacks against all the nations they consider to be their enemies."

"So, we're going to see a nuclear war from orbit?" asked Billy. "Please tell me that's not why you brought us here."

"We don't know," said Jessica. "Like I told you before, we don't know what's going to happen in the future. No one knows what the future holds. You can tell, just by listening and watching the three of us, that this is the most poignant and critical moment in the history of this world. I know you don't understand the language, but just watch these astronauts and their interactions. You can see the tension growing. You can see arguments. You'll probably see tears, I'm sure. The reason they're all sitting together now is that the announcement is scheduled in the next few minutes on whether or not peace talks have been successful."

"So, let's observe a moment of silence and send good thoughts and prayers to the people below who are trying to keep peace on this world."

A few moments later, the tenth astronaut occupying the space station came around the corner. Based on the insignias on his uniform, he appeared to be in charge. What he told the other nine astronauts seemed to please them. There seemed to be a sigh of relief from the astronauts as well as the five of us.

A few moments of calm followed.

Then Jessica spoke. "I'm sorry to tell you this, but there's a nuclear payload on the way and this could get ugly real fast. These people in the space station don't know it."

Again, there was silence.

Dana said "The missile evaded the defense system and is about to hit a major city. Keep your eyes on the upper right continent along their western coast."

We all trained our eyes that way. Then we saw the mushroom cloud. Even though it was small from outer space, the impact had to be enormous. I could see that the sisters were upset. Finally, one of the astronauts pointed it out to the rest of their team and they put their noses up to the glass and started to argue back and forth.

After a few minutes, other mushroom clouds started to appear. First, just a few. Then, with each minute that passed, more and more appeared. At first the astronauts were quiet. They were saddened at what they were witnessing. We were in disbelief at what we were witnessing. This went on and on and on.

Alison put her back against the wall and slid down into a seated position behind the back row of chairs. She covered her face and wept. I sat down on the floor next to her. I was shocked and numb and at a loss for words. The explosions finally stopped and an enormous amber cloud covered 90 percent of the world below. Only the small continent at the equator seemed untouched.

Holding back my tears, I pointed out the window and asked, "Why did no one strike that continent?"

Jessica said, "that's the one impoverished continent I was talking about. They have no nuclear weapons. They have no fossil fuels or minerals, nothing that anyone wants, except there are people living there that have great value. They were ignored by the people who could've helped them. However, there was no reason for anyone to attack them. Unfortunately, the nuclear cloud and nuclear winter will eventually destroy their vast green vegetation and will kill many with radiation sickness."

"I have to tell the both of you that the horrific deaths of the physical bodies of so many people at the same time is utterly debilitating and painful to the three of us. Please forgive me if I need time in between to answer questions." Billy then asked the last question in the world I would have ever asked, but I'm not Billy.

Billy said "Can we go down there?"

I stared at him. I thought it was the craziest question I had ever heard. Then I heard the craziest answer.

Dana said, "Yes."

"Yes?" I yelled. "Are you all insane? Forget about just the physical destruction by nuclear weapons that we will be walking through. I can imagine the amount of dead bodies we're going to see that haven't been incinerated. I can imagine the dying people we're going to see and we are not going to be able to help them. I don't want to go down there."

Alison turned to me and said, "Miles, we need to go down there, if even for just a brief time. Trust me, this needs to be part of the trip. We knew that if this situation went bad, the two of you would need to go through this whole learning experience. Trust us, we will not be injured in any way and we won't make you stay longer than you can take. So, let's just get this over with."

I saw tears coming from her eyes again.

Dana said "Grab hands."

In the blink of an eye, we were on the surface of the planet, though there was no life to be seen. Apparently, we were on the edge of a blast zone and bodies had not been totally incinerated. I heard screaming nearby and then more screaming in the distance, people in excruciating pain. Eighty to 90 percent of the buildings around us had been leveled. There was smoke everywhere. As I looked up, the sky started to glow red in the distance, blood red. We looked up into the heavens and saw swirls in the clouds, strange swirls like miniature tornadoes.

Billy had seen them too and asked, "What in the world are those swirls?"

Alison answered, "Those are the infinite essences of people who just had their lives taken away from them, in an instant, when it went from 70 degrees to 10,000 degrees. It's a shock even to the infinite world."

The smells around me were nauseating.

Alison said, "Even though this area was not directly hit, it was heavily populated, and I hate to tell you this, but you are smelling what happens to life when it's ended in this manner."

Just then a dog that had survived the initial blast came racing out of a demolished building, squealing because he was on fire. He dove on the ground and wriggled around and tried and tried to save himself.

I screamed, "Can't we help him?"

Jessica shook her head no.

I turned to Billy and unleashed my wrath on him.

"God damn it, Billy, I want to get the fuck out of here now. What in the world do you want to see down here? Haven't you seen enough? This has nothing to do with you being a fucking scientist so don't give me that horseshit. Ladies we need to get out of here **now**!"

Billy responded "I'm sorry, I'm sorry, I don't know what I was thinking."

Dana said "No, Billy, we would have brought you down here even if you hadn't asked. Miles, that's just the way it is, but we can get out of here now."

We grabbed hands and bang, we were out of there and back in the space station.

Jessica turned to us and said, "What's going on up here is this. There are two space stations from different countries in orbit around this planet. Both captains have been talking on a secured line. They agreed that they were all going to die anyway and they made a private pact to put the stations on a collision course about a week from now, while both crews were asleep. They could end their suffering that way, rather than starve or suffocate to death over a long period of time. They both knew that no one was coming to save them, and if they did come, where would they go? They said they would lie to their crews and tell them that both stations agreed to do what they could to survive in the coming weeks."

That was all I needed to hear. I was completely devastated. I could see Alison looking at me like I was a stranger. She had never seen me this way. I had never been this way. I didn't know what to say. I started to do my deep breathing to calm myself down.

I looked outside the window and now the planet was totally covered with red glowing smoke. I fully expected the planet to light on fire like a candle wick at any moment.

I sat back down against the wall and Alison joined me. I didn't look up but I said to the group "I'm okay. Anytime we're all ready to go, I'm okay to go."

Billy asked "Alison, how many, how many people lived on this world?"

"About 4.8 billion people."

I finally looked up and I am sure I had a zombie-like expression on my face. The astronauts on the station were crying and screaming at what had happened. I stared out the window at the planet below. I couldn't get the images of the dead people out of my mind. I couldn't get rid of the excruciating image of that dog burning. We were standing there and could do nothing about any of it. Then it occurred to me that the sisters had told me many times, that each planet is on their own, that each planet has to make their own decisions and live by the consequences. We had witnessed the consequences of this world. It left me broken. I was hollow inside.

Jessica said "guys, you're going to get through this. Make sure you are writing in your journals."

About 10 minutes later, Dana took us all back to our homes.

I couldn't keep my body from waking up instantly. It was about four-thirty in the morning and I usually got up about six, so I decided to stay up. Alison was awake as well. I told her to come over to me in bed so I could hold her. We just lay there speechless until about five. During that time that we lay there, I was emotionless. What I had just witnessed had sucked all the joy out of me, to a level I had never experienced before. I hoped and prayed that I never had to witness anything like that again. I hoped and prayed that our children and our children's children would never have to be a part of anything like that in the future.

Then I kissed Alison on the forehead and said, "I'm going to get up, Sweetheart. I'll make some coffee."

"Miles, wait," Alison whispered.

"We are going to be taking you to a lot of wonderful places. Don't let yourself be destroyed by today's trip. It was a necessary learning experience. We really didn't know what would happen, but we knew they were on the brink of self-destruction. Even if the nuclear holocaust had not happened, you would have at least experienced the tension of the moment. The bad news is, as horrible as what happened today was, there are worse places in the universe. Please don't try to imagine them, because it'll take you into areas of your mind where no one should go alone. Remember, you've got some notes to write over the next couple days. There's an important reason for that. Once you have written about all your feelings and observations about a trip, you can just close the journal and leave them. They will be there if you want to revisit them. Does that mean all the pain will instantly go away? No. But some of it will. As we continue our journeys, you will see how important your journal is, and that it will help you move past what happened today and other moments in the future. However, we all will never forget today. You know it and I know it. It was horrific."

We both got out of bed and we held each other and rocked back and forth for a few moments. Alison's words of wisdom were profound and they helped, but I was still a hollow man, void of emotions and staring off blindly into the distance.

I would normally have kissed Alison before I went to the kitchen, but I just ended the embrace and walked out towards the coffee maker. It was as if I was mad at her and her sisters for putting Billy and me through this.

Then I realized I had just been naïve to think that we were going to be exposed to one paradise after another. Then I said out loud, but quietly, to myself, "Stupid Miles, you're just stupid."

I had done that a lot when I first started teaching and coaching, when I made mistakes in the classroom or in the gym. With each experience I had, I said it less and less over the years.

However, it applied today.

When Alison came down in her robe, I grabbed her and held onto her.

"Today is going to be the hardest day of my life, because I have to go to school and practice, and I won't be able to talk to anyone about this. "

I had never carried a burden as enormous as this. I carried that burden around with me all day, like a 500-pound backpack.

7. Miles Away

When I came home from school that night, I couldn't remember any part of my day. I didn't remember making eye contact with anyone. I didn't show the enthusiasm that a classroom teacher needs to make students care about the day's lessons. I didn't have energy for my basketball players at practice that night. I excused myself a number of times during practice. When I left the gym, I found the nearest out-of-the-way wall, sat down and just gazed into the distance. I got in my car, drove home, and pulled into my garage, and in all that time I might have run every red light and every stop sign on the way home. I just didn't remember.

I came into the house and I could see in my peripheral vision that Alison was looking at me, but I didn't make eye contact with her. We said our hellos, but instead of giving her a kiss and a hug, as I did every night, I asked her to excuse me and I kept walking into our small home office.

Alison was right behind me, but there was silence between us. I knew she wanted to talk, to make sure I was okay, but I didn't want to talk. She watched me put my things away and start preparing for the next day at school. A couple minutes later, she turned, left the room and went to the kitchen to make dinner.

Dinner with the kids went fine. I spoke as little as possible. The kids really didn't know anything was bothering me. Alison didn't force the issue. We each had our after-dinner clean up chores, and when they were done, I returned to my office.

A few minutes later I sensed Alison standing at the door. Without turning my head, I said "Alison, is that you?"

She said, "Yes Miles, it's me."

"I've got my journal out and I'm going to try to start writing my thoughts, but if there's something you need from me first..." I just kept staring down at the desk.

"Well, okay then," Alison replied. "I'll leave you to your writing." She turned and quietly walked away.

It took almost an hour before I picked up a pen. Then I started to write.

Planet 2

Today I witnessed death, killing, and murder on a global level that no one on earth has ever witnessed. Four billion people lost their lives in what seemed to be the blink of an eye. I'm searching for the lesson that I learned today. People are evil? People are arrogant? People are hateful? People are ignorant? People are greedy? People are innocent victims? The answer to all those questions is yes. If it was only the awful people that perished, would I feel like this? Most of the people that perished were innocent. I don't understand it. I'm thinking about my children. I'm thinking about all the kids in my school. I'm thinking about all the good people I know and my family and friends. When I think about them, it was people like them who lost their lives today. I don't understand why I'm not breaking down in tears. Is it because there's something lacking inside of me? Has this experience destroyed who I was? Am I destined to live out the rest of my life with the images of Planet 2 swirling in my head, replaying them over and over again, until I end up in a mental hospital? Then, when I tell my doctors what's bothering me, they'll never believe it and they'll start giving me schizophrenic medications and put me in a straitjacket.

I quickly stood up, threw the pen down, and pushed the journal away from me.

I started talking to myself.

"Miles, get a grip, maybe today's not the day to do this writing."

I stood there for a couple minutes. I closed the journal and put it in a drawer that I locked every night. I had made up my mind that that was enough and I would revisit my writing tomorrow.

I pretended to be watching game film until I knew Alison was asleep. Then I crawled into bed saying nothing. My eyes were wide open staring at the wall next to my bed, facing away from her. I lay there for a long time without logical thought, just images frozen in my memory. Finally, in case Alison was awake, I whispered her name softly.

"Yes Miles?"

There was a long silence.

I finally said "I want to hold you close, but there is something that's stopping me. It's the guilt that I **can** hold you close, **and** that all of the people on Planet 2 can no longer hold each other close. For some reason, because I witnessed the destruction of their world and did nothing to prevent it, I feel like I don't deserve to hold you or anyone close."

There was more silence.

"I know there was nothing that I could do, but that doesn't make it better."

More silence.

Then I uttered the last words I would say before falling asleep. "Good night, Sweetheart." I didn't hold Alison. I didn't touch her. I didn't kiss her. Alison whispered "it's okay Miles. Remember that I love you and a lot of other people love you. You need your rest, so fall asleep and I'll still be here in the morning."

*   *   *

The next couple days were a replay of the previous day. The only difference was I didn't even take my journal out of the desk.

On the third day, after dinner, Alison came into the office, closed the door and said to me, "Jessica and Dana wanted to make a trip tonight, but I told them it was too soon. I just wanted to let you know. You have to work through this. I am here for you if you need to talk."

"Thank you. But before I can talk, I need to be able to feel again."

The next morning came and I was still going through the motions. Right before I walked out the door, Alison called out from the other room, saying, "Miles, your mom called me yesterday and she's going to join us for dinner tonight and stay and visit for a while. I just wanted to let you know."

"Thank you," I said and walked out the door.

I came home that night and dinner was on the table. My mom was there and the kids were all in their seats. The kids were happy and smiling from ear to ear, because that's how grandma made them feel.

My mom came over to me and grabbed my face with both hands, as usual, and kissed me on the cheek. I hugged her squeamishly, as if she were a dead fish. I knew Alison hadn't said anything to her, but she didn't need to. My mom stared into my eyes and I couldn't look away. She said, "Are you okay? Are you sick, or have you had a long day or a long week?"

I looked at her and said, "Yeah mom, it's been a long week and I'm sorry I seem so tired. It's so great to see you as always."

Both she and Alison knew those words didn't come out of the real Miles. That's just not how I spoke to my mother.

One of the greatest things that Alison ever taught me was about my relationship with my mom. It wasn't anything she said, it was what I saw in how Alison interacted with my mother over the years. The two of them had gotten close so quickly that my mom treated Alison like she was her own daughter. Alison ran up to her every time they would see each other and Alison hugged her so tightly and told her she loved her. My mother would be all aglow. Then, one day, I realized that Alison showed more genuine affection to my mother than I did. That was the last time I gave my mother a halfhearted welcome—until this night.

After dinner was over and the dishes were done and grandma told the kids some bedtime stories, we three had time to visit. We were sitting around the living room on our old beat-up furniture. The television had some inconsequential basketball game on, with the volume turned all the way down, because my best girls both knew I loved basketball. They granted me that indulgence whenever they could.

As I sat down and looked at Alison and mom on the couch, I felt the slightest bit of life crawling back into my body. Not much. But some.

Alison said, "Miles, your mom was just telling me the story of her family and all the generations that owned and farmed their land in Hungary. Did you know that their family lived in the same home for 300 years before the Russians took their land away after World War II?"

I looked right at Alison with embarrassment and said, "No, I didn't know that. Mom, why didn't you ever tell me that?"

But I knew the answer before I even asked it. Neither my mom, nor my father, nor my aunts and uncles ever talked about World War II and what had happened to their family and friends. However, Alison could get anyone to talk — and anyone included my mother.

"Keep going Mom," Alison said.

"Yes, it was in 1729 when a number of German families purchased land in and around the farming village of Mucsi. We ate what we raised on our farms. Everyone in town knew each other and got along. Our kids learned both German and Hungarian at the one school in town and everyone in the village went to the same Catholic Church. Our town had stayed out of the way, for the most part, in World War I. They took some of our men for the Army, but not too many.

"World War II was different. They took many of our men to fight on the German side, including your grandpa. Then, after the war, the Russians took over the Hungarian areas.

"As the war was coming to an end, Russians came into our town and took some of the teenage girls, including your Aunt Anna and Aunt Gotto, my two older sisters. They had to work in the Russian coal mines. That left me home as the youngest of the family, with my mom and my grandma. When the war finally ended, the Russians came into our town and issued orders in our town that every family had to declare whether they were German or Hungarian. If we were German, we had two hours to take whatever we could carry and start walking to a railroad line that went to Frankfurt, which was in the American-controlled sector. If we declared ourselves as Hungarian, we could stay.

"Ninety-five percent of us were Germans. We gathered what we could, with no idea where we were going or where we would end up. My sisters were still gone, working in the coal mines in Russia, and your grandfather had still not returned from the war, even though the fighting was over. No one could even tell us if he was dead or alive."

"It was on the third night of walking to the train yard, which was three towns away, that the Russian guards who were accompanying us got drunk. They came over to the women and started to make advances. My mother told me to just shut my eyes and pray. I did what my mom said. She held me tight and put her hand over my eyes. Our prayers were answered. The captain of this platoon was a good man and ordered the drunken Russians away from us. The next day we climbed into cattle cars, 32 to a car. The train cars had no bathroom and the roofs leaked whenever it rained. The only food we had was what they gave us when the train stopped, one time a day. It was mostly potato soup and a piece of bread.

"When we got to Frankfurt we were taken into the countryside, to the small towns around the city. German people whose homes were still standing had been told to take us in as boarders until we could find a place of our own. The order was taken so seriously that the mayor of each town went from house to house to make sure that each family was hosting at least one displaced family. We were lucky that we found a kind family to take us in and give us one room to live in. We found whatever work we could and tried to save our money.

"The Salvation Army would come to town once a month with new information about loved ones. Alive or dead? That's what everyone needed to know so the process of putting families' lives back together again could continue.

"Eventually, your grandfather came home alive and uninjured. My two older sisters came home from the coal mines. My oldest sister, Aunt Anna, had a severely injured hand where a coal car had run over it. A couple years later, we learned that Aunt Gotto had black lung disease that would cut her life short, and she wound up dying in her late 30s."

Alison and I sat there spellbound as mom told the story. I didn't know any of this. What kind of son was I to not know this?

Alison said respectfully "Mom, that was quite an ordeal. I never would have guessed that we would hear that story from you tonight. Thank you so much for sharing it with us."

"I do have a question. During all that time, and all that pain, what is it that got you through? I mean, was there something that you focused on that kept your hopes alive—that everything would turn out okay?"

"My faith in God," mom said.

"In the German town we settled in after the war, there was only one church. Because there were people of many faiths, the church had to be shared by all the different faiths. On Saturdays, the priest that Rome had assigned to our area said a Catholic Mass. All of us looked forward to that. In a way, it gave us the ability to pray to God to deliver us good news. So, my faith in God and my hopes lived from Saturday to Saturday to Saturday."

"After your Aunt Anna and Aunt Gotto were released from the coal mines in Russia, they had gone to Mucsi and were told that we had gone to Germany. With help from the Salvation Army, they tracked us down in Germany. They were like walking skeletons. Your Aunt Anna—even though she was happy to find us—the ordeal had pulled all of the joy out of her soul. One night in bed, I turned to her and asked her if God had helped her get through her ordeal. She told me that, for the last 18 months of her life in that Russian hell, she went through every day like a robot. She just assumed that she would fall over one day and die. She didn't talk to anyone, just existed. Aunt Anna told me she stopped praying, because she felt forsaken by God. I snuggled up close to her, I brushed her hair back behind her ear and whispered to her 'That's okay Anna, I was praying enough for the both of us.' I told her that it was a miracle that she and Gotto had found their way back to us. She cried for a long time. The next morning when she got up, and every day after that, her old self came back a little at a time. We were all thankful."

My mom stopped for a moment to take a drink of ginger ale.

"Miles, that's where I fell in love with your dad, who was in the American Army. To see young people in love, to celebrate weddings with flowers and dancing and to see and hold newborn children again, helped all of us a lot. When our family was finally back together, we all decided to move to the United States, because there were German families and company owners there that wanted Germans to come to the United States and work for them. That's how we got here. The records are all at Ellis Island of the day that we came through."

Alison said, "well, if you had never come to the United States, I would've never met Miles. I can honestly say that I can't imagine my life without him, Mom."

With that, my mom and Alison hugged and cried. Alison ran out of the room for a box of tissues as they hopelessly tried to stop crying and save their eye makeup.

Alison looked over at me. Even though I sat silently, tears were streaming down the side of my face. She came right over to me, wiped the tears from my face and held me. Then my crying started in earnest. I was crying so hard I thought my heart would burst. My mom got up from the sofa and stood next to us with her arms around both of us, shushing us, stroking our hair like a mother telling her children everything is going to be okay. Little did she know that I was crying as much for all of the families on Planet 2 as for our family.

When my mom left that night, I made sure I was the one hugging her and kissing her the hardest, the way Alison had taught me. That night, I held Alison close to me all night long. The next morning and throughout that day, I felt more and more of my normal self returning.

Still, I'll never forget one of the last things mom told us that night. Alison had asked her how everyone around them had survived all of this physical and mental abuse.

My mom told us that during World War II, over 60 million people died. Not just in Europe but in the Pacific and all around the world. The world had never seen anything like that before and she hoped we would never see anything like it again.

"However, when something horrific happens to you," Mom said, "there comes a point in each person's life, where you have to choose to live on and live life to the fullest, or you will just shrivel up and die. Those who could not make that choice to live on, did shrivel up and die. That type of person would live a very short life of depression."

Mom said "Even though we tried to help them, they couldn't let go of the horror and the images. It was not their fault. It was pure evil that had forced that horror upon them. They were not the ones that started these wars, but they became victims. So, we chose to live. Just remember, that whatever tough situations you go through, the situation ends, and you have to pick up life and you must choose to keep living it to the fullest."

On Sunday night I was downstairs listening to my bootleg version of Neil Young at Massey Hall. After that night with my mom and Alison, one of his songs, Don't Let It Bring You Down, suddenly had a whole new meaning for me, especially the line "just find someone who's turning." Well, I guess that was my own mom.

8. Is this Heaven?
No, It's Mayberry On Steroids

Monday morning came and Alison told me that it was important for all of us to have a normal week. So, that's what we did. On Wednesday night, I called Billy in California. We visited on the phone for an hour about our journal entries. I shared the emotional roller coaster that I had gone through. He told me he was happy that I had made it back to my normal self.

While he shared some of the same emotions, he had become more focused on the technology of Planet 2. He had come to the conclusion that although their technology surpassed what we had on earth; their technology was next to useless without peace in the world.

We agreed that we were grateful for Earth's current nuclear treaties. However, we also agreed it wasn't enough. The world had to take larger steps forward to assure that we wouldn't blow up our planet. Complete elimination of nuclear weapons had to be the goal. We both agreed on that.

On Wednesday night, at about 2:30 a.m., I woke up with a violent shudder from my recurring nightmare. Alison said "Miles are you okay? Did you have another nightmare?"

My breathing was very labored as I answered "Yeah."

"Was it about Planet 2?"

"No. After all of the horror I just went through on Planet 2, who would have guessed that I would dream about my old fear — knowing that someone was dead and being unable to remember the details?"

"Miles, I've been married to you for a long time now. I love you. Your family and friends love you for who you are. What you went through on that planet didn't change who you are. I hope and pray that someday we can figure this out and you can stop this recurring sense of dread in your life. Now turn around and let's go back to sleep and you stop worrying, I'm here."

I gave a deep sigh and Alison curled up to me and in about 10 minutes I was asleep.

Friday night came and Alison and I went out and to split a burger at our favorite railroad car diner. After the waitress took our order, Alison reached across the table, grabbed my hands and leaned into me as close as she could.

"Miles, remember that first night in the park at Iowa State?"

I was taken off guard a bit, but said "Of course Alison, you know I'll never forget that night. Why are you asking me about that night?"

"I want to ask you a question that's been on my mind a long time. When I first met you, you told me that you were in love with Rebecca who lived back in your hometown. You went into great detail talking about her during the time we spent together. Even though we both felt ourselves growing in our relationship, I really didn't know if either one of us would ever make it to that moment in the park under that full moon, and finally talk about our feelings for each other. After all, I did love Jack and had been dating him longer than you had been dating Rebecca."

Alison had my attention now. I don't know why she brought up the subject, but I was all in. I was more than willing to talk about it because it was one of the sweetest memories of my life.

"I have to wonder why you're talking about it tonight after our game. Did something happen today that made you remember that night? Is there a specific question you want to ask me?"

"Right now, it's not important what made me bring up the subject. What's important is the question I want to ask you," she said.

"Okay, go ahead."

"For the last week or two leading up to that walk on the nature trail, I could feel that you were being overcome by a sense of guilt. It seemed like you were battling against falling in love with me because you were betraying Rebecca."

"Well, didn't you feel the same guilt regarding Jack?"

"No Miles, I didn't. For me, falling in love with you didn't mean that I stopped loving Jack."

I was perplexed for a moment. Then, the memories came rushing back from all those years ago.

"Oh yeah, that's right. I remember when you told me about the phone call you had with Jack. That you told him that you still loved him, but that I was the one that you wanted to spend the rest of your life with. Wow, I'm going to have to think about this for a while to get my arms around it. I understand it, but I guess it was just in my DNA to feel guilty about falling in love with you before I told Rebecca."

"Miles I need to ask one more question. I want you to take your time and think about your answer, to make sure it's the real answer from that moment."

I drank from my water glass.

"What **exactly** did you feel guilty about?"

"Well..."

"Stop," Alison said.

"Just be quiet and think it through. I don't want you thinking out loud and then looking at the reactions on my face."

Now her voice went into a whisper. "Close your eyes if you have to."

I did close my eyes. Through my mind's eye I took myself back and I saw us walking down the nature path towards the park. I dove inside that moment and quickly connected with my feelings from all those years ago. With each step I took in memory, I fell deeper and deeper in love with Alison. Then, I was at the park, facing Alison, and the feeling of guilt jumped right up.

I said "Alison, at my age, at that moment in time, it was pretty normal for college guys to think about having sex with any beautiful woman, whether they had a significant other or not. With some of my friends, that's all they could think about. But most guys wouldn't feel guilty about that, or most of us would have been walking around feeling guilty all day, every day."

"Oh, I see," Alison said, looking a bit crestfallen.

She gathered herself and quickly retorted, "I've told you many times, Miles. I don't mind being told the obvious, but you don't have to tell me the incredibly obvious."

I chuckled. She got me on that one. Then I said "Wait, I'm not finished."

"But that's not why I felt guilty that night. I felt guilty, not because I wanted to sleep with you. I felt guilty because I wanted to kiss you, and I had never felt like that before in my life about any woman."

Alison and I locked eyes and she smiled, her face just radiating.

"Miles, that's what I hoped way back then, but I was afraid to ask you and have my bubble burst. I love you so much and I will for as long as my earthly body will allow it. Then, I will love you for eternity in the infinite world, but there's something you need to know. It's okay if you still love Rebecca. For a time in your life, she was your world. That's a beautiful thing. Don't ever let go of the good memories that the two of you had together."

I was a bit perplexed, but it was the best perplexed I had ever experienced. Somehow, I immediately reshuffled the memory cards in my brain and put my relationship with Rebecca in the loving and satisfied deck. In a strange way, I felt a sense of relief that Alison made me talk through it, but I couldn't say just why.

"Alison, I feel like you're holding something back about bringing this up tonight. Am I right?"

"Miles, everything that you and I talk about helps us with **our** relationship and **all** of the relationships in our lives. That includes our family and friends and people that we have yet to meet. It's a learning and growing process."

"There is an important reason that I brought this up. You coming to terms with your relationship with Rebecca was very important. Now you've got it in the correct perspective."

"Wow," I thought. Alison had led me to the right place, and she had gotten from me exactly what she was looking for. I was happy that I came up with the right answer. I was thankful to Alison for helping me get off the hook I had put myself on for all these years and reminding me how much I loved Rebecca. Most important, I felt relief that still loving Rebecca was okay.

As we split our burger, fries and shake, Alison let me know that we were going on a trip the next night. I was both excited and apprehensive.

Saturday came and the day seemed to drag with my anticipation of the trip. The time finally came when we were lying in bed, and then we left Earth to meet up with Jessica, Dana, and Billy on Planet 3.

Oh, what a planet it was, Planet 3.

We were standing at the edge of a farm field, looking out over the crops. In the opposite direction stood a white farmhouse with a green roof shaded by a ring of 80-foot oak-like trees. The latticework around the roofline and gables gave it character and suggested to me that generations had taken care of this building. The crop fields behind us stood at least 15 feet tall and they were filled with something that looked like corn. The air was so clean it had a sweetness to it. We were standing on a high spot and I could see other farms all around the area. Some also had groves of trees with fruits colored orange, green, yellow, pink, and purple. The sun had just risen, so it was casting long shadows everywhere.

Jessica said "Let's walk up to the farmhouse."

We started to walk the 50 yards or so to the farmhouse, while taking in everything around us. The grass at our feet was a bit thicker and softer than the grass on earth and I felt like I was walking on a mattress. As we got closer, we could see the beautiful flowers that had been planted all around the farm house. They were plentiful and in full bloom in many colors and shapes. We walked around the entire home and saw that it had a porch that wrapped around two sides, with plenty of chairs, a couple swings, and some children's' toys.

Jessica led us in through the back door. What we saw was a mother and a father gently waking their children from their sleep by stroking their hair and softly kissing them on their foreheads. Once everyone was up and dressed, they gathered in the modest living room. They formed a circle and held hands. The mother began to speak and when she finished, the father had his say. They looked around to see if any of the four children wanted to add anything. The tallest boy said a few words. His mother and father looked at him and then looked at each other and smiled. Then they all spoke, in unison, in what sounded like a prayer, a Pledge of Allegiance, or a traditional morning greeting. When it ended, the two older children went outside and started to ride down the road on their bicycles. Their bicycles were similar to Earth bicycles except that there were two wheels at the back.

The parents began to make breakfast, as the little ones set the table.

I said "So Jessica what is it we just witnessed?"

"On Planet 3, this is a typical lifestyle. The planet is mostly agrarian by choice. When the family got together the parents gave thanks for their family, they gave thanks for their friends, and they gave thanks for the peace that permeates this world. Lastly, they expressed thanks for the love that the people of their world share for each other. Then their oldest son added that he and all his siblings were thankful for and loved their parents. Then they spoke a traditional planetary prayer, giving thanks to the creator of their beautiful world. The two older kids drove down the road to see if their elderly neighbors were up and to provide help if needed."

"We'll come back in a few minutes, but let's go to town."

Then we were in the middle of the town square. It was fairly large and the park in the middle was beautifully manicured, with tall trees and gazebos surrounded by colorful flowers and play areas for children.

Dana said, "Down here are all the stores that these people need. They can get groceries, clothes, and all the things that you would find in our own homes back on Earth. There's also a doctor's office and a small hospital, but it's not used very often. There is also a place of worship over there." She pointed to an old but very well-kept wooden building with woodcarvings and painting on the outside.

The town was beautiful; the temperature was perfect, and the clouds were islands in the azure sky. I broke away from our group and started to run through the park as fast as I could, like a little kid, running for the swing sets. When I got to the playground, I got on one and then I saw that Alison was right behind me running and laughing. Alison said while she laughed, "Miles, what are you doing?"

"I'm tired of standing and being lectured to, so I felt the need to experience some of this world on my own," I replied as I pumped the swing with my legs, going higher and higher. Alison laughed and said "Well, you sure have come a long way in a short time from that night with your mom and me, and I couldn't be happier."

"Push me Alison, I want to go as high as I can!"

Alison pushed me until I was laughing so hard, I thought I would cry. By then Jessica, Dana, and Billy had walked over to us.

Dana said "Miles, the first time I came to this planet I did the same thing you did. I guess we both still have a lot of kid in us."

"Well, my grandpa always told me 'keep thinking like a kid and you'll never grow old,'" I replied.

Jessica said "We need to go back to the farmhouse, because something is going on that you need to witness."

We quickly returned to the farmhouse. One of the children apparently had fallen off her bike and injured her arm, which may have been broken. As she lay on her bed, her parents and siblings sat all around with their hands touching her. Their eyes were closed and they were in deep meditation. I looked at my companion's faces as they stared intently. Then I looked back at the bed. I didn't understand what was going on, but no one was saying anything, so I remained silent.

Five minutes passed. I saw the bruising go away and the arm straighten out and I realized what had happened. The broken arm was healed. I couldn't believe it!

Alison said, "On this planet, everyone understands their infinite nature. They understand that their physical bodies are temporary but are powerful channeling instruments. Their essence, in connection with each other, and in connection with the universe, can heal someone's injuries or sicknesses, physical or mental. They also understand that this healing power is limited to the lifespan of the human body. In other words, they just can't keep healing each other and live forever. No one here fears death. They understand that death is just the inevitable shedding of the physical body and a permanent entrance into the infinite world."

The girl got up from her bed smiling and addressed her family. No one needed to explain to me what she was saying. She was thanking them, and that scene became etched into my mind forever. When she finished, they all started to go about the business of the day, eating breakfast and going out to work on the farm and to school. It was wonderful to watch their lives.

Billy said "So ladies, we just witnessed another non-ordinary state of reality? Is our civilization on Earth capable of doing the same thing?"

Dana said "Yes. There are miracles that happen in our world all the time that we just don't know about. If you pay closer attention, you will see them all around you. Where there are two or more of us, with the correct focus, miracles can happen."

I said, "So can Billy and I achieve this?"

Jessica replied, "you are not there yet. You both have a long way to go, but you might get there someday."

Dana said, "there's one more place I want to take you before we all leave. It's one of the old barns near the back of the property, so let's just walk there."

We went into the old building and what I saw was something I would never have guessed in a thousand tries. The old barn was filled with technical devices covered in dust, soot and tarps. There were devices large and small. The only things that seemed recognizable to me were what I would guess to be televisions or monitors.

"Ladies, what exactly are we looking at?"

I sensed a long explanation coming.

Jessica said "this world has been peaceful for over 1,000 years. During their history, their technology had advanced to a point about 300 years beyond Earth's technology today. You see that television monitor over there? Well it not only can show you a picture in three dimensions, but it could provide smells, simulate wind, and for the brave-hearted viewers, it could actually disperse water, fire and smoke into the scenes of the movies and into your family rooms. Many of the smaller devices you are looking at were for communication between individuals and groups."

"Here's a summary of what happened. The civilization on this planet realized that all the technology they had created had dehumanized people. It was a movement that started small, and it took many generations, but they eventually decided that just because they could invent something, that didn't mean they had to use it. They slowly began to turn their back on what we would call 'pop culture technology' and only kept the technology that was necessary for the health and welfare of the population."

Billy said "that brings back to mind an old professor that I had in college. He had a singular vision that many of us would laugh at outside of the classroom, but now I get it. He told us that in any decision-making moment, choosing to do nothing was a decision. Now I get this. I really do."

Billy then said "What I saw here explains what my professor said, that a society that blindly accepts every new technology without making a conscious decision eventually becomes enslaved by those technologies."

Billy looked right at me and we were both smiling and nodding our heads. It had been a great trip.

Soon after that we returned to Earth and into our bodies at home, where Alison and I were in bed. It was about 2:30 in the morning. We were awake, but calm and wrapped in the glow of a peaceful joy that came back with us from Planet 3.

"Thanks for that trip," I said in a hushed tone.

"I love you, Miles. I love everybody, Miles, and I understand everyone doesn't love me, and that's okay," Alison replied impishly.

I started to laugh, because I remembered back to Iowa State when she first said that to me. However, now it meant so much more to me. Now I understood that she was trying to lead me to that condition of the heart that she always had. Now I knew that was part of the journey, and now I was looking forward to our next trip.

Just to be playful with Alison, I said "Actually, I do know somebody who doesn't like you."

"You can't bluff me, Miles. You don't know anyone who doesn't like me. Do you know how I know that?"

"How?"

"Because all the people who don't like me would never tell you. Gotcha!"

"Don't worry, I know pretty much all the people who don't like me. I love them anyway, because, as you know, that's okay—that they don't like me."

9. *I Just Love Elevators*

It was Friday night. Alison and I went to a big hotel by the freeway to attend a fundraiser for the school district's special education programs. We did this a few times a year and made it into a date night by having the kids stay over with friends or having a babysitter stay overnight at our house. Then we could stay over at the hotel.

The evening included a silent auction, dinner, then music and dancing until midnight. My beautiful Alison still fit into her little black dress. She had put her hair up and was wearing the diamond heart necklace I had given her years ago. Before we left the house, she came over and asked me to smell her perfume and tell me whether it was too much.

"Yeah, you kinda smell like a hooker," I said.

Alison tilted her head and smiled. "Thanks a lot. By the way, how do you know what hookers smell like?"

I deserved that, but that's what made our relationship work and I loved every bit of it.

Actually, she smelled like fragrant lilacs. I didn't say anything else, but she looked at me and smiled and she could tell that I liked it. What I really liked was her smile. Everything else about Alison was second to her smile.

After dinner Alison dragged me out on the dance floor as she always did. I had learned how to let her be the star, just dancing around me. I couldn't keep up with her, but just being her partner made me look good.

We returned to our table. As usual, a stranger came over, complimented Alison on her dancing and asked if I would mind if he danced with her. As always, I said "I love being with the most desirable woman in the room, as long as she comes home with me."

I always said it was up to Alison, because she might be tired. When Alison danced with these poor fellows, she held back and never really cut loose like she did with me. She would limit their time to one or two dances.

That night, after they danced, he led her back to her seat and thanked her. As he left, we looked at each other and snickered, as usual.

"You know, my dear, you look really great in that black dress," I said.

"Why thank you, Miles. It's always nice to hear you say that."

"So, have you had enough dancing for the evening? Would you like to head up to our room so we can relax?"

"Sounds good but give me a couple minutes to talk with Jenny over there about something that we have going at school," Alison said.

I chatted with the others at the table. The event had thinned out quite a bit. Alison was back in a few minutes and we said our goodbyes and our nice to meet you's to our new friends.

Just watching Alison say goodbye to complete strangers was one of the joys of my life. No one could resist her magic wand of happiness. She cast a spell on everyone, no matter what frame of mind they were in. In that moment, I felt so lucky—the luckiest man on earth. I was sure that without her, I could have grown up to be a bitter old basketball coach who lived in my office next to the gym. With her, I felt joy that no earthly man deserves to feel.

I had a lot of friends who were married. Most of them were happy in their marriages to one degree or another. I thought, is this happening with all my friends? As the years go by, do all of us love our wives more and more? Or am I one of the lucky few having this experience? Guys just didn't talk about these kinds of feelings with each other. Whatever the answer, it didn't matter to me. I loved Alison more year after year, hour after hour, minute by minute. When I thought about it, that was truly amazing.

After we left the others, we walked to the elevators. I pushed the call button and, in a moment, we walked in. I pushed the button for 18, our floor, and we turned around and faced the closing doors.

Our doors sealed tight and that moment of upward movement began.

Now that we were alone, I turned and faced Alison. I reached down, grabbed her hands and interlaced our fingers. I leaned in to kiss her but stopped just before our lips touched, then slowly pulled away. I could hear her sigh. I slowly pushed my body against hers until I had her trapped against the elevator wall. Then I took her hands and slid them up against the wall until they were above her head, pinning her in that spot with my hands and my body.

I moved my head towards the right side of her neck and whispered "We could be discovered at any moment." I kissed her neck three times, with each kiss getting longer.

She sighed again.

The elevator continued to go up.

Finally, I came face-to-face with her and said "Alison, in this moment, there's no way I could love you more."

I moved my lips to hers as slowly as possible until we kissed.

The elevator kept going up.

Moments later the elevator bell rang.

Neither one of us moved. Alison was still pinned up against the wall and we were now gently making out as if on our wedding night. Our kissing and breathing were in perfect harmony.

The doors opened and I heard a voice say "I guess we'll take the next one."

The doors closed and we continued upward. We said nothing.

Suddenly, I felt an enormous warm rush connecting us at our lips, at our chest and all the way down to our toes. I saw the stars in my mind. It was ecstasy. It was love. It was perfect.

Then I heard the bell and the doors opened at the 18th floor. We walked down the hallway hand-in-hand, without a word. We walked in and I turned on the lights. As the door closed behind us, Alison turned off the lights, then locked the door.

We could see each other in the dim light coming through our hotel window. Alison put her finger over her lips as she pushed me slowly towards the bed. A second later she put a finger over my lips and whispered "Shhhhh Miles, don't talk. Trust me."

Suddenly, Alison grabbed me, but what I thought would be a hug instead was a tackle that took me down on the bed. I started to laugh, because she had never done that before. She climbed on top of me, straddling me tightly. Then she started to roll us toward the end of the bed. I could feel we were only inches away from dropping off the bed and in the darkness, I yelled "Alison, stop!"

We didn't stop. We rolled off the bed and I braced for the crash on the floor.

But we didn't hit the floor. We didn't hit anything.

We kept falling and rolling into darkness. I didn't know what to do. I yelled "What's going on?"

"Just breathe and you'll be fine," Alison said.

We started to pull up from our fall, like an airplane pulling up from a steep dive. We leveled off. The next thing I knew, we were hurtling through the cosmos at an incredible speed. I could see galaxies and nebulas. I could see single and binary stars. I could see shockingly bright colors jump out of the darkness, like fireworks on the Fourth of July, and all the time I held on to Alison for dear life.

We were banking right and banking left through the universe. Then we started what felt like a dive and slowed down. We headed for a planet, reached its atmosphere and slowed down even more, then plunged into a brilliant blue ocean.

We flew past a wild assortment of fish, mammals and brightly-colored plants, all underwater.

Before I knew it, we popped out of the ocean like a missile launched from a submarine. In the blink of an eye we were back among the stars, flying past a dozen planets.

We stayed just outside the atmosphere of each planet, close enough to see the dark sides that were lit up artificially by their inhabitants, and the sunlit sides, which showed mountains, lakes, forests, and deserts.

My goosebumps had goose bumps that had goosebumps.

Alison calmly said "And you just wanted to have sex."

I said nothing.

In a minute, we entered darkness and came to a complete stop. There we were, me lying on the hotel bed with Alison on top of me. She rose up, put her hands on my chest, looked me in the eyes and said "Not bad for a girl in a little black dress, eh?"

I stammered out "What? What was that?"

Alison began to giggle and said "English teacher forgot how to talk, Miles?"

My eyes were bulging out of my head. I had never seen anything like that, nor had I ever imagined I could see anything like that.

"Let me try to answer all of your complicated and intellectual questions.

"What? I took you on a special tour of the cosmos.

"Where? Round-trip, we probably covered 500 light years.

"How? Just like all of our trips. Except this time, I went much slower so that you could enjoy the view.

"Why now? That's actually the best question of all. The answer is because of what happened between us in the elevator tonight.

"It was the first time that both our essences became one. When we connected completely in perfect love, it is the purest of joy. You need to know that I felt the same strong intense feelings that you did. It was wonderful. At that moment, we were in perfect harmony with the universe and our bodies would have looked like a starry night to anyone who saw us. It happened in an intimate moment between us, but it doesn't always happen in that way. And it's not always just between two people. It can happen with many people coming together at once in unconditional love. When that occurred, it allowed me to take you on the type of trip that we just experienced. You have officially passed one of the mile markers on your journey."

I replied "So, that's what it was? That's the feeling that we both had in that moment on the elevator?"

It was a rhetorical question. Alison didn't need to answer.

I took some deep breaths and tried to relax. I was starting to get it. I let my mind wander through the events of the evening. Alison had just taken me on a ride that no one could have imagined. As I reflected on the whole experience, from the elevator to this moment, I felt the universe and the planet getting smaller and smaller. At the same time, my life before me was getting larger and larger. Even though I still felt the immensity of the universe filled with a billion Earths and a billion civilizations, I remembered the words that Alison had uttered that snowy night in the train car diner: "Miles, the world is what's around you." It was all starting to make sense to me now.

Later, as we were trying to doze off from an extraordinary day, my mind wandered, going back through our entire life together.

Then it popped into my brain and there was no way to stop my mouth.

"Alison, there's a question that I've been meaning to ask you for a long time. I hope you don't feel like it's an awkward question. You told me that you were married in your previous physical life, but we have really never talked about it. Can you tell me a little bit about it?"

Right after the question came out of my mouth, I was sure that I had spoiled the moment. If I could've taken it back, I would have.

Alison was lying on the bed facing me, with her arm across my chest. After a few moments I could sense that she was okay with my question.

"Miles, where and when I lived before was nothing like Earth. I am living a human life with you. We live in the 21st century of this world and we do what human beings do in the 21st century. The planet where I was first born was at least 500 years farther down the evolutionary road than we are on Earth. The social mores there were very different than they are here and now."

"Yes, I did have a husband or partner, for lack of a better word, in my previous physical life. I also had a family. But right now, I don't see or talk to them. That way I can be in total focus on this life and on the here and now. I need to immerse myself in my mission of helping you and helping our children grow in the right direction. When all of our lives are over, we will be together in the infinite world."

I thought for a while about what Alison had told me.

Then I asked the logical question "Well, which one of us will be your husband or partner in the infinite world?"

Alison started to laugh.

"Miles, I'm sorry to tell you that the infinite world isn't like that. When you and I are finally together there, you will get to know and love everyone from my previous life and you'll love them just as I do now. You can look forward to that, rather than being jealous."

"That's all I can really tell you. We are allowed to let you visit planets right now. You can learn how they function, but until the end of our journeys, I can't tell you too much about the other life that I lived all those years ago. You would become consumed with it and lose all focus on what we're doing here. It's possible that we can visit my home world, just as we visited Dana's home world. If we do, then I can tell you more about the first physical world that I come from."

I said "I don't understand. Why are you not allowed to tell me about the important things in your life that happened before you met me?"

"Miles, you have to trust me. You will get to the point where you will either discover answers to mysteries, or we will tell you the answers to mysteries. You need to focus on two things and two things only. Our life together here on earth, and the journeys that we take you on. It will all take care of itself in the end. Trust me."

I was on my back and staring at the dark ceiling. There were a lot of directions I could go. Would I succumb to simple human jealousies? Would I become angry that my best friend wouldn't tell me more about her other life? Would I just clam up and pout? Or would I trust Alison?

I turned towards Alison and with my right hand I gently traced around the edge of her lips. I whispered to her as quietly as I could "I trust you."

Then I pulled her close. Then sleep slowly and softly descended upon us, like being covered by a blanket of pure new snowfall.

10. The Journal

A couple days later the three sisters, Billy and I met and discussed how to proceed with future trips to other planets.

Alison reported that Tommy had been staying in touch with us. We told the others what a delight it was to talk to him on the phone or when he stopped by the house. Alison said she wanted to include Tommy in our future trips. Dana and Jessica agreed. It became Alison's job to bring Tommy into the fold.

I said I wanted to include Michael. I fully expected a pushback from the ladies and even from Billy. To my surprise, no one said anything for about 30 seconds. Then Jessica told us that Michael had been staying in touch with her and she was thinking the same thing. There was a 10-minute debate about the pros and cons of including an impetuous Michael.

Alison reminded us that we were planning to take our children on these trips when they got older. Then she said "So, bringing a child like Michael along now shouldn't be a problem."

We all smiled and nodded in agreement. It helped that Jessica and Dana both volunteered to bring Michael up to speed.

Over the next two weeks, Tommy and Michael were told the short version of what had happened and what was planned. Together they made their first trip to Dana's planet, exactly as Billy and I had done. They were both just as excited as we had been.

We began making more trips, and each time we made a trip, Alison and I would visit Tommy before the three of us left to meet the others on the latest planet. Dana and Billy would pick up Michael in the same manner.

As the weeks went by, we visited more and more civilizations. It got to the point where we were taking three or four trips a week. To make it easier for us to absorb what was going on in each world, the sisters gave us, in advance, briefings on how each world had developed. That helped a lot.

Billy, Michael, Tommy and I started to have problems keeping up with our journal entries and keeping our information straight on each civilization. We told the ladies our homework was excessive. That was when we took a break from taking new trips and spent time revising our journals. Sometimes we would call each other in the evenings to make sure that we had the right information on the right civilization.

This was a labor of love for all of us. For me, some worlds were completely unforgettable. Sometimes I would go back and re-read my journal entries about those places, even though I had finished writing about them. That's probably why I was the slowest at updating my notes. I didn't care.

I asked Alison to look at my notes, but she said that she would enjoy it much more if I read my journal entries to her. So, after the kids were asleep, we would get ready for bed and I would sit in the chair in our bedroom and read to Alison, who was already in bed.

About the third night, Alison got silly with it.

"Tell me a story, daddy," Alison said, perfectly mimicking our little ones.

I laughed out loud. "Have you been a good girl today?" I said.

"Yes daddy, I did all my homework and put all my toys away, so I've been a good girl and I deserve a good story."

"Okay, I'll tell you one of my favorite stories. Ready? "

"Yes."

"Once upon a time: The End."

That joke really made the six-year-olds laugh! When our kids were pouting at bedtime, I would pretend to read that story out of a book. It got them in a better mood before I read them a real story.

Alison saw it coming, but laughed anyway and said, "Okay, okay, I'm ready for you to read me some of your journal entries, Miles."

"Ready, here we go."

Planet Seven

About 30 years before our arrival, the planet had reached a point where the people on most continents were thriving. Of course, there were wealthier and poorer countries, but even the poorer countries had begun to use medical, communication, and business technologies and they were starting to join in the global economy.

On this planet, exploration of space took priority over all other scientific research. There were 12 planets in their solar system and the other 11 were uninhabitable. Scientists had already sent manned missions to three of them and unmanned missions to another six.

However, a near Extinction-Level Event occurred well before we got there.

The astronomers saw there was a meteor coming that would pass close by their planet, but they were in no danger because the meteor would stay a safe distance away. Their main interest was to acquire specimens from the meteor.

There was no way to land on it. Their brightest minds came up with a plan to launch a spaceship to intercept it, armed with the largest conventional missiles that existed. It would fire at the meteor, breaking off smaller retrievable pieces that could be harvested and returned to Planet 7 for study. A fleet of 12 space shuttles would follow the path of the meteor to collect smaller debris.

Simply stated, they thought they could blow up Mount Everest and then have people stand around with fishing nets and catch the small pieces of rock as they fell to the ground.

That didn't sound like a good idea to me, and as it turned out, it wasn't.

The attack ship accomplished its mission of delivering four large missiles that struck the meteor. However, something unaccounted for happened, as the meteor apparently contained a number of minerals that were ignited by the missiles, and it blew up like a nuclear bomb.

The attack ship was incinerated, killing all 20 astronauts on board. While the debris field did not put the planet in jeopardy, the fleet of specimen-gathering ships was in big trouble. Even at maximum speed, they would not be able to escape from the large incoming debris field. Eleven of the 12 ships were destroyed and the crews—12 astronauts on each vessel—perished. One ship was badly damaged but survived, and managed to retrieve a dozen pieces of rock from the meteor.

That ship returned home. While most of the inhabitants of this world mourned the loss of the brave astronauts in space, the scientific community considered them collateral damage and was exuberant about the 12 pieces of rock. It took only a short time to realize that 11 of the specimens contained nothing of interest to the scientists.

The 12th rock, now exposed to the moderate temperatures on Planet 7's stable environment, began to grow a non-indigenous fungus, which quickly evolved into a number of small plants. The scientists were elated. After about a year of study, the scientific community announced that the new plants had secreted a gel like that inside an aloe plant on Earth. That extraterrestrial gel would make skin perfect, as clear as a newborn baby's skin. All moles, acne and other skin blemishes, including skin cancer, would vanish within a week or two. It was soon mass-produced and spread across the world quickly.

However, it had not undergone long-term testing and a grave side-effect appeared two years later. Users developed a viral infection that would lead to a horrible, painful death. The virus became airborne and devastated this world with a mortality rate higher than that of the Black Plague on Earth. A world of 5 billion people saw 4.5 billion die in a period of eighteen months.

Before his own passing, one highly-regarded scientist made a public plea to those who would survive: "return to the simple life!"

He said their ambition to reach the stars was unattainable and they should focus on medical research and on keeping the planet as healthy as possible, because one day an Extinction Level Event would end their civilization. He told them that nobody knew when that would happen. It could be in 100 years or 100,000 years, but it would happen. He told them most importantly, to cherish and love each other. Finally, he described a non-ordinary reality he had experienced while battling his imminent death. He said his deceased father came to him in a dream and told him that his desire to search for meaning in life was correct. However, the search should be inward, not outward, into the human heart, into the infinite essence.

With all that as background, we started to explore Planet 7 as populated by descendants of the plague survivors. We visited a settlement that reminded me a great deal of what the 1800s looked like in paintings and photos of America or Europe. People were well-groomed and dressed in modest clothing. Men wore formal hats and women wore hats or bonnets. There were horse-drawn carriages and bicycles.

We were there to watch the festivities of a holiday that was much like our Thanksgiving. People gathered in their homes and held prayer services or attended one of the local churches to worship with their neighbors. The goodwill and love expressed among the settlers was inspiring.

There was a marketplace teeming with fresh food, arts and crafts, and musicians and street performers entertaining the crowd. The elderly were helped as they got ready for the communal dinner. Everyone worked on putting together the feast.

There were no televisions. There were no cell phones. There were no modern-day appliances such as stoves, dishwashers, washing machines or blenders. However, there were a lot of books, musical instruments, and musical technology left over from earlier times.

By late afternoon, everyone in the settlement gathered in the large hall.

The meal consisted of large roasted birds like turkeys; large roasted meats that looked like beef and pork; dishes and dishes of multicolored cooked and raw vegetables. But the smell of the breads and the other baked goods overwhelmed me to the point where I was dying to join in the dinner, which was made by hand and cooked in wood-burning stoves and ovens.

When the feast was complete, one of the elders gave a 45-minute reading from a book. Everyone sat, spellbound. When the reading was done, all applauded politely.

The musicians played their hearts out and people danced joyfully, seemingly until they might drop from exhaustion. There were games for the children. The elderly were given prominent places on the sides of the stage, where they could enjoy the merriment even though some could no longer dance.

Just before the night wound down, we followed a young couple outside the hall. The young man, who looked like a white person on Earth, was talking in measured sentences to his beautiful girlfriend, who was olive-skinned, looking like a Hispanic or Middle Eastern person. Even though I couldn't understand him, I could tell he was nervous. It was cold outside and we could see the steam coming from his breath as he spoke. With each word that passed his lips, the gleam in his girlfriend's eyes grew brighter and brighter.

Dana whispered "he's telling her that he loves her and he's asking her to be his life partner." When he was done talking, she grabbed him with both arms around his neck, smiled and spoke to him. We could all tell that she had happily agreed. A tear trickled from my eye, one that I quickly wiped away before anyone saw it.

We all looked at each other and smiled.

After about five minutes, the couple ran back into the building to tell everyone the good news. We knew it was time to leave, but I asked if we could stay for a few minutes more, because I really enjoyed the music. I had never heard anything quite like it, but it had grown on me very quickly— a combination of Latin, Brazilian and Middle Eastern harmonies and rhythms that I never could have imagined.

The more we listened, the more everyone else wanted to stay and listen.

I could think of only three songs I knew that combined some of those multiple flavors. Led Zeppelin wrote Kashmir; Shakira wrote Ojos Asi, but it was Basia's haunting duet with Mietek Szczesniak in Wandering, that was closest to what I was hearing.

So, we did stay for another hour just to take in as much music and merriment as we could.

Out of the rubble, the disaster, and the pain, this world had begun to thrive again. It was taking small steps. This time it would not forget that the most valuable things were people's relationships to each other, to take care of each other, and to take care of the planet that they had been given.

Planets 39 and 40... Two for the Road

Today we went planet hopping. In our preparations for the trip, we're told that planet 39 was coming to an end because of the eruption of seven super volcanoes. Planet 40 was coming to an end because their sun was about to go supernova in the next 10 years.

Planet 39 had never progressed beyond medieval societies. Tribal wars were everywhere on the planet, for any reason— race, religion, land, power, different sexual practices. All seemed to be valid reasons to go to war with the next town or village. The battles we witnessed could be compared to the Roman gladiators in the Coliseum, but with no limits or rules. Men and women who had been trained to fight their entire lives went to battle in the most personal type of war. The ferocity, the severed limbs and heads, the blood that coated the battlefields made it look as if a heavy red rain had just fallen.

Volcanos already had killed many with explosions and lava. The survivors continued tending their crops in hopes that the ash-filled skies would one day clear up.

Dana told us that life on this planet would be over in 36 months because of the volcanic eruptions.

This planet's population had been here for thousands of years. Only once did an enlightened movement start, but within two years, the leader and his followers were crushed by armies from surrounding areas. We were told that in less than 10,000 years, nothing tangible would remain from this civilization. What a waste.

Planet 40

The next planet in our travels was Planet 40, where scientists had determined that their sun was going to become a supernova within a thousand years. At that time, the planet was on the edge of enlightenment. Their science was very advanced, but they knew they could never reach the stars and repopulate another world. This revelation brought the civilization of this planet together into full enlightenment. Love and peace reigned over the world. They started planning for the extinction of their civilization. Scientists did their best to create permanent records of the world's existence so that if it were ever visited in the future, the visitors would know that a beautiful civilization had once existed on this world. They knew they had to leave something of a grand nature that would have the best chance to survive. They knew that technology crumbled over the years so they turned to granite and stone. The entire world worked on the project. Giant granite symbols were put together starting at the top of the world and working down. It started with a sun and sun rays near the North Pole. Just below that was an image of a man and a woman standing next to each other.

Just below that was the same image, with the figures holding hands. The next image, showed the man and woman standing together holding an infant. Next the man and woman were holding hands and had two children on either side. It went on like this all the way to the equator, which was filled with symbolic humans holding hands in peace with each other.

The pattern reversed itself from the equator to the South Pole. There, at the South Pole, stood the final man and woman, with no children. And the final symbol was the same sun surrounded by sun rays, but with a giant X covering it, symbolizing the extinguishing of their sun. We hopped around the planet and saw a dozen of the couples that were still alive. None of them mourned their fate. You could see by the way they looked into each other's eyes and by the way they took care of each other that there was a beautiful love they shared and that they felt lucky to witness the end of their civilization. Their population control had worked. No young children or babies were left to suffer the extinction of their world. The few people that remained were proud of the giant symbols they were leaving on the planet surface. They believed that anyone visiting would know that the people once lived here loved and cared for each other.

Planet 44

In our prep for this visit, we had learned that this world had reached an even playing field, from North to South, and from East to West. The people that lived here had plenty of food to eat, shelter, and technology everywhere. We noticed right away that everyone seemed to be in great physical shape and that they had meticulously perfect appearances, hair, clothing, makeup and so on. The cities were clean and there was relatively low violence or crime. I noticed right away that almost everyone carried multiple technical devices, much like our own cell phones, and they constantly had their heads buried in these devices. There wasn't much person to person interaction.

Jessica told us this world was dominated by three things: technology, sex, and political correctness.

People of all races, political affiliations, gender, and other type of group identity could present whatever grievance that they had to the government for disposition. All cases, including crime, assault, or civil action, were referred to the ultimate governmental authority which Jessica called The Department of Rationalization. Whatever disputes or crimes happened were ruled upon and the rulings became part of the permanent laws of this world.

Jessica gave us some examples.

Left-handed people complained because they were in the minority. The Department of Rationalization eventually ruled that even though right-handed people could not be forced to become left-handed, as a gesture to recognize the suffering of left-handed people, all people in public places who were putting on coats or jackets must first put their left arm in the coat or jacket. All offenses meant a minimum of five days of incarceration and reorientation to the sensitivity of left-handed people.

Another example was in the area of sports. Fans had become so irate with the officiating of sports events that the Department of Rationalization ordered that every single play of every game would be subject to instant replay. Additionally, 12 times a game, the head coach or manager of a team could cross-examine one of the officials on live television. The final decisions were made at the television center at the Department. If a referee or official made more than three errors in a game, they were imprisoned for up to one year.

I asked Jessica if she was serious.

She told me that there was a game on this planet that is similar to soccer. On earth soccer is played for 90 minutes, consisting of two halves of 45 minutes each. However, the record time for the longest game on this planet was 17.3 days, because of the constant replays and hearings.

I just shook my head in disbelief.

Jessica told us that sex was in the forefront of most people's minds. People meeting each other for the first time just headed into buildings that were provided by the government for citizens to have sex whenever they wanted, in a safe and clean environment. She told us that while some people still married and had children, the population of the planet was quickly decreasing. Many chose to have themselves permanently sterilized so they would never have to take care of a child and they could have sex with anyone they wanted without unplanned pregnancy.

As we watched, we saw gay and straight couples, threesomes, foursomes, fivesomes and even a group of six that included a dog, enter the building. I assumed the dog was not a part of the sexual activity, but it made me cringe to think about it. After all, anything goes on this planet. I watched one particular group go in and come out 15 minutes later. They weren't even talking to each other. They went in different directions without even saying goodbye. However, they were using their devices to communicate what I assumed was their recent adventure. Clearly love was not part of the equation for intimate relationships on this world.

There was only a very small province that shunned this Sex/Tech/PC world, as Jessica had labeled it. They were descendants of the ancient tribes, much like our North American Indians, who for 5,000 years had maintained their beliefs in both the physical and infinite states of the universe, in spite of the distractions of technology. Alison told us that more than 99 percent of the planet's population did not even know this tribe existed, much less that it thrived without technology.

Everyone spent their days obsessed by either sex or technology, though most worked a job that helped keep the world fed, clothed and sheltered. However, on breaks at work, Sex/Tech was dominant. If you couldn't get laid on your break, you went right to your computer games.

Billy asked "so, with all of their experience in sex, has it improved?"

Dana told us said that on Earth the average female orgasm is 18 seconds and the average male orgasm is 22 seconds. And the averages on Planet 44 are exactly the same. Dana said that technology was being used to improve entertainment and communication, as well as people's sex lives. So, while this world had reached a high level of meeting people's material needs, it was just spinning its wheels as far as development in other important areas.

When people got older, they became more and more frustrated because their bodies wore out and they could not partake in sex as they did in their youth. The suicide rate here among elders was astronomical, apparently because of the lack of real spiritual or emotional growth of its inhabitants.

Just before we left the planet, Alison told us that sexual relations across the cosmos progress through similar cycles. Almost all planets, including Earth, have a sexual revolution. But revolutions end. The danger was in entering sexual evolution.

We on Earth were now entering a tipping point. She told us that the evolution of a healthy civilization was when people's perspectives evolved to understand that sex does not equal love. Yes, intimate relations could be a beautiful moment between two people, but selfless love and caring that two or more people show for each other was 1,000 times more important than any sex act.

Jessica ended our tour with remarks that I paraphrase as "For those of you who believe in A Creator, on the Creator's list of things that we should care about, how and how often you decide to get off, is at the bottom of the list. As for technology, people have to understand that technology should serve them. Technology could do amazing things to make life and a planet better, but technology has limitations. Science fiction writers' dreams far surpass what science and technology could ever possibly achieve."

She emphasized again that we were all stuck with the planet that we were given.

Jessica said "Nobody's coming, and we ain't going anywhere."

Just before we left, Alison and I wandered away from the group and she reminded me of our night starting in the hotel elevator. I remembered how wonderful the connection of our two spirits had been. She looked at me like she was about to tell the punchline of a joke and said "that night you learned your 22-Second Lesson" and started to laugh. I laughed as it clicked in my mind that the mindless pursuit of those 22 seconds over the years had sure wasted the time and energy of a lot of guys, including me.

As I write these lessons in my journal, it's clear to me that the time we spend in a vertical position in our lives is much more important than the time that we spend in a horizontal position.

I closed my journal and looked up at Alison.

"Miles, you are really starting to become a good writer."

I smiled at her as I put the journal down. We were both tired, so I headed over to join her in bed. I had read from my journal for a long time, so dreamland was just around the corner.

11. Planet 97

The next day, we had a trip scheduled for the first time in a long time. I couldn't believe we had already been to 96 different civilizations. As always, in the blink of an eye, we were standing on a planet that was millions of light-years away. The rush you get when you open your eyes never gets old.

This was a world of peace. The technology in this world, we were told, was about 300 years ahead of Earth technology. They had used it wisely. Medical science had cured most diseases, except for a few rare strains of cancer. People lived productive lives through their 80s before old-age maladies crept in. The average lifespan on this planet was 99 years old! Alzheimer's had been defeated and many of the other problems that came along with aging had been minimized. Most people were physically active, comfortable and mentally aware into their 90s.

The environment of the planet was well-balanced. There were no countries at war with each other. All of the ancient grudges had been forgiven and a view of a peaceful future was shared by everyone.

We visited four different continents and witnessed a world that had chosen the path to love and peace, a path that was out there for everyone. Music, the arts, and sports all flourished. The people here were conscientious and happy. They prospered in a world full of energetic enthusiasm and love of life and most importantly, love of each other. Their maturity and intellectual developments had equaled their physical and technical developments.

Technology on this planet was thought of as a tool: nothing more, nothing less. The people cherished their personal development above everything. It didn't matter where we visited because to me, there seemed to be a quiet hum in the background that made me feel in harmony with this world. I was not looking forward to the moment when it was time to go.

On our last stop before returning to Earth we were standing downtown just after nightfall in a small city. As we walked the streets we noticed, as we had all day, that there was no problem with diversity in this world. People of all races, people of different types: black, white, short, tall, overweight, skinny, and even the beautiful and the not-so-beautiful, were very friendly to each other.

We were all alarmed when a siren went off from the top of a tall building nearby. Jessica asked us to stop and wait to see what would happen. A message was broadcast across the downtown area. Dana told us the message was delivered by the city's Chief of Security, who asked people to immediately enter the closest building, and for the buildings to be locked. The message ended there.

Alison, Dana and Jessica looked at each other.

Tommy asked "what's going on?"

I think we were all surprised when Jessica said "we don't know."

A sense of unease fell over me.

Half a dozen vehicles left the Security Department building and sped down the street.

Alison said "it's best for us to wait here until the vehicles arrive at their destination." I sensed a shaky tone in Alison's voice for the first time in a long time.

Jessica and Dana left us to follow the vehicles. Alison told us "nothing like this has ever happened on our previous visits to this world. We have visited here a number of times and it is one of the most peaceful worlds in the universe. Because of that, Jessica and Dana went to see what is going on."

None of us were satisfied with that answer, in part because we had been told that we were not visible to any of the people on these worlds.

Before we could ask Alison any questions, Jessica and Dana were back.

Jessica said "it's time for us to leave."

We were having none of it.

Billy said "I don't understand why we can't go to the site of the disturbance." All of us agreed with him. We wanted to go to the site.

Dana said "It's not safe for us."

There was a terrible silence.

All of us were probably thinking the same thing: that the sisters had never been afraid of anything. After all, they were part of the infinite universe and had already passed into their infinite lives.

Billy asked "What could the three of you be afraid of?"

In the most chilling moment of my life, Jessica said "Evil."

Jessica said "The universe contains great powers of evil. Left unchecked it can reap havoc and destroy a world. A planet that is prospering like this one is a prime target for Evil. Evil is not allowed to roam unfettered throughout the universe, but when concentrated, it can be focused on a world like this one. The scene of the disturbance is a small subdivision just outside of town, where 22 people have been killed, and not just killed, but brutally mutilated. From listening to the officials discussing the matter, the senseless killings started about six months ago, and are beginning to happen all across the planet. Evil was able to creep into the minds of individuals who felt alone, who felt hopeless, with no sense of direction or moral beliefs. These people have been totally consumed by Evil. They live in the darkness, in the shadows, and their sole purpose is to destroy the world, a world that in their minds, isolated them and turned them into what they are now. These individuals don't understand it as Evil."

I said "why can't we go to the scene? After all, no one can see us."

Jessica said "when Evil strikes in this manner, there is at least one individual in these dark groups that has the power to see into the infinite world, and therefore, to see us. While the sisters are safe, the rest of you are not. You are not strong enough to ward off Evil's overwhelming power and all of you are in danger of being consumed in the blink of an eye, and lost forever."

With that, Jessica immediately transported us all off Planet 97, but instead of being back in our separate homes, we were all at Billy and Dana's farm house in California.

Jessica said "I wanted to make sure we were safe, and it was taking too long to explain everything."

We still didn't understand. Tommy said "Evil exists on Earth and on all of the planets we visited, but the three of you have never been afraid of it before tonight. Why is that? What makes tonight different?"

Dana replied "yes Tommy, there is Evil on other worlds including our own, created by people with self-centered motives. The Evil that was on Planet 97 was directly from The Evil One. The Evil One has not been allowed to visit Earth for decades but left enough poison that we are still fighting through what was left behind."

Michael said to the sisters "you are talking about The Evil One as an individual, and not Evil as a concept, right?"

Dana said "yes, there is an Evil One, and there are lesser Evil Ones that exist in the universe."

We still didn't understand it.

The sisters looked at each other and finally nodded in agreement. Jessica asked us to close our eyes and keep them shut. She told us they had the ability to project images into our minds and that she was going to show us about 60 seconds of the scene on Planet 97.

She showed us the mutilated bodies of husbands, wives, and children. We saw heads cut off. We saw hearts cut out of bodies and strung together and nailed against a wall just below a symbol that was written in blood. We heard the Chief of Security tell his officers that he suspected it had been done by the same group responsible for school shootings and suicide bombings in their province over the last six months.

From the vantage point of an attic window, we saw the dozen terrorists of Evil hiding in the woods. They were dressed in black and wearing face masks as camouflage on this overcast, moonless night. They watched, knowing the good people of this world were unable to deal with the horror before them.

We saw one individual standing behind the others, and his eyes were fire-red in the darkness. With that, the vision ended.

Dana said "once we identified an individual consumed by the Evil One, we got out of there immediately."

"At one time in the early stages of the universe, before humans and their planets existed, the Evil Ones were banished from the universe forever and thrown into prisons from which they could not escape. Even though they cannot individually escape, if they concentrate their Evil energies the prisoners can target different worlds and disrupt progress by planting the seeds of Evil in the minds of directionless people. They only need one strong leader who would recruit others to join.

"Their modus operandi is usually the same. They choose a race, religion, political or ethnic group and they turn a few members of this group into zealots who commit murder and other atrocities on the rest of the world, and claim they are driven by their belief system. Even the most peaceful civilizations eventually will become wary and distrustful of that entire group, even though most members of that group have nothing to do with the killers. You have seen it many times on earth, where entire groups of people being blamed for the actions of a few. This is how the Evil One operates."

Needless to say, we were all speechless, but had a thousand questions. Before we could ask them, Jessica told us that we had to end the evening, but that tomorrow night we would not be visiting another world. Tomorrow night we would be visited. We should stay patient until that time, when all of our questions would be answered, before we even asked them.

Alison said "you have reached a stage of learning at which it is time to meet one of the great teachers in the universe."

With that, our crazy night came to an end.

12. Heaven and Earth

The next day seemed to drag on forever. First of all, the previous night's trip was extremely unsettling. I am sure we had all felt completely safe on all of our visits until yesterday. Of course, we all knew there was evil in the world and in the universe, but we didn't know that there was an Evil One who was so powerful that we needed the sisters to rescue us from its powers.

I was excited about the meeting, but I was also extremely frustrated that Alison wouldn't answer any questions about what was going to happen. When we finally made it to our bedroom, I pushed the issue one more time.

She turned and said "Miles, just read your book or fall asleep. I'll let you know when it's time to go."

With that, my level of frustration had reached its limit. I gave a heavy sigh as I rested my head on the pillow, just staring at the ceiling. Alison turned off the light on her night stand and the room became dark.

It wasn't long before Alison grabbed my right hand. She knew I was awake, so she just said to me, "It's time to go."

I had no idea where we were going. All I knew was that we were going to meet someone new. My excitement squashed any frustration about how long it had taken to get to this moment.

When I opened my eyes, we were all sitting around the bonfire in the backyard of Dana and Billy's vineyard. No pleasantries were being exchanged. Everyone was quiet. I think we were all surprised to be sitting around the bonfire. I thought we might have gone to some magnificent castle, where we would be among the many sitting before a great Sage, a cosmic intellectual who would teach us about the universe.

My question was quickly answered.

"We brought everyone here tonight, because it was the most comfortable setting for you. We've all been here many times for joyous reasons, so we knew that all of us would be at ease and able to learn from our visitor," Dana said.

I asked "So Dana, will we have to wait much longer?"

"No," she said, "I see the Teacher coming, walking up the hill."

We all looked into the distance and saw a figure slowly walking towards us. As the Teacher came closer to the firelight, I could see that she was a very young Hispanic girl with wavy black hair, about 12 years old. She was wearing an ornate white lace dress and her hair was filled with flowers, which made her look like a bridesmaid. We looked at each other in amazement and then looked back at her as she came close enough to address the group.

The girl seemed surprisingly wise for her youthful appearance, and a sweet but firm voice said "Greetings Miles, Billy, Michael, and Tommy."

All of us had remained seated around the fire. She shook hands with each of us. And as she did so, she placed her left hand at the back of each person's head and looked directly into their eyes in a gesture of love. Then the Teacher went to each of the sisters and hugged them and we could see that the ladies had been set aglow by the embrace of this little girl.

She finally sat on a rock and faced us.

"Alison, Dana and Jessica let me know that it was time for me to visit the four of you. Relax, because I have come here to tell you the story of our universe."

I didn't know what to expect, but I was as excited as a child on Christmas morning.

"I would ask that you please let me tell my story and not have you interrupt me with questions."

With that she began her tale.

"The greatest one of all has been known by many names. The Creator, God, The Divine Intelligence, but to keep it simple, I will refer to the great one as the Creator. The Creator has no beginning and has no end. The Creator and the infinite universe have always been here. There are two parts to the universe. The infinite part, which occupies the entire universe, is endless. The second part, the physical universe, does not occupy the entire universe, and while being enormous, it does have a limit to its size."

"Billions of years ago, the Creator became lonely and decided to create sentient beings with which to share love, beings that were immortal. On this planet, it would be easiest to refer to them as Guardians or Angels. The Creator made billions and billions of Guardians, who were powerful and interacted with each other and the Creator. They took love, joy, and happiness from their existence and their relationships. For millions of years the universe existed peacefully, with only the Creator and the Guardians as sentient and intelligent beings."

"The Creator had made a pledge to its creations that they would have free will and that the Creator would not interfere with their actions. However, one Guardian decided that their immortal, infinite existence and power, when grouped together, was probably as great as the Creator's powers. That Guardian began to recruit other Guardians into thinking likewise. That group of rebel Guardians grew large enough, because they each had their own free will, and so a great cosmic battle began between the rebels and the Guardians loyal to the Creator.

However, after thousands of years of fighting, the Creator realized that what had been made was imperfect, in that Guardians had not been given enough purpose to their lives. Hence, thousands of years of battle had occurred, as a form of evil which was at odds with the love the Creator had given them. To end the battle, the Creator ripped many holes in the fabric of the universe and cast the rebellious evil Guardians into these holes, from which they could not escape.

"Your planet has evolved enough for me to tell you that these are the black holes that you have discovered in your scientific research. As you know, the gravity inside of a black hole is so powerful that anything entering from the physical universe would immediately be crushed. What you don't know is that the gravity inside black holes is so great that it keeps the evil Guardians inside them, trapped—for eternity."

"The billions of Guardians that remained faithful to the Creator were given a greater purpose to their existence."

"The Creator first made the physical universe and millions of years later, after the physical universe had stabilized, the Creator made the human race. First, there was an enormous burst of energy. Then, billions of solar systems that included Earth-like planets were created in smaller explosions. You could call that the Little Bangs Theory. Once these planets had stabilized, sometimes after millions of years, the Creator made human beings to occupy and take care of these worlds but, more importantly, to take care of each other."

I was so mesmerized with the story that I had failed to realize that our small girl had slowly morphed in form to a young black man in his twenties. He had short black hair, brown eyes and flowing white robes. He stood up and began to walk before us as he continued the story.

"The Creator placed these worlds far enough apart that they could never interfere with each other in the physical universe. The Creator wanted each world to survive or fail on its own values, judgments and priorities. The Creator provided these worlds with moral and ethical teachings of love and forgiveness and guidelines on how people should live together."

"Most importantly, the Creator told the legions of Guardians to watch over humans and to do what was necessary to keep them out of harm's way, so that they may fulfill their purpose. Each human being in the entire universe has a Guardian watching over them, helping them, and sometimes protecting them when needed.

"It is time for you to meet your Guardians."

I was in utter amazement. Right before my eyes, a being that looked just like a human being appeared, as others appeared before each of us. My Guardian looked incredibly like me. I stood up and my guardian immediately approached me and we embraced. I had never felt safer in my life. This was not a human being. My guardian was an otherworldly being and engulfed me with peace and love. It was overwhelming.

After we all greeted our Guardians, the Teacher continued the story. However, now the Teacher appeared as a beautiful Asian woman in her early 30s.

She had long black hair and green eyes that sparkled like emeralds and she said "Angelic Ones, please stand behind your humans. Humans, please sit. Know that your Guardians have been with you since the day you opened your eyes and will be with you until the day that you close them for the last time and enter the infinite universe. They will then be assigned to new humans, on different worlds, to continue their work."

"I must tell you that while the physical universe and the people in it are imperfect and impermanent, they are all interconnected to each other through the infinite universe. All of your physical worlds will one day end, as will the physical universe. However, the infinite universe will last forever."

"The infinite universe, when you arrive there, will be like nothing you have ever known. It is one day of infinite joy followed by another day of greater infinite joy, which will go on forever. You will be able to understand much of this when you finally cross over."

"Most importantly, as it pertains to the physical and infinite universe, you need to know one thing, that all of us, including the Creator, serve one master, and that master is Linear Time. The Creator is all powerful and all-knowing, but even the Creator does not manipulate, reset, and travel backwards and forwards in time. As it pertains to the Creator, no one knows if that is by choice or not. But the fact is that time moves forward everywhere, and the choices we make are the choices we live with. There are no do-overs, not even for the Creator."

This was too much for Billy to take without asking a question. So, unfortunately, he said "But Teacher, our science and mathematics have shown us that it's hypothetically possible to bend time and space." The Teacher cut him off in a booming voice, saying "Quiet! At the beginning of our lesson I asked you to be quiet and now I see I have humans who cannot respect my wishes. I have made you mute and you will not be able to speak again until I leave."

"Now, I want you all to stand up and turn around and look at your Guardians again."

We all stood and turned around, and what we saw was unbelievable.

Our Guardians had grown to three times the size of a human being and had enormous wings. Some were carrying spears and some were carrying bows and quivers of arrows. They now looked like the Angels depicted by the great artists of the world.

The Teacher, in an even louder voice, said "Turn around and sit down, humans."

The Teacher was standing with her back to us, and we all sat down. She slowly crouched down and started to turn around to face us.

As the teacher turned, crouching, we could see that the teacher now was a man in his late 50s. He had his left index finger extended and had long curly black hair and a long beard. With a disheveled look and baggy clothing, he resembled a homeless person.

"Hear me!" he screamed.

"Do you know why your Guardians need to be powerful? It's because the Evil Ones, though they cannot escape their eternal prisons, **can** concentrate their evil thoughts on a world and can destroy that world through the evil actions of its inhabitants. They have done that many times, even with Guardians fighting them."

"You came from a planet yesterday where the Evil Ones had sent their thoughts. If not for the sisters, you might have come under their influence and been lost forever. Even now, we don't know if they knew of your visit or if they have been able to trace you back to this world."

That notion sent a chill up and down my spine.

Before I had time to think about it, the Teacher looked up into the sky and screamed, in a voice that could be heard around the world, "The Evil Ones are coming!"

He grew into a gigantic magnificent winged Guardian, ten times the size of our own Guardians.

"Guardians and Protectors of the Earth arise!" he screamed.

The Teacher and our Guardians flew up into the sky. We could see Guardians rising into the sky for miles around and heard the sound of gigantic wings flapping. I didn't know if it was real or if it was a show done for our learning, but in either case, it was the greatest display of physical power I had ever witnessed. These otherworldly beings filled the sky and completely surrounded the earth like an Angelic force field.

Alison said "The Evil Ones have traced us back to this world from the planet we visited yesterday, but the Teacher and the Guardians will not allow any more of their evil to enter this world. The Evil Ones have already visited this world many times, but the Creator has deemed that they will never again enter this world, which is at a tipping point of whether or not we can work our way out of its problems. That's why the three of us are here. That's why the Teacher came tonight."

Jessica said, "It's time to go."

Before I knew it, Alison and I were lying in our bed and I looked at the alarm clock and realized it was morning.

My senses were on overload. I got up from bed, walked over to Alison's side and sat down.

"Well, if you wanted to scare the living daylights out everyone, I think you sure succeeded."

"Miles, we never promised you that this would be easy," Alison said. "Frankly, I was surprised it took this long for us to visit a planet where Evil was trying to change its course."

"I have so many questions, but the Teacher is gone. Can I ask you my questions? Are you allowed to answer?"

"It depends on the question. Go ahead."

"Give me an example of when the Evil One has influenced Earth."

"Stalin, Hitler...they were both under the direct influence of the Evil One. Their disciples still exist in our world to a much lesser degree, but thankfully the horror of the 20th century is behind us and I hope we learned our lessons."

I was taken aback by the notion. But not surprised.

Alison said "Also, you need to know that there are times when the earth experiences hurricanes and typhoons, and these are a result of battles that are going on in the infinite universe, above the earth. Some of these events are the result of battles, but sometimes they are just meteorological events. I don't want you to think that we are constantly under attack."

"Wow. I guess I'll pay more attention to the weather."

"Also, if you look at UFO reports, the majority of them involve bright lights. These are guardians or individuals moving between the infinite world and the physical world. Others are secret aircraft developed by First World countries. Then there are hoaxes that people perpetrate for the fun of it, such as crop circles."

I shook my head and smiled, but I still had other questions.

"The Teacher said that our Guardians were here to protect us from harm. However, people die every day of accidents and illnesses. If they are here to protect us, then why do bad things happen to good people?"

Alison said "Your Guardians all have a sense of what contributions you need to make to your world. They cannot see the future, but they know who you are and that you are not done with your contributions to society. If you have not completed your contributions, then the Guardians are allowed to intercede."

"Give me an example."

"Okay, remember that time that we parked in Canada near Lake Huron and there was not another person around?"

"Yes, I remember."

"Well, remember the lake was really wild, but we felt safe to walk out on the pier because it was concrete? Don't you remember what happened when we came back, stepped onto the sand and turned around to look?"

"Yes! A huge wave came crashing over the pier and if we hadn't left when we did, we would've been swept into the freezing waters."

"We probably would've died, but our Guardians held the waves back until we could reach shore. If we had died at that moment, we never would've had our family. I would have never been allowed to take you on these trips. Understand?"

My mind started to rummage around in the memory bank for other close calls.

I said "So the time on that icy bridge when that car came spinning at us from the other lane and barely missed us? That was our Guardians protecting us?"

"Yes," Alison said.

"What other questions do you have? I expect to hear the kids shortly."

I stared into Alison's eyes and said "What about Tommy's brother Danny?"

Alison looked down. She was upset. I saw a teardrop hit the bedspread. I put my hand on her shoulder and said "You okay?"

Alison looked up at me. "Yeah, I'm okay. It's just that this is the hardest type of question to answer. Not because I don't know the answer, but because you might not like the answer. Danny's death, while extremely tragic to all of us, served the enormous purpose of making everyone deal with it. From Tommy and his parents all the way down to the guy sitting in the last row of the bleachers. Everyone knew about the tragedy. Everyone had to deal with it in their own way. The span of reactions, from anger, despair, rage, all the way to acceptance and love, taught so many people so many lessons about the world. More importantly, it taught them about themselves. If you really think about it, Danny's short life affected so many people in such a profound way that it would be totally wrong to say that Danny didn't matter in the world. As I always tell you Miles, the world is what is around you. To me, Danny is a hero."

I turned away. I was breathless. Her explanation was painful and profound. I knew she was right, but it didn't make the pain go away. I sat there for a moment and tried to accept her explanation.

My sadness was starting to swallow me up. I knew I had to move on to a question that was less painful.

I said "Well, the Teacher said that the infinite universe was like one day of infinite joy followed by another day of greater infinite joy and so on for eternity. I'm not a scientist or mathematician, but I guess my question would be how there can be one infinite thing greater than another infinite thing?"

Alison lightened the mood with a smile and said "Great question, Miles. I'll have to let Billy and Dana know that you have become a professional mathematician.

"If I asked you to compute the amount of numbers, using decimals, that exist between the number one and the number two, what would your answer be?" Alison said.

"Um, there would be an infinite amount of numbers if you're using decimals. Right?"

"Right. If I asked you to compute the amount of numbers, using decimals, that exist between the number one and the number three, what would your answer be?"

I replied "There would be an infinite amount of numbers."

"Yes, but the number two is only twice as large as the number one, and the number three is three times as large as the number one. So that would create a greater number of infinite values. In that way, tomorrow's infinite joy can be infinitely better than today's joy."

I wasn't enough of a mathematician to refute that theory and it appealed to my common sense.

"One more question and then we have to get the kids up and start the day. We can talk later again if you want."

"Okay. Why did the Teacher's form continue to change? From a 12-year-old Hispanic girl to a 20-year-old black man to a 35-year-old Asian woman to a 50-year-old homeless-looking white man preaching fire and brimstone?"

"That's what you saw, Miles. Yes, the teacher changed form, but the different forms appeared differently to each of us. This way, the students learn that there is knowledge to be gained from the diverse people on their planets."

Alison got out of bed, put on a robe, and came over so we could hug. After we embraced, she stepped away from me and cupped her hands in front of me, palms up.

"Miles, don't worry about the Evil Ones getting through to our world. We are as safe as if we were in the palms of the Creator's hands."

13. Let's Play My Turn

"Excuse me, excuse me," I said to Jessica. "I'm sorry to interrupt, but I have something to say to the group before you brief us on our trip today."

No one had ever interrupted Jessica before she gave us the background on the next planet we were to visit, but I was determined to have my say. My journal indicated that we had already visited 98 different worlds. After that fantastic fire and brimstone experience in California, I had an epiphany.

"Go right ahead if you have something you want to share with us," Jessica said.

I had the floor.

"Well, after what happened a couple nights ago, and skimming through my journal, something occurred to me and I wanted to share it with the group and see what all of you thought about it."

I had everyone's attention now.

"What I'm asking is can we go to a planet of my choosing?"

Dana said, "Really Miles? Where do you want to go?"

"We have been to all types of worlds in our first 98 trips. You're trying to teach us about the right way and the wrong way to live our lives. I think we all get that. However, in reviewing my journal entries, there is one world that we haven't visited."

Billy said "Go ahead Miles, I'd really like to hear what you think."

"Thanks Billy."

The sisters were standing just to my left as I looked right at them and said, "Ladies, I want to visit a world that is very much like our civilization here on Earth. I want this world to be on the verge of learning all the important lessons of life. I want to see a world close to the edge."

Alison turned to her sisters, smiled and said, "Okay, I had Miles in the pool, so I win on that one. Who had the over 100 and who had the under 100?"

The sisters laughed at me, but all in good fun. We knew they were just messing with us so we laughed along with them.

"We were starting to worry about you guys," Alison said. "It took you 98 visits to different worlds to ask this question. Miles, thank goodness you had an epiphany after last night. We were getting to the point of taking you, but it's more powerful if you ask. You are now more focused and I think you will get a lot out of it."

"Any questions before Jessica gives you the background on our visit?" Dana asked.

We looked at each other and shook our heads no.

Jessica began by saying "This will probably be the longest introduction to any civilization we have ever visited, so sit down and relax while I go through it."

"The history of this world is extremely important. As Miles put it, they are close to the edge of full planetary evolution. The planet has survived its industrial phase and is being cleaned up because most of the countries abide by strict environmental laws. Technology is about 50 years beyond what it is here on Earth. There are no great world wars going on. There is urban gang violence in countries that are not enlightened. The violence is either being controlled, eradicated, or isolated, but these countries are not doing enough to cure themselves of their unenlightened lifestyles."

"Now, I need to take you back about 15 generations, when this world's turnaround began. I remind you that no two worlds have ever evolved in the same way, but you asked to visit a world on the brink of survival, and this is their way."

"On this world, they refer to this story as: **Rimitto, Dare, Ignosco, Utamor,** which are the names of the four main individuals."

"There were two young, very accomplished financial executives named Rimitto, who led the accounting division, and Dare, who led the internal auditing division, at the government bank in their country. Like our Federal Reserve Bank, this is the bank to which all other banks report. Their country was going through an economic downturn. Families were losing their homes because of the lack of employment, as happens in low periods in the United States. People bought homes and started businesses using mortgages, second mortgages, home equity loans, and commercial loans. Both of these young men had previously worked at smaller institutions, so they were aware of the horrible anxiety that families go through when losing their homes and their businesses. The two of them came up with an idea to save these families from economic destruction."

"The two of them had come to the conclusion that their entire planet and their entire country's economy were all just based on what they called 'numbers on paper.' It was held together by something they called 'mutual consensus.' They set up an account at the Federal Reserve labeled Debt to Foreign Countries and told their superiors they had consolidated all separate debts into one large account to make their balance sheet look cleaner. They added an additional amount into that account. Since they were in charge of accounting and auditing, their superiors never added up the separate accounts that were consolidated.

They felt like economic anarchists. They were convinced it was worth going to jail if they were caught."

"Since all the other banks reported to their Federal Reserve Bank, they were able to see the loans that each bank owned—the loans that were being paid on time, as well as the loans that were in default. So, one bank at a time, they started to pay off all the delinquent loans. They sent a letter to these borrowers stating that a benevolent benefactor had heard about their problems and that this benefactor had chosen to step in and pay their debt off for them, on the condition that they would not tell anyone. Each time one of these transactions was made, the other side of the transaction was a credit to the account labeled Debt to Foreign Countries. They got through all the delinquent loans in their country and paid them off without anyone saying a word. The directors of their Federal Reserve Bank simply looked at this large account of foreign debt and saw that it was decreasing daily by large amounts, so no one ever questioned it."

"Hold on a second," Billy interrupted.

"Michael," Billy continued, "You're the business expert on our team here. Is something like this even remotely possible?"

"Well everybody, let me answer that question with this urban legend that most veterans in business or finance have heard. Whenever you interview accounting firms to determine who you are going to hire, at the end of each interview, the president of the company asks each accounting firm one last question. That question is 'How much is one plus one?' We all know the answer to that question. But the accounting firm that gets hired is the one that answers 'What do you want it to be'?"

226

"So, yes. If you are working at the Federal Reserve you are the ones auditing all the smaller banks. No one is auditing you. So, if the head of the Federal Reserve auditing department and accounting department are in cahoots, it could take quite a while for it to be uncovered. I have to say, I completely agree with their assessment of numbers on paper, and mutual consensus. You could clearly make an argument for that viewpoint here on Earth as well. After all, when you calculate your net worth, all you end up with is a number on a piece of paper."

"Does that answer your question Billy?" Michael asked.

Billy answered "yeah, I get it. I don't know if I like it. But I get it."

Jessica continued.

"When the two completed their initial mission, they came to believe that the holders of non-delinquent loans, who were paying on time, deserved to have their debts extinguished as well. So, they used the same process they had used with the delinquent mortgages. However, this amount was much larger, so when they were through, their activity was discovered."

"All of this was kept hidden from the public. They were hauled in front of the President and Vice President of that country, named Ignosco and Utamor, as well as the directors of the bank. Everyone in that meeting was sure that they would go to jail for the rest of their lives."

"The President got up and walked around the table to face them and asked them why and how they did it. Their explanation about how their country's economy, and the entire world's economy, was all built on the concept of 'numbers on paper' and 'mutual consensus' quieted the room. Everyone there expected an explosion or tirade from the President. Instead, he walked back to his chair and sat down.

"The President asked them, 'Why did you do this? Neither one of you benefited'.

"They answered in unison: 'to end our citizens' economic suffering'.

"Others tried to talk, but the President shut them up right away. He walked around the room and finally settled back down in his chair. He turned to his Vice President and they talked in whispers."

"He then turned to the two and said '**Well done**'.

"There was a gasp around the room.

"The President said that their country had not reached economic independence. He reminded the board of directors that their government owed a lot of money to others, which created a great tax burden on their citizens.

"He turned to his two young executives and asked 'Can you also make that debt go away?'

"Rimitto and Dare turned and looked at each other and smiled and said of course they could.

"They adjusted the numbers in a new bogus account to five times the national debt and proceeded to systematically pay off all of the nation's debt over the next two years until the country was debt-free, with an enormous surplus in their treasury.

"When they reported the completion of the project to the President, he already had been mulling over his next move. He asked the two, 'Who's the richest person in our country and how much are they worth?'

"To make this explanation easy to understand," Jessica said, "let's say they told the President that the wealthiest individual in that country was worth $100 million. The President responded by telling them to issue checks to every single citizen of our country, including the wealthiest, for $100 million. The president had already passed a law that froze wages and prices. He also decreed that people remain in their current jobs for the next three years. He gave everyone $100 million so the wealthy could not complain that there was injustice in this, because they were still $100 million wealthier than the common man. However, the common man was now so enormously wealthy that it had rendered money moot in their society. There was almost nothing that couldn't be purchased or owned by anyone.

"On the day that all of this happened, the President made a speech to the nation explaining the logic of what had happened. Once he had explained 'numbers on paper' and 'mutual consensus' he went into the most important part of his speech.

"He stated that everyone's debts had been forgiven.

"Everyone had been given a fortune.

"But the most important challenge lay ahead.

"He said each and every citizen in this country had to take the next week and reflect in their hearts and write down all the injustices that had been done to them in their lives. They had to remember all the grudges and hate and disdain that they had had for their fellow man, living or dead. Just like their debts had been forgiven, each citizen had to forgive their ill will towards others, in order to move forward in their lives.

"A week later, the President made another address to his country. He told them that he was sure everyone had made great efforts towards forgiveness. He declared that every day at noon, all of the church bells of all of the denominations would ring for 30 minutes, reminding them of their forgiveness pledge.

"He then asked all of his citizens for one final thing.

"He asked everyone to give of themselves, but more importantly to give love to their brothers and sisters. He asked everyone to help someone in physical or emotional need, or to help someone to learn and to better themselves. He reminded them that they all still had to perform their jobs for three years. They could not just quit their jobs, because if they did, their country's economy would quickly fall apart. He stated that all work was noble. He reminded them that they had to feed our populace, take care of our sick, and educate our children. He reminded those who were wealthy and thought they had nothing to give, that they had great education, experience and knowledge about the arts, music, business, and sports and that they could teach those who wanted to learn."

"Of course, natural selection always has a part in social and environmental engineering and changes. Some people could not control themselves and their newfound wealth. Drinking, drugs, gambling, and despicable lifestyles took the lives of those people in just a few years.

About 70 percent of the nation was able to successfully change in their thought processes. The 30 percent that struggled were mostly people at the upper income levels and the lowest income levels. The wealthy fought against the abolition of the caste system in their country. They wanted to continue to be served hand and foot, as if they were royalty. Many of them moved out of the country. The people at the lower income levels struggled because of lack of education, lack of employment skills, and lack of functional family units.

The 70 percent identified this problem immediately. They ignored the wealthy. But they got to work on educating and teaching job skills to their lower income brothers and sisters.

As a byproduct, these lower income families began binding together more closely and created structured and lasting family units. It took almost 100 years of adjustment, but the country finally worked its way through their challenges.

"The process soon spread to other countries. Over the next 15 generations, the majority of the planet had accomplished forgiveness of all debt, and had given riches upon riches to their citizens, rendering the use of money moot. They succeeded in forgiving each other as people and forgiving each other as countries, which ended the primary motivation for future wars."

"Life in these countries began to simplify. People only desired the things they needed, not the things they wanted. People no longer strived for physical possessions. The scientific community realized the irrelevance of discussing trips to the stars and refocused their greatest minds on improving the human condition. The scientific community realized that their planet and their civilization would not last forever and accepted that. All they could do was to make their behavior as humane as possible in the time they had in this physical world. Even with vastly improved medical technology, these evolving people no longer feared death, because they knew that what came next—the infinite world— was not something to be feared. Individuals, with the help of their Guardians, were able to understand other languages without a second thought, which helped in the forgiveness of long-time grudges and military skirmishes between the smaller countries. These places became like paradise."

I sat there in the quiet when Jessica paused for a couple minutes. I realized that this story, although in a much different fashion, moved me just as much as the display from the night before.

"You probably have a lot of questions, but it's time to go. We will be visiting a meeting of their United Nations. The majority of countries have reached this positive plateau and their agenda is to convince the minority of countries—those that still have economic caste systems; that still have all types of ethnic, racial, religious, identity politics and violence in the streets; that still have many directionless citizens following lives of greed, depravity and hate—to change their ways and join them in lives of contentment. The countries still clinging to the old ways are doing so because their wealthiest classes, including the governmental ruling classes, are clinging to their caste system. They want to continue to be served hand and foot by lower class citizens. They don't understand the selfless joy that they are missing."

"We will witness this meeting, but quite frankly, the outcome really doesn't matter. A great migration has already begun to the enlightened nations of the world, nations governed by love and forgiveness. Within a few years the servant classes of these greedy countries will move to the enlightened nations."

I stood up, looked at everyone, and said "Here we go."

There were 12 countries in all. Nine of them had reached enlightenment and were trying to convince the others, the three wealthiest countries, to follow suit. The three displayed indifferent body language at times and when the meeting broke up, I wasn't sure that any minds were changed.

Shortly after adjournment, I noticed that two female heads of the wealthy states sought out the Chairman for a private discussion. We listened in and were pleased to hear that they had been moved by the presentation and that their countries were considering changing their cultures.

On our tour of the planet, we found that people in the enlightened countries all had similar modest homes and everyone was industrious and caring for each other. However, the wealthiest three nations' large cities still had both decadent mansions and ghettos where the working class and poor lived. Gangs roamed these ghettos at night, people who saw no hope in their lives, who were selling hate, drugs and weapons. It was all too familiar to us after visiting so many worlds.

After our trip we didn't go right back to our homes, but first we came together for just a few minutes.

Jessica said "I did want you to all know an interesting fact about the nine enlightened countries. The leaders that were here today were not long-term leaders of those nations. They had discovered over the generations that placing one person in charge of a large country for a long time could not possibly serve the differing needs of the different people spread out across such vast regions. All these countries had adopted The Rule of Seven. They divided the country into seven states and each state had seven regions, and in each region, there were seven counties. Elected leaders each served on their county, state or regional board for seven years, including a one-year stint as chairman or chairwoman of that board. These people realized that the saying 'power corrupts and absolute power corrupts absolutely' was true, so they actually did something about it. I ask you to remember our trips to worlds that found enlightenment. I ask you to remember that these worlds had little or no government because they were not needed."

Then, all three sisters said "don't ever run for office. All great change comes from the grassroots level and happens over generations!"

Jessica continued saying "The residences of the powerful leaders of the past have been turned into museums as a reminder to never go back to those selfish ways."

The idea fascinated me. I could understand immediately that a system like that could work in our country and other countries on Earth. I recalled that Harpo Marx in his autobiography, Harpo Speaks, told of being one of the first American entertainers in communist Russia immediately following the revolution. He was taken on a tour of the Kremlin Palace of the overthrown royal family, the Romanovs. They had amassed such enormous wealth that, in his words, "it made the Hearst Mansion look like a collection of souvenirs from Atlantic City." His tour guide showed them a room that had nothing but snow blowing through a broken window, with snow and rocks on the floor. Those stones were the first ones hurled by street fighters during the Russian Revolution. He said that the symbolism of that room was more valuable to the people of Russia at that time than any of the gold carriages that the royal family had possessed.

However, the metamorphosis we had witnessed by the nine enlightened countries included three things that the Russian Revolution lacked—selfless love, forgiveness, and self-driven industriousness. Without those, the Russian experiment turned into an example of "meet the new boss, same as the old boss" as millions suffered or died.

Jessica looked at me. Her glare was penetrating into my soul.

"Miles," she said, "You are so close. It's not about the money or wealth. That's just the way they got to this point. The barriers crumbled, and the walls fell. I can't say any more than that."

Why was Jessica talking in metaphors? What barriers? What walls? Why can't I understand? She is taking us this far and not giving us the answer.

Frustration.

Then, Alison and I were home. It was the weekend and we needed to recover from a long week. It was good just to get back to the grind of taking care of our family.

The next day, after lunch, Alison suggested that I go to into the basement and listen to some music to unwind. She specifically said to listen to the first three Yes albums. She also told me to follow lyrics and to study the other-worldly artwork that went along with these fabulous pieces of progressive rock music.

I did as she asked. It was a labor of love to listen to all that music again and to look at the beautiful images on the albums. I suddenly realized that I was looking at the artist's renderings of some of the worlds I had visited.

As the last record started to play, Alison came downstairs. I turned and said "Alison, did the band members and the artist, Roger Dean, reach individual awakening? Did they make similar trips to these worlds, with help from friends of yours?"

"Yes."

I held up the cover of their album Fragile.

"Did..."

Alison interrupted me. "Yes Miles. And you and I need to sit down and relax and listen to the music. Okay?"

Of course, I understood her reference.

We both sat down on the beat-up Southwest sofa and I put my arm around Alison as she pulled her legs and feet up under herself to stay warm. I had played this music many times, and had never understood it the way I did now, revisiting this music after the powerful experiences we had had during the last two days. Suddenly everything snapped into place.

I took a deep breath, exhaled and rested my head on Alison's head as the music played on...

Part Three

1. Fool Me Twice

We stood in a circle holding hands. The talking ended when Jessica asked us to please be silent for the entire trip. She looked at us and asked, "Do you trust me?"

We all nodded yes.

Jessica said, "Unlike our first 99 trips, I will be in total control of our travel to the next planet. There can be absolutely no talking during this trip."

We all looked at each other. I was surprised that after 99 trips we were going to change the methodology for this one. Jessica had piqued my curiosity.

We closed our eyes and away we went.

Unlike what happened during our previous trips, this time we could see blurred images in our peripheral vision, while straight ahead there was light. We reached that light in about five seconds.

It was daylight and we were standing halfway up a hill, overlooking a village. We saw aircraft fly overhead, then heard loud explosions.

We were swept away again and found ourselves at the edge of the village. We saw uniformed soldiers shooting the men and older boys of the village, who were unarmed. There were cries and screams coming from inside the bombed-out homes, where we could tell that women and girls were being raped. Outside one home lay the bodies of two dead women whose breasts had been cut off.

I told myself to breathe.

There was a community water well in the distance and we could see soldiers pouring large buckets of white liquid into it. The men of the village were protesting, but their protests were met by machine-gun fire.

We could see children being rounded up and forced to walk away from the village while crying for their parents.

We were off again.

This time we were in a jungle, on the outskirts of a village where soldiers in uniforms were fighting poorly-armed villagers. The villagers were quickly defeated and the men were lined up. The ones who had fought back were beheaded as the rest of the men stood there, weeping. Screams came from the huts where women and children who were hiding saw the massacre. After five men had been beheaded, the rest of the men were shot to death.

We were off another time and then we were standing atop the only hill for miles around. In the distance we could see that this was rich farmland, ready for harvest. At the edge of each crop field, there were fires being lit. Soon, I could see that a dozen fields had been set ablaze, with all the crops soon to be disintegrated into useless ash. I turned to Jessica. She looked at me and shook her head slightly from right to left to tell me not to speak.

We were off again.

We saw a battle between two armed forces in a jungle, about 100 yards from where we landed. The fighting was intense, including automatic weapon fire and mortar or rocket fire that was hitting targets with deadly accuracy. Ten minutes later, the battle was over, and Jessica moved us into the middle of the battle zone. The victorious soldiers walked from body to body and killed anyone who was only injured, so as to complete the massacre. We looked down at the dead bodies and could see that some of them were 11 or 12-year-old boys who had been taught to fire weapons.

I was starting to get sick to my stomach.

We were off again.

We were standing in the last row of a choir loft of a church filled with men and women who were crying and children who looked terrified.

Jessica quickly moved us outside the church, about 50 yards away. We could see three soldiers fire rocket launchers at the church, which brought the roof down upon the people inside. The terror and screaming from inside was making me feel faint.

I didn't faint, and we were off again.

This time we found ourselves in the middle of a small, impoverished village that was home to emaciated people who moved very slowly.

Jessica quickly took us to another village, then yet another village, and then a small town. At each place we saw people living in horrible conditions. In the town, the streets were lined with human filth. Buildings had no windows left after they had been shot out or smashed. We came upon the body of an old man who had died and had been left there in hopes that someone would take him away and bury him. There were famine-ravaged mothers trying to feed their newborn babies, but they could not produce enough milk to satisfy the babies, who cried out from hunger.

Next, we found ourselves standing on an upper loft of an old school building that had been converted into a makeshift hospital. The wails and moans of the suffering and dying had finally overcome what I could tolerate.

Michael beat me to it as he screamed "Jessica, please, that's enough!"

At that, she nodded, and we were all back on the porch of Billy and Dana's home in California. Dana and Alison left the group and went in the house. We stayed on the porch with Jessica.

Michael said "Jessica, I know you told us not to talk, but I had reached my limit."

I said "Michael, if you hadn't said what you did, I was going to, so don't feel bad, I think we had all reached our limit."

Billy said "Jessica, out of the hundred trips we've been on, it's not like we haven't seen atrocities before, but I don't understand the reason for taking us on this kind of intense, horrific trip, one of human evil and human suffering."

No one had paid attention to Tommy. He was sitting on a swing on the porch but wasn't moving. His feet were planted on the porch, elbows upon his knees. His hands covered his face as his tears ran down his bare arms. I quickly walked over, sat next to him, and put my arm around him. He was our youngest and had become our beloved little brother.

A few moments passed and the explosion of emotions had calmed. Dana and Alison had brought out food and drinks, but no one was interested after all we had witnessed.

I turned to Jessica.

"I think Billy had a good question, but I also have a question. Why didn't you give us any background on the planet we just visited?"

Tommy had gotten himself under control and Alison was sitting next to him on the porch swing. He looked up at the group and spoke, saying "I know why Jessica didn't brief us on our trip ahead of time. She shouldn't have needed to brief us, because we never left Earth."

We all looked at each other in silence. We had visited worlds that emulated many of the aspects of our own world, that I had stopped questioning the similarities and dissimilarities of one world to another world, or the latest world to Earth. I thought, "could Tommy be right?" I know he was a really smart kid and graduated with the highest of honors in college, but I still thought, "please don't let him be right."

Jessica said, "That's right Tommy, we never left Earth.

"Here's where I took you."

"We started in Sudan, where 250,000 men, women, and children have already died from the genocide taking place there. The government is trying to kill or drive out the three ethnic groups known as the Fur, the Masalit, and the Zaghawa. The liquid you saw being poured in the community water well was poison."

"Next, I took you to the Democratic Republic of the Congo. The estimated dead from the fighting in this country is anywhere from 3 to 5 million people. Many of the killers and rapists moved into the Congo when they were run out of Rwanda, after the genocide there ended in 1994."

"We then visited Burma, which has been suffering from decades of persecution and abuse from the military junta that rules that country and renamed it Myanmar. There is genocide and rape and forced military recruitment of children. Younger children are used as slave labor until they are old enough to fire weapons."

"Nigeria was next, where there is genocide and a religious war. Worshipers are being killed and churches demolished to break the spirit of the country's inhabitants."

"Finally, I took you to Burundi, which has been the site of genocidal conflict since 1962, when Belgium granted independence to its former colonies of Burundi and Rwanda.

You could see from the villages and towns that we visited, what decades of hate and despair are doing to our brothers and sisters there."

As Jessica explained the route of our trip, my emotions were welling up. I felt anger at what I saw, hopelessness and sadness at what was happening to these people, and embarrassment that I didn't really know the extent to which these atrocities were happening across my own world.

For the next hour, it was very somber on that porch, with not a lot of discussion. If it was Jessica's intent to get our attention, she had succeeded. I know we were all thinking the same thing. We were all thinking we needed to do something about what we just saw, but we all felt helpless, because we didn't know what to do or what to say or where to start.

Jessica had been quiet for a long time, but now she turned to me and asked, "So Miles, what did you take away from our trip today?"

I took a deep breath and exhaled slowly. I leaned back in my chair, looking at the group with my hands clasped in my lap.

"Sadly, the lesson I learned, is that you don't have to travel to a galaxy far away, to find Evil that inflicts suffering upon our brothers and sisters, who need our help."

2. Michael's Mission

On the last day of our trip to Dana and Billy's, we were all sitting around the porch and chatting after breakfast and waiting to depart for the airport.

Alison stood up and stretched, and then turned to us and said, "Well everybody, I know it's been a bit of a roller coaster weekend, but I hope by getting the tough part out of the way early, you were able to get some rest, at least for a short time."

"I need to tell you something on behalf of my sisters and me. We've taken you to 100 different worlds in this miraculous universe, to give you an idea of how your brothers and sisters have met the challenges of life. Today, I'm telling you that there will be no more trips. Today, I'm telling you that you need to go back to the beginning of your journals. You will find that some of the things that you observed in our early trips will be understood differently by you, now that you have completed the grand tour."

"Dana, Jessica, and I will teach/educate all of our children in the same manner as we have taught you. They will have their own trips to take, and their own journals to write, when they become mature enough to understand what's going on all around them. Mostly, they need to understand what's important, and what's not important."

Alison paused. My mind was trying to digest whether I was feeling angry that our trips had ended or that I was feeling relieved. After all, our last trip gave birth to a new drive in me, to do whatever I can do to make our world a better place. I knew about living in the United States, a First World country, with selfish First World problems, but I was a neophyte when it came to figuring out how to help people a half a world away from me. That was my challenge.

The weekend ended and we all went back to our lives trying to make a difference. Every night I reviewed and rewrote my journal. It became a labor of love for me. I felt that I had been given a vast perspective of the universe that only a few living individuals had been privileged to receive.

About a month later, I received a phone call from Michael. He told me that he left a ticket at the airport for me to fly in for the weekend. He wanted to talk to me about the rollout of his new company policies.

Just before I left for the airport, Alison told me "I can't wait for you to get back and tell me what Michael has cooked up." We both laughed as we hugged and kissed goodbye and I was off on my trip to the President and CEO of one of largest defense contractors in the world.

I got in Friday night in time for dinner. Michael and I went to one of our favorite dives called Bumpers, one that we frequented in college. I had been waiting a long time for him to use the company for the good of the whole world, as he had promised me years ago, when he called himself an undercover anarchist.

As we were finishing dinner, we were laughing at the old stories that only Michael and I knew about over the years. Michael's tone changed as he came back from the jukebox.

"I know you've had a long trip Miles, but I ordered one more round before we leave. I put some money in the juke box and found some old Neil Young to keep us company."

"Miles, I want to share with you something about the relationship I have with my dad. When I was young, I worshiped him as the founder and CEO of a huge company, one that gave our family enormous wealth and privilege. When I got to college and started to learn more about the world, I challenged him to explain the ethics and morality of what our company did. He was always very patient with me and he is an extremely intelligent individual. The bottom line of his argument was that someone had to provide these military products to countries around the world, and that at least he could control what countries received what type of advanced military weaponry."

"He told me that grandpa and grandma had been hippies way before their time. They believed in nothing but peace and love and helping thy neighbor. He adored his parents. Anyway, I objected vehemently to his arguments, but he never got cross with me or lost his patience. I accused him of being no better than his Bilderberg Group and Trilateral Commission buddies, who were trying to rule the world in their covert meetings, and he always laughed at my conspiracy theories."

"As I got older, my dad's patience with me grew thinner and thinner. He told me that if I ever had any intention of inheriting this company from him, that I had to show him some semblance of thoughtful, well intentioned maturity. Thank goodness I met you Miles, and by meeting you, I met Alison, Dana, and Jessica. While I was going through our many trips together, my father and I grew closer, even though we still agreed to disagree."

"A year before he fully retired, he relinquished one of his titles to me. He was still Chairman of the Board, but I was the President. I know he wanted to leave the business to spend more time with mom, but we weren't really able to cross that final bridge of trust until late one beautiful California afternoon."

It wasn't like Michael to spin these long yarns. He was a jokester and while I knew he was an intelligent person, he never took the floor and sermonized. He liked being the fly on the wall. When I used to challenge him about not speaking out more, he would quote Mark Twain, saying "It's better to be quiet and thought the fool, than speak and remove all doubt." Tonight was different. Tonight was a different Michael.

He continued "I went into his office and sat down. After I gave him an update of the week's activities, I asked him if he had a few minutes more, because I had something to share with him. I asked him if he had ever heard the story of the Mexican fisherman. He told me he didn't recognize it by title, but that I should start telling it, and if he had heard it before, he would let me know.

"The story goes something like this. There was a successful American businessman on vacation on the coast of Mexico. One day he decided to walk through the seaside town alone, just to take in the commerce that went on in a sleepy tourist village. He came upon a man dressed in a hat, T-shirt, swimming trunks and sandals. He was holding a fishing rod with one hand, and slung over his back were three good-sized fish that he had caught that day. He introduced himself and asked the fisherman about his life in the village. The fisherman told the businessman that every day, he got up, and went to the ocean to catch food for the day's meals. During the day, he could spend time teaching and playing with his kids, and spending time with his wife. The businessman was impressed by the skill of the fisherman. The fisherman told him that it was very easy to catch three fish a day because the fish were plentiful in the ocean there. With that, the businessman told the fisherman that he had an idea that could make him a multimillionaire. All he had to do to start was to purchase one fishing boat. Then, he had to save his money, so that he could buy a fleet of fishing boats. Once he had a fleet, he could build a cannery and export fresh fish and canned fish all around the world. Then he could take his company public and become a multimillionaire on the sale of the stock. "

"The fisherman asked 'Why would I want to do all that?'"

"Why would you want to do all that? Because then you could do anything you wanted to do in life and spend the rest of your life enjoying it," the businessman replied.

"The fisherman shook his head, stepped up to the businessman and said, 'You mean like having a house on the ocean, and spending all day with my wife and my children, teaching and playing with them?'"

"The businessman replied 'Well, never mind.' Then he walked away."

"My dad stood up from his chair and walked over to the window and gazed upon the late afternoon sunlight, the palm trees, and the waves that were rolling up on the long stretch of beach, which went south all the way to Mexico."

"I got up and I walked over to him and asked him if he was okay."

"He turned to me, and for the first time in years, he embraced me."

"He said, 'Son, I love you. I'm so sorry that it took me so long to figure out who you were. I didn't recognize that story till the very end, when I realized that the only other person that ever told it to me was my own father.' You are ready to take over. I'm sure you're going to make the world a better place, however it is you see fit.'"

"He hustled over to his desk and put everything away."

"I said, 'Dad, are you late for something?'"

"He said, 'No, I just need to buy a fishing rod before the stores close. Mom and I always eat fish on Friday nights.'"

I had never seen Michael like this. I was so proud of the man that he had become. I sensed he had more to tell me.

I said "Michael, that's a great story. I'm so happy to hear that it tied three generations together in your family again. I know you didn't ask me to come out here just to tell me that story. So, what else is going on?"

"Yeah, I want to tell you about my new mission for this company."

"This week I had a meeting with the ministers of defense of all of the First World countries. They all use our hardware and software. They didn't have a choice but to attend, because it was at the risk of me cutting them off as clients. When I got them in the room, I kicked out their assistants, and closed and locked the door."

"I told them that their existence as the most powerful military countries in the world wasn't doing the world any good. I told them that from now on, their countries all had to take on a greater mission, that mission being, protecting the innocent in the Third World nations around the globe. At that point, I handed them the only piece of paper they would get during this meeting. Here's a copy for you, Miles. Frame it and maybe someday it'll be famous and worth something."

Michael handed me a piece of paper that said the following:

"Genocide is happening all over the world in the following countries and more. As a start, please choose one of the countries on the accompanying list and have your troops clandestinely enter these countries and protect the innocent people there. All killing must stop. There is to be as little bloodshed as possible and the perpetrators of evil should be put in prisons in their own countries, but these prisons must be monitored by your country."

Syria
Sudan
Democratic Republic of the Congo
Ethiopia
Burma
Nigeria
Chad
Equatorial Guinea
Yemen
Kenya
Central African Republic
Burundi
Iran
Mali
South Africa
Rwanda
Angola
Sri Lanka
Iraq
Somalia
Afghanistan

I looked at the piece of paper for a few moments. Then I turned to Michael and said, "So how did it go?"

"At first there were foot-stomping objections by many of the nations. I let them talk until they were tired. I turned to them and I said, "Look, my company and I will be calling the shots on this and here's how we are going to do it. We are never going to give any of you the most state-of-the-art weaponry and software. You will never know whether what we are selling you is one generation or 10 generations behind what we could sell you. If you don't do what I'm telling you to do, I will give more modern weapons to the countries in this room that **are** doing what I'm asking you to do."

Michael started laughing and said "You could've heard a pin drop in that room. I knew I had them all by the balls. I told them as a first order of business, that their priority must be to return all children from military service and labor camps to their parents. I told them to provide decent homes, schools, hospitals, and villages for people to live in. I told them to provide any medical and educational systems that these people would need to start thriving as a community. However, I told them **not** to do any nation building! I want them to be there as a safety backstop, but each country deserves to build their own peaceful brand of government, if they choose."

"Then I told them the good news: for every dollar they spend in accomplishing these directives, I would credit them a dollar on the purchase of weaponry or software that they need from us."

I was floored. I couldn't believe what I just heard and while I had great feelings of reservation, I couldn't wait to see this begin to happen.

I said, "Wow, that's incredible—what you have set in motion. Is there more?"

"Yes," Michael replied, "The United States hasn't agreed to move forward on my plan, but it has given my company a huge piece of public land where I will be building a small city, to start taking in the orphaned children from these countries, as well as kids from our own country that are in tough situations."

I shook my head in amazement. "So, what was the toughest objection you had to deal with?"

"When they asked me the one tough question that I was ready for: 'So, what are we supposed to do with all the prisoners in these prison camps?'

"Here's what I told them: I want you to train everybody in those camps to play the most popular game in the world—soccer, or futbol, as it's known outside the US. Then, once everybody's in good shape, I want you to hold games between the opposing prison groups. Yes, there will be fights early, but I'm sure they'll eventually get down to playing soccer. As incentive, tell them that if they win the upcoming three-month tournament, the winning team will be set free and the players can go home.

"I told them that I was sure this would work and that they had to trust me. I let them talk amongst themselves for a few minutes and then I asked for their attention again. Right away, as I had predicted to myself, a number of them said they would have to get back to me once they had talked to their Prime Ministers or Presidents back home."

"I told them no.

"I told them that they had the authority to agree to this deal, and that if they walked out of the room without signing the agreement, which I held up in the air, that they would not be receiving any further equipment from my company. I told them in no uncertain terms that it had to be the goal of all of our countries to bring peace to this planet.

"I told them that their goal should be to put my company out of business. They all signed."

"They did?" I said.

"Yes, they did. When they did, it was as if a weight was lifted from all of their shoulders and they suddenly became much friendlier to each other.

I still had great reservations about his plan so I said "Michael, do you really think all of these nations will implement your plan?"

"Oh, hell no. I would say that at least half of these defense ministers will be fired immediately after they report to their country's leader. But Miles, I only need one country! If I can get one country, and I let the espionage grapevine know that I got one country to do this, the rest of these countries will know that this one insightful country is receiving our most advanced technological warfare products. Then, they'll start second-guessing whether they should join in. I'm not that naïve Miles, but I do know how all these jokers work, and I can play them against each other. If I just get one brave nation, it may start the dominoes to fall worldwide."

"Well, I'm sure your dad is smiling from ear to ear right now, Michael."

"I hope so, and I hope he reeled in a big one this afternoon for dinner tonight."

And Neil Young's voice rang out across the restaurant, singing the haunting lyrics "four dead in Ohio."

Michael came up with a great name for his initiative: the Protect the Innocent Project.

About three months into it, I called Michael one night, and he had just gotten back from Sudan. He told me that one country had agreed to clandestinely send troops into South Sudan to stabilize the region. Michael was not going to believe reports unless he could verify them with his own eyes. He told me that he had walked about 25 miles across a stretch of the country that formerly had been considered unstable and dangerous. It was nothing like that now.

When the evil-doers from the north approached at night, the soldiers from the one country cooperating with Michael were more than happy to carry out their mission: protecting the innocent. They had sent messages telling the would-be killers to leave the people alone, and that if they attacked, the soldiers would make sure they would reap their eternal reward. Despite these warnings, the evil-doers tested the highly trained soldiers, who had state-of-the-art combat equipment. It was a bad choice, as the soldiers fought off the attackers and protected the defenseless families. It only took about a week for the attacks to stop and the building to begin.

Michael told me about one specific conversation that he had had with a sergeant who had been in the military for 18 years. He told Michael that for the first time in his life, he felt an enormous compassion for the people he was defending and helping. For the first time, he wasn't fighting for some political issue, economic issue, or retaliation. In his words he was "keeping the bad guys from killing the good guys, who couldn't defend themselves."

The people took to these soldiers as if they were powerful Guardian Angels sent by their God to bring hope and peace back into their lives.

I found Michael's story, and the way he told it, quite moving.

3. The Magical Jessica Tour

Meanwhile, Jessica had become a scientific and medical celebrity. Her campaign to try and refocus scientific and medical research on the here and now had really picked up steam and she was in high demand on college campuses and in the media. She had authored three books on the subject and with each book, her followers grew in number. The last book was aimed at college and high school aged individuals and it had an enormous effect on helping them to start refocusing their worldviews.

Jessica rarely made media appearances. She knew the media tricks of taking statements out of context and twisting them to suit some agenda other than her own. She had strict rules for accepting any interview. The interview had to be live and it had to be broadcast in full until she said the interview was done. The interview could not be replayed except in its entirety. In any interview, Jessica's staff would have to be included, and they would be ready to show any information that Jessica wanted seen or heard. In essence, her people got to take over half of the control booth.

Billy had become her go-to producer in the control booth, because she could trust him and she felt that he was incorruptible.

I remember in one of her early interviews when asked about landing a man on the moon she replied, "the astronauts and people working as a team that put them on the moon, and brought them home safely, showed a tremendous amount of human courage, courage that is often-times missing in today's world. Once we achieved reaching the moon, however, we should've stopped there. The missions themselves brought back very little evidence that advanced science in any meaningful way. These ongoing missions were driven by political reasons, to show other countries our perceived technological and military might. The same goes for the old Soviet Union. The massive funding of these projects could have helped so many that were in need here and especially in the totalitarian Soviet Union." That made the front page of a lot of papers around the country.

Jessica loved to use psychologist Abraham Maslow's Hierarchy of Needs chart to help television audiences understand the suffering in our world.

She said "There's no perfect way to explain the human condition in our world, but Maslow does as good a job as anyone. If you could please put your mind in a state of considering the world in its entirety, and not just your home, or your hometown, then you and everyone else might better understand what I'm trying to get the world to focus upon. Here in the United States, along with other First World countries, we have for the most part achieved Maslow's levels three, four, and five, depending on the individual. In the rest our world, our brothers and sisters are struggling with providing their families with the two lower levels—physical needs and safety—every day, every hour, every minute, as we sit here in our comfortable existences and do very little about it. Mostly, because we know very little about it."

Many times, I saw hardened news people fall under Jessica's spell, which was very easy to do. She was one of the smartest people on earth, and only a few of us knew the reason why. Her enormous empathy, coupled with her beauty, made her, as one Pulitzer Prize winning writer said, "The angel and champion of the world's innocents."

But one of my favorite interviews was her response to the statement "But Doctor, I don't think it's fair to make us all feel guilty because we have achieved some level of success when others have not. Granted, many have not had the opportunities that we have here in First World countries, but even Jesus Christ himself said 'The poor you will always have with you.'"

She replied as tersely as I had ever heard her speak "Yes, yes, I have heard you and other commentators use that phrase from the Bible to defend your ambivalence to the fate of your brothers and sisters across the world. Christ was talking to his disciples and knew his crucifixion was imminent and he was trying to teach them as much as he could before he left this world. Then Christ became angry with them because they were not listening to him and when he said 'The poor you will always have with you,' he meant the poor people of the time in which they lived, not all poor people ad infinitum. You and all of your friends who take this out of context should be ashamed of yourselves. You're helping to make my point, that the poor do **not** always have to be with us, unless we don't do anything to save them from poverty and oppression. Secondly, I am not here to judge anyone. I am NOT trying to make anyone feel guilty, but if you feel guilty, then do yourself a big favor, and forgive yourself. We want you to join us. I am trying to make everyone aware, and I am trying to tell everyone that it is our responsibility to save our underprivileged brothers and sisters in the world.

"I am here to make as many people as possible aware of what's happening in this world. We are not getting the job done, that job being: bringing everyone up to an acceptable living standard, and doing that with as much love, kindness, empathy and understanding as possible."

When Jessica got on a roll in that way, no one was a match for her.

One of her funnier moments was in replying to a question about her politics when she said to her interviewer, "I am a political agnostic. I have severe doubts of the existence of any honest politicians in this country. I am not a Democrat, I am not a Republican, I am a sister to the rest of my family in this world, and that includes you."

That phrase "I Am a Political Agnostic" became a bumper sticker all around the country.

Jessica was once on a panel that was discussing the theme of Sentient Life Throughout the Universe. Because of all the things that the sisters had taught me, and knowing the things that Jessica knew, I watched it as if I were watching a comedy show. Of course, Jessica held her cards close to her chest, but the zingers came when she told everyone "it's a scientific and mathematical certainty that there is sentient life throughout the universe. However, if you put the metaphorical gun to the head of any competent astrophysicist, they would tell you that it's impossible for us to travel the enormous distances that lie between us and any of these other earthlike planets. To summarize it for our audience: We ain't going nowhere, and no one is coming to save us."

Another comical comment Jessica shared that night was in her response to the Big Bang Theory when she said, "I think it has a lot of merit, but a great deal of work must be done before it could become a more credible part of scientific knowledge. One of my interns came up with an interesting analysis of it. It goes like this: Give me one miracle and 11 dimensions, and I can almost make the math come out. Almost."

The nationally renowned cartoonist Jill Spencer, who had become an avid supporter and friend of Jessica's, had created a thought-provoking cartoon, which was printed in all the major newspapers across the country. It depicted Jessica as a mother, entering a room where her three sons had been playing. Jessica had arrived just moments after they had thrown one of those magic eight balls, one that predicts the future, against the wall. There were bits and pieces of it flying everywhere and the liquid from inside was covering the wall and the desk in front.

Jessica asked her boys "what is it you're doing in here?" They replied "our school science project was to investigate and discover how the magic eight ball was able to tell the future. We decided that we needed an atom smasher to find out the answer, and well, it didn't turn out to be such a good idea."

When asked about her cartoon's meaning, Jill Spencer replied "the message I was trying to send, was that just because we can do something doesn't mean we should do something. Like splitting atoms, and like trying to re-create black holes, at the CERN supercollider. A lot of that money could have been used to feed and clothe and shelter the poor."

Jessica was definitely having an effect on the psyche of America and First World countries around the globe. She started the ball rolling, and my concern was whether or not it could keep its momentum through the generations that were to follow.

* * *

One morning I received a phone call from Billy, and he told me that he was an hour's drive away from our home because Jessica was doing an interview this afternoon. He asked me if I could grab some dinner with him tonight. So, we agreed to meet at a diner called Skelton's which was about halfway between our home and his location. After we exchanged pleasantries, I saw Billy's face take on a seriousness that I hadn't witnessed before. I knew it was my time to be a good listener.

I said "So, what else is going on?"

Billy replied, "Miles, I know Dana tells people not to ask me about why I never finished my dissertation. She thinks I don't know that, but I do. Anyway, I recently ran into my astrophysics professor, Dr. Arrowsmith, after one of the news shows in New York where Jessica was being interviewed. After the show, I saw him in the distance but I didn't approach him. But our eyes met and when they did, he started walking over to me."

Billy had my attention.

"Miles, I was almost done with my dissertation and Dr. Arrowsmith, had looked at some preliminary drafts and said that it looked very promising. I knew that he had said those exact words to others before me, others who had received their PhDs, so I was sure I was on the right path. I had maybe a month to six weeks more to work on my final draft."

"He was kind enough to invite Dana and me to dinner one Saturday night. All four of us had a great time with good food and wine and lively conversation. Dana was working on her Masters in physics at the time and he told me how he found Dana to be quite delightful before we left the restaurant."

"Then he offered to take us to the observatory, even though it was after hours. He wanted us to see a new celestial body that had been found, one that was 20 million light years from Earth and might be able to sustain life. As we drove there and walked to the telescope, Barbara and I were quiet. Dana had challenged him by saying that, while discovering lights in the sky was interesting, it would never amount to anything, because we would never be able to travel fast enough and safely enough to visit these planets. The conversation went on as we all took a look through the lens. When we all finished, he turned to Dana and said, 'So what do you think of that, little girl?'

"He said it in such a demeaning way, that quite frankly, it pissed me off, but Dana wasn't going to back off her argument because of his lack of manners and his superiority complex."

Billy continued with his story.

"Dana replied to him, 'Dr. Arrowsmith, I have a genuine affection for you and I respect you as a person. I'm sorry that you feel it necessary to address me in such a condescending manner, but I forgive you. I just have one question for you.

"Then Dana stepped right up to him face-to-face and said 'So, what is more likely the purpose of your life Doctor, that little speck of light that we all saw through these enormous lenses, or loving your wife, who is standing three feet away from you?'"

As I sat there, all I could think was how great a story this was and how cathartic it must be for Billy to tell it to me.

"Go on Billy, I'm with you, I'm standing next to you in that observatory all those years ago."

Billy took a deep breath through his nose and exhaled it through his mouth and it did help them relax before he continued.

He said "I told Dr. Arrowsmith to answer Dana's question. His wife Barbara was standing next to me and the both of us watched. He argued that the question was unfair, and it wasn't even stated within the realm of a scientific inquiry. He went on for five minutes before he finally gave Dana a chance to reply. She said to him again: 'What is more likely, that the meaning of your life is that little glimmer of light at the end of that telescope, or loving Barbara, who is standing three feet away from you?'

"Dana and I had been dating for quite a while, and we had a number of philosophical discussions about how my degree in astrophysics could be a waste of time, if not used in a productive manner. That was the moment, at the observatory, that I knew that there were more important things to do in this world, than look for planets that we could never visit in whatever time Earth has left as a civilization. You know it and I know it. Ninety-nine percent of all species that once inhabited earth are now extinct. Why would human beings be spared the natural process of extinction? An extinction level event should occur in the next 35,000 to 50,000 years, like the one that killed all the dinosaurs.

"I stood there and looked at Arrowsmith and saw him for the first time as he really was. I knew that I never wanted to be like him, and that's why I walked away from my final dissertation. I realized that the most important thing in my life was Dana, raising a family, and helping those less fortunate than myself."

Billy stopped talking. But I knew he was just taking a break and gathering himself.

Twenty seconds later I asked, "So, what did Arrowsmith say to you that night in New York that your paths crossed?"

"Dr. Arrowsmith told me that the next morning after our dinner Barbara packed her things and moved out of our house. She couldn't understand that I was just trying to win an argument. He said it took them over a year, but they eventually came back together as a couple. He told me that he felt guilty because he never reached out to Dana and me, because he was embarrassed to admit he was wrong. Then he thanked Dana and me for bringing them closer together."

My mind now quickly took me back to that moment from years and years ago, when Alison had told me to never ask Billy why he didn't finish his PhD. Now, I got to hear the answer. Billy seemed incredibly relieved to tell the story, and I could almost hear the albatross fall off his neck and onto the floor.

"I told Dr. Arrowsmith that Dana had forgiven him a long time ago but that I had been carrying around this baggage for years. I told him that I really appreciated that he had come over to me and talked with me."

"As we were about to part ways, I told Arrowsmith that I would be talking to Dana later and that I would give her your apology and best wishes. Then he asked me if I would mind calling her right now so that he could personally apologize to her. I thought it was a good idea, so I did call her."

"I could only hear what Dr. Arrowsmith was saying and it went something like this:

"Dana, this is Dr. Arrowsmith. I want to apologize for my boorish behavior all those years ago. I am sorry. You never said anything to me that deserved disrespect. In fact, in the end, you were right, but I didn't understand it at the time. I had taken my wife Barbara for granted, and because I did, I almost lost her over a speck of light. I wish I could've taken those words back, because they almost cost me the only thing I had ever truly loved."

"Dana said something in return to him."

"Dr. Arrowsmith replied 'Thank you, Dana, I appreciate that you accept my apology and I'll follow your advice. All the best to you and Billy, and your family, in the future.'"

So I asked Dr. Arrowsmith "What was Dana's advice?"

Dr. Arrowsmith said "She told me that she had forgiven me a long time ago, and to tell Barbara exactly what I had just told her. I plan on following **that** advice."

Billy sat up straight with his back against the padded booth and looked me right in the eyes. It was a look of great relief that he had gotten the whole story out. I loved him as if he were my real brother and I was happy for him that he had finally moved beyond those moments all those years ago.

4. Weddings, Anniversaries & the Brotherhood

It had been six years since Marco played point guard for me during his senior year at Kennedy High School in Peoria, Illinois, where I had accepted the head coaching position and was teaching honors English. And now I was coming to Marco's wedding, as was Tommy, who had become my assistant coach and was teaching sociology, and many others from that year.

Neither Tommy, nor I, nor the players will forget that year we spent together. It was the greatest coaching experience of my life and it really had nothing to do with the fact that we that had finished second in the Illinois state basketball championship tournament. It had everything to do with the fact that the players and coaches kept company with each other for three to four hours a day, six days a week, for four straight months.

Marco and his running mate at guard, Craig, both multi-sport stars, were destined to become Division I college soccer players, having signed letters of intent with colleges in what is now the PAC 12 Conference. They were seniors and they both understood the game at a level greater than any players I had coached before. As any good coach can tell you, if you ain't got guards, you ain't got shit. But I had great guards, and that gave my team the chance to win every game and a shot at winning a championship.

Craig was lightning fast, about six foot one, and could dribble with either hand at top speed, come to a complete stop, and then take off at full speed again. Defensively, it wasn't just that he had an innate ability for stealing the ball. It went beyond that. I would say that at least a half dozen times in the last minute of a close game Craig could sense when the **other** team was about to steal the ball from us, and when they did, he left his man and stole the ball right back. Then he would dribble out of danger or call a timeout. That wasn't something I had ever seen, from any player, at any level.

Marco, on the other hand, was like a cross between Pele, the soccer legend, and Curly Neal of the Harlem Globetrotters. He could do otherworldly things with the ball just by changing speeds and the direction of his dribble. The list of amazing things that he did could go on forever, but this one always stuck out in my head.

There was a loose ball bouncing in front of the other team's bench and Marco ran full speed toward the ball, then did a pop-up slide, a soccer or baseball move rarely seen on a basketball floor. As he slid to the floor, he put one hand out and began dribbling the bouncing ball while still down, then popped up to his feet and dribbled full speed in the other direction.

The other team's coach screamed at the referee standing right in front of him that Marco was traveling. The official looked at him with his whistle stuck in his mouth. He put his arms out, palms up, and shrugged his shoulders, indicating to everyone that he hadn't seen that before either, but in his opinion, it was not traveling.

Because they were soccer players, Marco and Craig not only had a great understanding of how to use the entire court, but they also had unending endurance. If they had to, they could play the entire game without a substitution. Most importantly, no matter how athletic or physical a game became, they were physically strong enough and mentally tough enough that they never got tired, and so they could find the order within the chaos and direct the team to victory.

Mark was our center at six-nine and he was a gentle giant and a great kid. He was the best passer on our team and understood that our set offense had to start with him inside. He understood that starting with him inside did not mean he was to shoot the ball, but that he had to read the defense and make the right decisions. His shot blocking ability, which he worked on after the regular practice, was uncanny. He had perfected blocking a shot and having it drop softly straight down to him. His senior year he had 65 blocks and he corralled 45 of them, which were considered steals.

Glenn was one forward and was the Thor of basketball players. At six-six he had a vertical jump that was amazing. He was immensely strong, quick, and he could shoot three-point shots and outrebound anyone. Six years later, he was playing defensive end in the NFL. I once told Glenn privately that he had the heart of a lion, and that he was the greatest competitor I had ever seen.

Last but not least was James. A six-two forward who could handle the ball, shoot threes, make unbelievable drives to the basket and finish. He could be counted on to make last-second shots in close games. James was very quiet, but he was one of our best overall athletes. His senior year I challenged him to guard the other team's best player, even though he was our leading scorer. He took on that challenge and did a terrific job every single game.

The rest of the team resembled our starters in that they were all great hard-working kids and each had developed certain skills that helped our team to be very successful, with a 29-2 record that season.

However, what Tommy and I were most proud of was the players' absolute sense of trust and love for each other, as well as for the coaches. That included things on the court and more importantly things off the court. They even named themselves the Brotherhood.

I told them at the beginning of the year, as I told the players every year, that Tommy and I would teach them all the valuable life lessons that had been passed down to us by our parents, family, coaches, teachers, mentors, friends, and our faith. I told them that by the end of the year, it was important to Coach Tommy and me that they became fine young men and that they learned to believe in something greater than themselves, because if they didn't, they would fall for anything after they left school.

As assistant coach of the varsity team, Tommy was the de facto assistant coach of the whole program, and I made sure he talked to the freshman and sophomore teams every day. His favorite story to tell the younger kids was that the United States of America was the only country in the world where men did not embrace regularly. A couple weeks into the season, he would have them form a circle before practice, hold hands and commit to giving a maximum effort that day. I told Tommy that without those small steps early on, our varsity teams would never have become as close as they did. By the time our kids were juniors and seniors, their team circles sometimes involved them putting their arms around each other. When former players came back to visit after a game, they would be welcomed into the locker room with sweaty hugs from the current players.

There were many standard lessons I tried to teach my teams, but one of my favorites was the Christmas speech. I told them that I found it interesting that young people could easily believe in vampires and zombies at the movie theaters, but if they just opened their eyes, they could see real magic and real miracles all around them. To prove it, I challenged them. I told them that on Christmas Eve to find a way to be alone with their moms. When they were alone, they were to hold her hands and look her right in the eye and say "Mom, thank you for all the things that you have done and that you do for me. I want you to know how much I love you." Then I told them to stand back and see what happens. Only a few of the mothers were dumbfounded. Most of them grabbed their sons and hugged them and many of them would start crying, as they told their sons how much they loved them too.

Not all the players did it, but the ones who did told us that they saw the magic of love happen right in front of them. Their mothers would begin crying and some wouldn't let their sons go. Sometimes, the player would start crying while telling the story to the rest of the team. I knew that the vulnerability of sharing personal stories would bond any group tightly.

Over the years I had a lot of notes and emails from moms thanking me, and that always brought a smile to my face.

At this point it was six years later and we had all been invited to the wedding of Marco and Kelly, his longtime girlfriend and fiancé. Most of the players made it to the occasion. Tommy and his girlfriend Anna accompanied Alison and me to the festivities.

The wedding was held in a beautiful church with ornate stained-glass windows that depicted the Beatitudes, the blessings that Christ had given the crowds during the Sermon on the Mount. The inside of the church was filled with white marble altars and beautifully crafted birchwood pews and a thick green carpet. All of this made it seem like a royal wedding, right here in middle America.

Once the ceremony came to an end and we pelted the bride and groom with rice, the guys and coaches started to gather together and it was as if we all just picked up where we had left off six years before. Alison was as much a part of it as I was, because the kids were always hanging around our house, either for pizza parties or to watch games with Tommy and me and my kids. There was playful pushing and shoving, neck holds, and messing up of hairdos, as was our tradition all those years ago, but no one got mad. We all just laughed harder and harder at the silliness. The playful love and joy was soaked up by everyone who had been part of or witness to the Brotherhood.

Tommy and I were happy to see that all the things we had learned over the years had paid off and helped make these boys into young gentleman. We were very proud of the fact that these young men thought it was just as important to prepare dinner at the homeless shelter, serve it, and clean up afterwards, as it was to attend a basketball practice.

Over the years there had been times when I felt we were a little tight coming up to a big game, so Tommy and I would skip practice the day before and take the team to the shelter and work. We were undefeated in those games, but as a group, we never told anyone, especially the newspaper reporters. We wanted our charitable work to stay among us. The players thus learned the difficult lesson of selfless humility.

A couple hours after the wedding we went to the reception, at a banquet hall surrounded by a huge forest. There were no other buildings around, and it was about a one-mile drive to the downtown area, where we had booked rooms for the evening.

The reception went beautifully. Feelings of joy, love and good intentions for the newlyweds filled the room. All the traditional ceremonies went on. The couple cut the cake and playfully smeared it in each other's faces. The traditional first dance was very sweet. The second dance saw the entire wedding party join the happy couple, who were loved by everyone in that room. The night then turned into fun and games.

About 10 o'clock many of the players joined Tommy, Alison, and me to talk about old times and all the fun we had. We talked about the legendary triple overtime semifinal state championship game that we won at the buzzer. Basketball people in Illinois still think of it as one of the greatest high school games played in the last 25 years, not just because of the skill of the players and the tension of the overtimes, but also because of the tremendous effort by both teams. We were down one point with six seconds to go and James drove the lane for a layup. Everyone was watching and holding their breath as it began to roll off the rim. Everyone except for Glenn, whose lion heart told him that the game was not over until there were only zeros on the clock. He jumped up and tipped the ball in with one second to go for the victory.

That's not the most remarkable thing I remember from that game. When I put my arms around each player as we walked off the floor, I found that their uniforms were drenched in sweat from top to bottom. That had happened to me once or twice before with one player from our team. It had never happened with seven or eight players from our team. It showed me that all the starters and several of the subs had left everything they had on the floor that afternoon.

However, winning that game meant we had to play the championship game later that same night and we were just too tired to come back and beat an outstanding Eisenhower High School team, though it was a tight game. With five seconds to go, we were down one. Mark was three feet from the basket when he caught a rebound with one hand and in the same motion tried to dunk the ball. However, it rattled out, an Eisenhower player grabbed the rebound and we had to foul with one second left. They made their free throws and we missed a last second shot.

We had given everything we could, so when we walked off that floor, our heads were held high. All except Mark, who was despondent over missing an almost impossible play. What happened in the locker room afterwards is what coaches yearn to hear, even it only happens once in a lifetime.

Mark's head was down, but right away Marco said "Mark you didn't lose the game for us. I had four turnovers and I should've had zero, and we probably would have won."

Craig said "Mark, I missed two free throws and if I had made those, we would've been up by one and not down by one."

Glenn said "I missed two easy tip-ins and that's four points we could've had that we didn't. "

Then James, the quiet one, stood up and said more words than he had in the entire season.

"Mark, we all played this game together. We all did the best that we could. Not one person in this locker room, including the coaches and trainers, has anything to hang their heads about. We won 29 games and finished second in the state of Illinois. But more importantly, I learned how to love each one of you as a brother. I learned to love my coaches as fathers. As time goes on, a lot of the things that happened during all of our games will fade from my memory, but I will never forget any of you, the time we spent together as a Brotherhood, and how much you cared about me. It's all the players and coaches in this room that helped me crack through my shyness, and to tell you all right now that I love all of you, and the thing I hate the most is that this is the last game we'll ever play together as a team."

Everyone stood up and put their arms around each other in our team circle. There were many tears shed, but for the most part it was brothers telling each other "great season" and how much they loved each other. In the middle of it, a shot of perfect love hit us in the middle of our chests. It was the love that Alison and I had experienced in that elevator years before. It actually made the lights in the locker room flicker briefly. We all looked up at each other and a number of the kids said "whoa."

The moment was perfect and I knew it couldn't last, but I still think about it. Every. Single. Day. So of course, we talked about it at the wedding reception.

Later, I made my way over to the DJ. He was a middle-aged fellow in a young man's job. We talked for a few minutes before I put in my request, which had never been fulfilled at any of the parties that Alison and I had attended over the years. However, today was different.

I asked "Can you play the Al Jarreau song We Got By? It was the first song that we danced to on our honeymoon in San Francisco. We were in a small jazz club in the wharf district where Billie Cobham and Al Jarreau were performing before they became famous. It's been our song for these 27 years."

The DJ said "My man, I've been waiting a long time for this request, and yes, I do have that. Which version would you like, original studio or live Montreux Jazz Festival with David Sanborn?"

"You have the Montreux version? Wow! Let's do it," I replied.

Then he asked me "Twenty-seven years? Are you kidding me? Is that your wife standing over there? Did you rob the cradle?"

"No, no, no" I said as we both started to laugh. "So, are you just working me for a tip, or did you want to meet my lovely bride? In fact, I can prove that we have been married 27 years."

I waved at Alison to come over to the DJ table. As she was walking over, I wrote on a napkin how many years we were married, 27, and what day our anniversary was, then gave it to the DJ. I told the DJ "today is our 27th wedding anniversary" and said I would not say one more word until he asked Alison his question.

When Alison arrived, the DJ asked his question and she confirmed the wedding date and year. He just shook his head and smiled. I put five dollars in his tip jar, but he quickly grabbed it and put it back in my hand. He said "I'm friends with Marco's family. So, I finally get to meet Marco's high school coach. You coached Marco and all these kids, didn't you? I remember you now from watching that triple overtime game on television."

I said "Yes I did, and it was a privilege and an honor to do so."

He replied "I've gotten to meet a lot of these kids tonight and I've been impressed with all of them." I turned around completely and we shook hands. As we shook, I slipped the five back in his jar with my other hand, so he couldn't see, and said "You're the best DJ I've ever heard." Then I grabbed

Alison's hand and quickly left before he could detect my sleight-of-hand with the five-dollar bill.

It was about 15 minutes later when I heard Marco's voice through the PA system.

"If I can have everyone's attention. There have been a lot of speeches tonight, so I'm not going to make another long one. Most of you know Coach Christian and Mrs. Christian, who are sitting over there on the right side of the dance floor. What you don't know is that tonight is their 27th wedding anniversary."

There was polite applause from the crowd.

Marco said "Coach, if it wasn't for our parents, for you, Coach Tommy, Mrs. Christian and all my teammates, we would've never grown up to be the people we are today. I think I speak for everyone when I say thanks for giving us such a great example of a teacher, coach, husband and father. Please know that we are all your adopted sons. If you would please do us the pleasure, the next dance is for the two of you, on your 27th wedding anniversary. And we are not going to let you get out of it. Come on everybody, keep clapping until they get out there on the dance floor."

It was a completely unexpected moment. I was caught off guard and I started to feel tears welling up in my eyes. I knew the old trick of staring up at the ceiling to try and suppress tears, but it wasn't working. So, I just got up and grabbed Alison. The fact that we were moving to the center of the dance floor returned my emotions to a normal state.

The DJ had started the song before we could reach the center of the dance floor.

I know Alison loved it, because she loved dancing, not because she loved the limelight. It was a beautiful moment, to walk hand-in-hand to the middle of the floor. When we reached the spotlight, Alison put both her hands around my neck. I put both my hands on the small of her back and pulled her close to me. We looked each other in the eyes and I saw in her eyes a quick twinkle—stars in the night sky. It had truly been 27 years of bliss, sharing a life together. The song reminded us of the huge leap of faith that we took and how hard it had been starting off, but that we had gotten to this point 27 years later, swaying back and forth on the dance floor at Marco and Kelley's wedding. As the song played on, I wished it would never end.

When the song ended, I saw that many of the people had circled the dance floor. I'm sure most of them had never heard that song by Al Jarreau and the soulfulness and love that it projected. It was a song that helped me learn the lesson that the little things that happen every day in life are the most important.

The song ended and everyone gave us polite applause and I pulled away from my Alison ever so slightly and said, "Thanks for putting up with me for 27 years."

She replied "Well Coach, it's been tough, but you're welcome. And by the way, all of these young men really love you, and so do I." We kissed each other as innocently as those two young kids did back in college. Then we turned and walked hand-in-hand off the floor.

At that moment, I realized that while life had shown me man's inhumanity to man, it had also shown me the great joys of life with Alison.

5. Letting Go

"So, which one of your old buddies was that?" Alison asked.

"That was Rich," I said. "Just catching up. We really haven't talked in about eight or nine months, but as usual, there were no cataclysmic changes in his life. Rich and Jenny say hi. Their kids are all doing great etcetera, etcetera, etcetera."

"Gosh, I haven't seen Jenny and Rich since your high school class reunion. What was that—four years ago?"

"Something like that."

Alison again asked "So nothing new?"

"Why do you keep asking me that? You listened in on my conversation, didn't you?"

Alison smiled and replied, "I never **listen in** on your conversations. I don't have to 'listen in' because you're so loud, everybody in the house can hear you. I'll still respect the so-called privacy of that call, even though I do know that Rich ran into your old girlfriend Rebecca, and what's her last name now, Badali?"

Alison was the least jealous person that I had ever known. It was part of her self-confidence, and of course, the fact that she had been around a lot more blocks than I had. So, I knew her request for an update on my old girlfriend was just out of curiosity, and nothing more.

"Rich ran into Rebecca at the drugstore last week, and to be honest with you, it was probably the reason that he reached out to me today. So, I was wrong. I guess there was something new," I said.

I continued, saying "They had a really nice visit. Rebecca and her husband have been married for 24 years now and have a family of their own and they're all doing very well. They talked about some of the old times and double dates we went on and shared some nice moments. She eventually got around to asking about how I was doing and Rich gave her a CliffsNotes version of our life."

"You have to remember, Alison, we were all pretty close back in high school and college. But I do want to share with you the one serious question that Rebecca asked Rich about us. She asked 'So, did it turn out that Miles found The One'?"

"Well?" Alison asked.

"Rich told Rebecca 'Yes, I can't think of a happier couple than the two of them.' His words, not mine. Rich said that Rebecca responded with genuine sincerity that she was really happy to hear that. Her husband, Tony, finally tracked her down in the drugstore and Rich got to meet him too. Rich said he seemed to be a good guy and that the two of them really seemed right together. I have to tell you Alison, that hearing those words probably helped dissolve the remaining bits of guilt that I was carrying for running off with you all those years ago."

Alison looked at me as if I had said all the right things and just smiled. She was whipping up something in the kitchen and I was sitting at the table flipping through the newspaper.

"Well, I didn't know you still had guilt dust hanging on you, but I'm glad to hear that you've been able to brush it off," Alison said.

I just shook my head and smiled as I kept my head buried in the paper. It took me about 15 minutes to get through the news and sports of the day. When I finished, I folded the paper up and threw it in the recycling bin. I couldn't help but think back to the time when I dated Rebecca.

Then, I turned into that guy defined by the phrase "how do I know what I think until I hear what I say?"

So, my ramblings to Alison started with "I really don't think about that relationship very often anymore, because I had worked through most of it when it happened, but today was different. I'm older and I hope wiser and I have seen a lot of relationship behavior over the course of my lifetime."

I quickly mentally scrolled through the time that I dated Rebecca, and something popped up into my head that I had never really thought about."

"When we first met, I was away at college and she was working and going to junior college at night back in our hometown. Even though we were a real item, the pressure on our relationship was minimal, because we only talked on the phone during the week and saw each other every other weekend.

Alison continued with her baking, but I knew that she was listening intently.

Alison finally spoke. "Miles, it amazes me sometimes the details in your memory. You've never talked about this as long as I've known you. Putting what you just said together with everything else you told me about Rebecca finally completes the picture I have of the two of you together. Remember Miles, we are all imperfect, impermanent, but interconnected. So, just remember the good stuff between the two of you. That's what you need to do."

I let out a sigh and replied "You're right. Yep. You're right. Thank you, Grasshopper, for your pearls of Buddhist wisdom."

I walked out of the kitchen and into the family room to see if there were any good basketball games on television. Duke was playing North Carolina and the second half was just starting. Needless to say, I became a couch potato for the next hour, watching one of the historic college basketball rivalries.

It was Saturday night and our kids were either at college or out with their high school friends, so we watched a movie and stayed up until our youngest came home safely and then we went to bed.

At about 2:30 in the morning, my old nightmare jumped back into my consciousness. I had learned to sit up more slowly, as I was now older than when this nightmare started many years ago. My breathing was labored, and what again came over me was the awful feeling of dread that somehow, I knew someone had died, and no one else knew about it.

Usually, Alison would sit up at that point and ask me if I had that same nightmare. Tonight, however, Alison was not in bed next to me. I figured she had gone to the bathroom or downstairs for some chamomile tea to help her sleep. So, I slung my feet over the edge of the bed and sat there and tried to calm myself down.

When I looked up, I was in our dark bedroom and saw through the doorway that there was light in the hallway. There stood a dark silhouette of Alison holding hands with a little girl who had pigtails. I rubbed my face to make sure I was awake. I wondered if we were overnight babysitting for one of our friends and that I had just forgotten about it.

In a hushed tone I said "Alison, who is that little sweetheart holding your hand? Couldn't she sleep either?"

Alison said "Turn on your bedside lamp, Miles. I don't want to turn on the overhead light. It's too bright for this time of the night."

I turned on the light and could see Alison's face and the face of a beautiful little girl, with blonde hair, blue eyes, and the most pixie-like smile I can ever remember seeing at 2:30 in the morning.

Alison and the little girl walked right up in front of me.

Without hesitation Alison said "Miles, this is your daughter, and little one, this is your father."

The little girl let go of Alison's hand and came up to me and stood there smiling. Then she crawled onto my lap, kissed me on the cheek and hugged me around the neck as if she would never let me go.

I whispered foolishly, as if the girl couldn't hear me, "Alison, I don't think this is funny."

"It's not supposed to be funny, Miles. **This is your daughter**. For real. This is your daughter!"

I said "What are you talking about? I don't get it."

The little girl stopped hugging me and looked into my eyes. She said, in one of the sweetest voices I had ever heard, "I love you daddy and I can't wait for us to play together."

In a stern voice I said, "Alison, just tell me what is going on here."

"What's going on is this. I didn't want you to keep suffering through these nightmares for the rest of your life. I'm taking advantage of the fact that I am both human and an experienced infinite being. I love you and I wanted you to have this moment sooner rather than later, and I wanted to stop your nightmares. After our talk at the kitchen table today, I knew it was going to happen tonight."

"What was going to happen tonight? You mean my nightmare?"

Alison said "Rebecca was thinking about her relationship with you and about the early term miscarriage that she had when the two of you first started dating. She didn't even know she was pregnant. She never told you about it. However, sometimes when she thinks about that, those are the nights you have this nightmare. When a child is conceived, the Creator puts an infinite spark into the unborn child, which helps mothers and babies get through the tough times of the birthing process. Needless to say, many times these children are never born, for many reasons, and in these cases, their infinite essence has to wait for their parents, so they can meet in the infinite world."

For a few seconds I thought I was dreaming all of this. However, when I looked to my little girl, I could see Rebecca's smile in her face and I knew that what Alison was telling me was true.

I said "This little girl is the person I've been dreaming about all these years. Rebecca kept it to herself and chose to wrestle with it on her own, about how and when or whether or not she was ever going to tell me?"

As I sat holding the little one on my lap, I tried to gather my poise, which had been severely shaken.

"Miles, the reason I brought your daughter to you tonight is because the first thing that happens in the infinite world when parents meet their unborn children is that they give their child a name. She's been waiting all these years to be named. Don't ask me how I know, but Rebecca has been able to move on from this experience, probably because she was the one that had to deal with it. She doesn't have nightmares like you, but I guess you get the honor of naming your daughter."

I thought, will the secrets of the universe never stop amazing me? There were days that I believed I was really starting to understand how everything worked, but to be confronted with this moment now made me realize that there was still a lot to learn.

I pulled my new daughter closer so we could sit face-to-face. If I had to guess, she seemed to be about seven years old.

"Okay little girl, your dad is so, so, so, so, so, so happy to meet you, and to hold you and hug you and kiss you. And love you." And that's what I did. I held her and hugged her and kissed her for a few minutes. Then I said, "let's see, your mom's name is Rebecca Susan. You'll meet her soon enough. Because you are very pretty when you smile, just like your mom, I'm going to name you after your mom, Susan. Or how about for tonight, I'll call you Susie?"

I started to tickle her under her armpits until she squirmed and laughed and a couple of happy tears came out of her eyes from the joy of the moment.

"Susie, can you stay and sleep with Alison and me in our big bed until morning?"

Smiling all the while, she said "No daddy, I'm sorry, I can't. I have to go in a couple minutes, but I want you to know that I do watch you and mommy all the time. I love you both and I can't wait to be with you. I liked spending time with you tonight, and feeling you love me for the first time has been wonderful. Susie. I really love my name. Susie. Thank you, daddy, for that beautiful name and I can't wait to play with you again soon."

With that she hugged me as hard as she could. There were no tears on her face, just the smile of a kid who just blew out her birthday candles.

"Can you walk me to the door dad? I have to go now."

"Of course, sweetheart."

I got up and walked with her to the doorway, right past Alison, whose arms were folded and who was crying at what she was seeing.

Susie stopped right before reaching the now-dark hallway and I went down to one knee. We hugged and kissed one more time. As she walked over the threshold from our dimly lit bedroom into the darkness of the hallway, she disappeared into the night.

I turned to Alison and said "Thank you. I'm speechless. Thank you. Thank you."

Alison grabbed my hand and said "Let's go downstairs and make some chamomile tea. I know neither one of us can fall asleep right now."

"I doubt it," I said and we walked down the stairs towards the kitchen. With each stride I took, I could feel myself finally letting go of my nightmare, one step at a time.

6. Alison's Smile

The plan was for me to retire from teaching and coaching, take a couple months off to recharge my batteries, and then go work full-time at Sunrise City. That was the city that Michael's Protect the Innocent Project had built in Southern California for orphans all over the world.

Alison, at 59 years old, had been diagnosed with breast cancer. It was caught early and the prognosis was very good. I asked Dana if the group could meditate and pray over her and cure her, but Dana said that the sisters were not allowed to do that on earth. However, she did tell me that the rest of us could meditate and pray over her and that it would indeed be helpful to her and may even aid in curing Alison, so that's what we did. In any case, Alison made it through, although she did have to have a double mastectomy.

Once we passed that challenge, Alison and I moved to Sunrise City, where we both began volunteering full-time as teachers. We adopted beautiful three-year old twin boys from Nigeria, Thomas and Matthew, and we raised them in Sunrise City.

Our girls, Jennifer, Maggie, and Laura, were all doing great. Alison and her sisters had seen to their galactic education by taking them on trips and having them write in their journals, so we were all on the same page in the way we thought about the universe. They would come to visit as often as their careers allowed. Our oldest, Jennifer, had married a great kid named Austin. He wasn't aware of the family Galactic Masters Degrees yet. Jennifer did tell us "the first time we kissed, Austin saw the night sky and twinkling stars in my eyes, just the same way that dad saw them in mom's eyes." We were happy for them, but I knew Austin was just starting his roller coaster ride and I made sure to let him know that I was always there for him to talk—if he wanted. I'll never forget the quizzical look on his face when I offered that assistance. His time would come.

Everyone in our group worked very hard over the next five years. The sisters told us that there were others on Earth, in different countries, going through the same education we were going through. They weren't allowed to tell us their names, but knowing that there was more help on the way gave us a much higher degree of confidence that we could turn things around. I could sense that there was a bubble of hope growing in the world and that we might indeed be able to save humanity from the narcissistic societies that had grown out of First World wealth, and from the hopelessness in the Third World. I knew it would be generations and generations past my own physical death before the final verdict on our planet would be reached. However, I have real hope in my heart and that's what gets me up every day.

Five years after Alison was declared in remission from her breast cancer, she came home from an oncologist appointment, kissed and hugged me and looked into my eyes and said "It's back."

I knew what she meant.

"Let's sit down. Tell me about your appointment."

"Miles, you know I've been doing really well for these past five years, but the older you get, the more chance there is that this might come back. The good news is that once again we've caught it early. The bad news is that it has started to spread to my lymphatic system," Alison said.

I knew exactly what that meant and it wasn't good.

In my mind, I never expected to outlive my beautiful Alison. When this happened five years before, it didn't change my opinion. I knew that she would be fine and that our lives would go back to normal.

Now, for the first time, I was having my doubts.

Over the course of the next six months, Alison went through all the recommended medical treatments. It involved terrible days of sickness and suffering with chemotherapy and radiation. We meditated and prayed for her. Every time we did, she felt better the next day. However, it would only last for a day or two.

Alison reminded all of us that our human bodies were frail and would not last forever.

Dana came to stay with us and she was a great help in keeping me calm and hopeful. Nevertheless, it was the first thing I thought about every morning when I woke up and it was the last thing I thought about every night when my head hit the pillow.

I thought to myself, how can this be? I had been picked to learn the secrets of the physical and infinite universes. Why was this happening? Why can't the sisters just take care of this, as I suspected that they had the capacity for healing. They kept telling me they weren't allowed to interfere with their own lives on Earth. Some days I was angry. Some days I was frustrated. Some days I felt hopeless. On the worst days, I was afraid. I was afraid of living out a life going forward without my Alison. I didn't have a clue on how I could possibly handle that.

As the weeks rolled by, the doctors told Alison, Dana and me about her progress, or should I say, the lack thereof.

Alison was starting to lose weight and they put her in the hospital. Some nights, I would stay all night with her, either sleeping in bed with her or in the lounge chair next to her bed. Other nights, she convinced me to go home, because our young boys needed a father, and I really needed to give Dana a break from watching them.

With each day that passed, Alison's condition became a little worse. Jessica, Michael, Tommy and the kids came into town to give Alison their full support. She was genuinely happy to see everybody. It did perk her spirits up considerably.

About the fifth day in the hospital, Alison became exhausted and the doctor told the family to take a day or two off from the constant visitations, so she could sleep and build up her strength.

At that point, he told Dana, Jessica and I that the prognosis was less than 50-50 that she could beat this.

Immediately after hearing that news from the doctor, Dana and Jessica asked to talk to me privately in one of the family rooms down the hall. As we sat down at a table, Jessica closed the door behind us. I was hoping they had something magical and positive to tell me.

Dana said "Miles, listen, everybody involved with Alison, from you to family and friends and the doctors and technicians, are doing everything they can to help her beat this. There's some things you need to know."

Jessica said "Miles, what you don't know is that Alison, and the two of us, have a much greater ability to fight off physical ailments and diseases than do normal human beings."

I said "So you're telling me that, without this extra ability to fight physical ailments, we might otherwise have lost her before now?"

There was silence, but the sisters looked at each other and then back at me.

Dana said "Miles, Alison is hanging on just for you. She is in a lot of pain, but she doesn't tell anyone. She can tolerate a great amount of pain, much more than normal human beings, but she is hanging on just for you."

I looked down at the floor and shook my head. Then I pulled myself close to the table and put my elbows on it and covered my face in my hands. Out from under my hands I muttered "I'm not sure exactly what you ladies are trying to tell me."

I dropped my hands onto the table and I looked up at Dana and Jessica. They remained quiet and still, but they looked at me with loving eyes, making me feel like I wasn't alone.

I finally said "You're trying to tell me that Alison is not going to be able to beat this, right?"

"Yes" Dana said. Her reply was like a dagger in my heart.

My thinking and my breathing stopped for about 10 seconds. Then I had to face the moment.

"Okay" I said, trying to keep myself together. "So why do you keep saying that she's hanging on for me, if she can't be saved?"

"She's waiting for you to say the words," Jessica said.

"What words?" I replied, frustrated.

"Only you know what words, Miles. Close your eyes and clear your mind and you will know," Jessica said.

I took a deep breath and closed my eyes and leaned back in my chair. I emptied my mind of the hundred and one thoughts that were clouding it. Once my mind was clear, I immediately changed roles with Alison, and asked myself 'what would I want to hear?' I felt the words coming. They started in my stomach and then moved to my chest and then up to my throat, just before I spoke them to Dana and Jessica.

I said "Alison's waiting for me to tell her that it's okay for her to go. Right? Alison's waiting for me to tell her that I'll be okay, that we will all be okay, after she's gone, right?"

Dana and Jessica said nothing.

They got up from their chairs and came over to me, sat on either side of me and held me, rubbing my back.

I started to cry.

My thoughts slowed down. I cried harder, all the while keeping my hands over my face. Then I caught my breath and the tears stopped. I was crying out of pity for myself, because I was going to lose Alison. She was enduring terrific pain because of my inability to accept the inevitable end of her physical life, an end that we will all face one day. It was selfish and I knew it. It didn't matter that I truly believed I would see her again when I got to the infinite world.

I needed to let her know that I would be okay, that our family and friends would be okay, and that she could be released from her suffering in order to pass on to the infinite universe.

"One more thing, Miles," Dana said. "Once Alison passes from this world, she will not be allowed to come back to communicate with you. She might be in the same room with you, watching you, like the others that have passed away do from time to time. You'll see her again soon enough. It doesn't give us any pleasure to tell you that Miles, but you needed to hear it because Alison is just too weak to talk much more.

"Miles, she's barely hanging on for you right now," Jessica added.

Dana, always prepared for everything, pulled clean tissues out of her purse and handed them to me. I wiped my eyes and blew my nose to regather some of my dignity.

I hugged them both and thanked them for helping me through that moment. Together we walked down to Alison's room. Jessica said "We'll be down in the cafeteria waiting for you." With that I went into Alison's room.

Alison was in one of those dreamy morphine-induced waking states. She watched me as I came to the side of her bed and pulled up a chair so our faces could be close.

She whispered "How are you doing?" as she brushed the back of her fingers against my cheek. "You know, I really hate this morphine. It's hard to feel like the normal me when they give me too much."

I calmly whispered "I'm fine, but in looking at you, I think I see the stars in the night sky in your eyes. When I think about that night, boy, was I glad that I mustered up the courage to talk to you about my feelings."

I could sense for the first time, that the cancer was eating her alive, and that now she was more an infinite being then a physical being.

"Ooohhh Miles," Alison replied meekly, "I was sure that you were the one. If you would've chickened out, I would've grabbed you anyway. After all these years, do you think I would've let you get away that easily?"

Alison used all of her strength to move over in the bed and I crawled in with her. We were lying face-to-face and I held her close.

"Alison," I said quietly. "Let me talk for a few minutes, I know you're tired. Close your eyes and rest. Just clear your mind and listen to my voice and I'll take us for a ride.

"Think about the stars in your eyes that night in Iowa. Remember that whenever we heard Stevie Wonder singing, Ribbon in the Sky, it would remind us of that night? Think about that crazy car trip to California. Join me and think about that special night we spent on the beach on Catalina Island, keeping each other warm, as the ever-so-soft ocean breeze and small ocean waves serenaded us to sleep. I remember how beautiful you were at our wedding and the fun we had on our honeymoon in San Francisco. Remember the birth of our children and raising them to become wonderful people. That was probably 90 percent you and 10 percent me, because I was always at basketball practice or a game. Remember that elevator ride? I think about it every day. It was the day that we really became one. Think about our anniversary dance at Marco's wedding. All I could think about that night, dancing with you in front of all those people, was how lucky I had been to be able to share my life with you."

Alison kept her eyes closed, but she began to smile like the healthy Alison I knew. I realized right there and then, that of all the beautiful things about my bride, her smile was surely my favorite.

But the time had come. I was saying all the right words, but I was having a hard time getting to the last few.

I whispered "Baby, I love you. I need to tell you, it's okay for you to go. We will all miss you. And I will miss you most of all, but we will all be okay."

Alison opened her eyes wide and continued to smile right at me.

"I love you too Miles," Alison said in a weak whisper, "You **are** going to be okay. Our boys need you to bring them up the right way, Coach."

She paused to gather some strength. I just lay next to her and held her, waiting for her to continue.

"Miles, my life with you has exceeded every expectation that I could've ever imagined in living a second lifetime. In my wildest dreams I never expected someone like you."

I kissed her gently on the lips.

"Please stay with me for a while, Miles, while I catch up on some sleep."

"Absolutely," I said.

She snuggled up to me as close as she could. Her eyes closed, but that soft smile that was only Alison's remained.

A half an hour later, I could see that her vital signs were dropping and the nurse came in, followed by the doctor. I faced them, held up the palm of my hand and mouthed the words, "It's okay."

They understood—that I understood what was happening. They stayed there with me, quietly.

A few minutes later, Alison's vital signs melted into nothingness, but the smile on her face remained.

I slowly made my way out of the room, found my family and let them know Alison was gone.

When I got home that night, I went right over to the book shelf in the living room that held a very old picture of Alison and me on our wedding day and I grabbed it. I took it upstairs and put it on my nightstand and got ready for bed. Just as I had pledged to think of Alison every time I looked at the full moon years ago, I made a pledge to myself that night that the last thing I would look at every night before I went to sleep would be her smile in that picture.

The next morning, my radio alarm clock came on with music, as usual. I'm sure it was Alison sending me a message. The song was Ribbon in the Sky. I just lay in bed. I fought back the tears for a few moments, and then smiled, knowing that Alison was here with me. If there had been any doubt that I could go on without her, that doubt was now gone, because I knew she would be at my side whenever I needed her.

7. Going On

Alison's funeral was enormous—attended by family, friends, coworkers, former students, former players and the like. The flowers that we received turned the church into a greenhouse. It was a lovely ceremony, with Dana giving the eulogy for her sister. She knew just how to take us to the edge of tears and then bring us back with a humorous moment from our lives with Alison. When it was all said, everyone there realized that Alison had lived a wonderful, selfless life full of joy and love, both giving and receiving love.

Our three daughters stayed for about a week. Jessica had to leave, but Dana had extra time to spend with us, even after everyone else was gone. She wanted to make sure I had myself organized, especially with our two young boys.

The week after the funeral, I sent Thomas and Matthew back to school, telling them that their mom and I expected them to do the best they could every day. I told them that on some days, their best might not be as good as on other days, but that's how life was always going to be. Dana and I made sure we spent a lot of time with them, with a lot of positive reinforcement about the short time that they had with Alison as their mother. One night, Matthew turned to Dana and said "So, Aunt Dana, are you going to be our mom now?"

Dana looked up at me and we both smiled. She turned to the boys and said "Yeah, Aunt Dana has now become your mom. Anytime you need me, you call me and I'll come running."

It was a godsend to have Dana there. It took about three weeks to slide into a routine. I felt that Dana would probably leave in the next week, because I wasn't feeling overwhelmed anymore. That was okay with me, I was ready to be a single dad.

It was our custom every night after homework to sit on the couch with the boys between us, find what baseball or basketball game was on television, and watch it together. I could teach them about the nuances of the games at an early age. I was surprised that Dana knew so much about basketball and baseball, but then again, being surprised about anything that involved the sisters was just my own stupidity talking. After we put the boys to bed, Dana would snuggle up to me on the couch and we either watched the end of the game or found some old movie to watch until we would get sleepy.

It was the moment I looked forward to each day, because it helped fill the crushing sadness in my heart now that I could no longer hold Alison.

One night after the boys were in bed and Dana was snuggled up to me with my arm around her, I asked her if she would mind if we talked a little bit.

"Of course not Miles," Dana said.

"Dana, my mom taught me a long time ago that even after she and my dad were gone, even after we lost other relatives and friends, I should continue to talk to them as if they were just in the other room, and to never think of them as gone. I've done that over the years. Now, I do it every day with Alison and it helps me a lot. I know that she won't be answering back and that's okay. It's made me think about my journal and my entries again, and I now know that I may have a few more insights to write. I want to ask you a couple questions."

"You know I'll answer whatever I can Miles. Go ahead."

I said "You ladies have always been very, what should I say, mysteriously politically correct, not answering specific questions about different religions and what to believe and what not to believe, as far as the theology of Buddhism, Catholicism, Hinduism, Islam, Judaism, and Christianity in general. That's okay and I understand. You want me and everyone else to find their own path, but here's my question: You always refer to the Creator, and I sense there's a reason that you choose that word. I have an idea of why, but I want to talk to you about it. Can you talk about it?"

Dana looked up at me with her smart aleck grin and a twinkle in her eye and said "We'll see."

"Okay, here's my question: Is the Creator God?"

"Why does it matter what word you or I use?" Dana replied.

I shot back, "Don't answer a question with a question, Dana. Just tell me if you can tell me the answer or not."

"I know that frustrates you, Miles," she said, "and I sense that you are really close to understanding everything, because losing Alison was the greatest suffering you've ever had to endure. Some people never get it, because they never suffered over anything. I know we all suffered when our parents died, but most of them lived long, full lives, so it's not the same thing as you losing Alison. Let me ask you this, Miles, why do **you** think I use the word Creator?"

I had to stop and think for a few moments.

"Well, I guess it's because you want it to be a direct correlation to Creation. Is that right?"

Dana smiled and I could see a lot of Alison in her smile. I knew Alison was in the room watching us, and I knew that Dana knew it for sure, but couldn't say.

"Yes. That's why we always use the word Creator. The Creator **made** all of creation. The Creator **is** all of creation. We, and everything around us, to the farthest ends of the universe, are part of creation and therefore, we are part of the Creator. That's also why we never use masculine or feminine pronouns. The Creator is not a being, in the sense that you and I are beings. "

I started to assemble the pieces of what Dana was saying. I tried to reconcile it with my own Catholic faith, as a "red-letter Bible" Catholic. I started to understand that there was a reason why Christ had to walk the Earth. He had to teach us and show us how to live a moral and ethical life. Most importantly, He had to teach us how to love and forgive. Then I understood that when He left, the Holy Spirit is said to be everywhere, which was somewhat consistent with what Dana was telling me.

I shared all those thoughts with Dana.

After I did, Dana said "Miles, you have seen for yourself that beyond our own planet, people have developed different types of faith, some of them very simple and some carried out with traditional pomp and circumstance, but when you drill down to the bottom, legitimate faiths preach the same thing, don't they?"

I didn't expect another question from her so soon. I had thought about this a lot. Billy and I had talked on the phone about it a lot, but now I had Dana right in front of me, seemingly willing to open Pandora's box in response to my questions.

The gears inside my brain were spinning at 100 miles an hour as I pondered her question. I was no expert on the theologies of the world, or of the universe, but I had certainly seen and heard a great deal more than most human beings. After we left Planet 66, we all asked whether Bellara was indeed the Daughter of God, in the same way that Jesus had claimed to be the Son of God, in order to teach their civilization the right way to live. We were told that that question was for the people of that planet to answer, and not for us. We had to make our own decisions on Jesus and the other spiritual leaders and prophets of the different faiths on earth.

"Alison, help me with this!"

Dana giggled at me, and then I laughed. I knew she saw it as a sign that I was coming to terms with the rest of my life in a positive way.

Dana looked at me right after we laughed and said "Miles, what is the meaning of life?"

I closed my eyes and emptied my mind.

It came out of my mouth without a thought, as if it were a product of all my life experiences.

"Every human being that will ever exist, and whatever planet they call home, is impermanent, imperfect, but interconnected by Creation itself. One day, all physical existence everywhere will end. However, while we are all here, we are to love, to forgive, and take care of each other and this miracle of a planet, the best that we can. Every single day."

Dana put her warm hands on both sides of my face, pulled me close, and kissed me on the forehead.

Dana said "Believe me, I've heard it expressed many ways, but your answer may be as simply and succinctly stated as I've ever heard. When enlightenment comes, as it has for you Miles, you must remember that everyone's understanding of the meaning of life is their own. But at its core, everyone's meaning of life is the same. Congratulations Miles, you've just graduated from the School of the Galactic Universe with a PhD."

I sat there and experienced a tremendous feeling of relief.

In coming up with that one statement, it seemed to validate all of the time I spent with Alison and her sisters. It was like winning a basketball game, but this was the biggest game of my life. I had just been asked the biggest question in the world and gotten the answer right.

Dana snuggled back up to me and grabbed the television control.

She said "That's enough heavy lifting for tonight, Miles. The Marx Brothers are on in Duck Soup tonight, and we're going to watch the whole movie. I don't care how late it goes."

So, as Groucho, Chico, and Harpo did their thing on the small screen, I started to laugh inside at the absurdity of the dovetail between stating my perception of the purpose of life and watching these knuckleheads. The Marx Brothers were brilliant comedians, and they never failed to make me laugh. Someone once said, when we're laughing, we are as close to God as we can get. The joy they had brought to me over the years, when I was watching their old movies with Alison, was inestimable.

I took a deep breath and let it out slowly. I put my arm around Dana and she rubbed my chest and said, "Attaboy Miles, let it out and relax. Let Groucho do all the worrying for the next two hours."

And that's exactly what I did.

8. Away Down the River

Six months after Alison left us, my youngest daughter, Laura, who had completed her degree in sociology, moved back in with us in our house in Sunrise City. Her fiancé followed her and got a small apartment. Based on the way that Todd looked at Laura, she had him under her spell. Believe me, I'd seen that look before, especially in the mirror. I was very happy for both of them and they were a great help to me in raising the boys.

Michael had visited a couple weeks earlier and told me that he had pulled off the Numbers on Paper banking scenario, by establishing a Federal Reserve Bank in South Sudan. He had amped up donations to the country through a huge Internet and telemarketing effort. However, with every donation, he added three or four zeros, and the country was quickly becoming one of the wealthiest per capita in the world. I told him that there may be handcuffs in his future, but he just laughed it off, telling me "I know people in high places." He wasn't worried about it.

On Palm Sunday, Laura, the twins and I were driving back from church. The passion of the Christ is re-created during the gospel on Palm Sunday and the congregation reads the part of the hostile crowd that wanted Jesus crucified.

Laura said "Dad, I remember years ago when I was about 14 and all of us were driving home from church and you said you were tired of being a part of the crowd that wanted Christ crucified. You even said that you refused to say the line 'Crucify him!' Do you remember that?"

"Yeah, I do remember that," I said. "I still refuse to be part of the crowd. I feel like at my age and my understanding, my faith has evolved beyond what they're asking me to do. Why are you all of a sudden remembering that day?"

"Because one of my last elective classes for my degree, was on Jack Kerouac, who I knew was one of your favorite writers. Anyway, in his autobiographical work named Lonesome Traveler, it turns out he had the exact same issue that you do. He was roaming around the small churches in Mexico City and in a stained-glass window saw a picture of Christ carrying the cross as the crowd was yelling 'crucify him.' Then he told his readers, 'I was not there, had I been there, I would've yelled 'stop it,' and got crucified too'."

"Apparently, it's true, that all great minds think alike," I said.

Laura giggled just like her mom and said "Dad, it's great to have you back to your normal self again. I know we both miss mom a lot, but she's laughing right along with me right now."

I was driving, so I could only glance at her for a moment, when I said, "I hope so kiddo."

Laura continued, "Also, in one of my last psychology classes, our professor talked about the collective unconscious. Are you aware of what that is?"

"I know a little something about it," I replied.

She said "Anyway, one of my classmates told the professor that they had read that there is a belief that during the time of Christ, because everyone was looking for a savior to be born, the collective unconscious is what brought him into the world. What you think about that?"

"What do I think about that?" I said. "I think it's just as likely that Dr. Frankenstein built him from spare parts."

"Okay, okay, so, you're on a roll this morning. I'll go with it," Laura said begrudgingly.

I wasn't in the mood for serious discussion about anything. I wanted to have a beautiful sunlit family Sunday with my daughter, two sons, and whomever else was destined to join us. We got home and I cooked out on the grill. We had a delicious lunch of hamburgers, hot dogs, bratwursts, relish, potato chips, lemonade, and a Corona Light for me, of course.

The fact of the matter was that I was getting a little older, so I asked Laura to spend time with the boys in the backyard while I cleaned up from lunch. When I was done, they were still having a ball. I sat down for just a few minutes to give my back a break and the next thing I knew, I had fallen asleep for the elusive catnap that we all seek, but rarely find.

When I woke up, Laura was sitting across from me on the sofa, holding my journal in her hands and reading it. We had been encouraged to share our journals with our kids as they were making their own visits and writing their own journals. Laura was almost done with her trips around the universe, so we were able to have some nice discussions.

I was in a better mood after my nap, and I was ready to accommodate Laura in any of her questions, no matter how serious.

"Don't try to plagiarize me now. I fall asleep for a few minutes and you're stealing all the great lines out of my journal," I said.

"Yeah Pops, like I'm not a better writer than you. The only thing I need to steal to be better than you is a pencil," she said as we shared a good laugh.

Geez, she's a chip off the old block, I thought as I smiled.

"You know Dad, Todd and I are talking about the possibility of getting married in the next year or so. The subject of finances came up and we are trying to figure out how much money we need to make. Dad, can you give me some advice on how mom and you handled that? More importantly, what were the things that worked for you and what were the things that didn't? I mean, are there one or two things that are more important than others?"

I looked at her and I was very happy that she shared with me that she and Todd were getting close enough to talk about setting a wedding date.

I replied "Yes. Make yourself rich by making your wants few. That's the best financial advice I ever got and it works. Remember those hot dogs and hamburgers at lunchtime? Good stuff, wasn't it?"

"Yeah, but dad, it's probably not the healthiest meal we've eaten."

"Oh, so you think you're going to live forever?" I got her on that one. She didn't know I stole it from her Aunt Dana. However, she knew that by simply not worrying so much and by focusing on the important parts of life, it was more likely that she would live a longer, fulfilling life than she would counting calories day and night.

While we were talking Laura had been skimming through my journal.

Laura said "Dad, it appears that you've gone a bit off topic here in this journal. Let me refresh your memory about this entry between planet 76 and planet 77."

Laura read from my journal.

"Was thinking about things that I would do once I retired. Definitely organize all my music and listen to it all day long. Gotta make sure I have the great works from the following artists: not in any order. They are all great to me.

The Beatles
Al Jarreau
Chicago
Alison Krauss
Carpenters
Peter Frampton
Prince
Basia
Yes
Neil Young
Stevie Wonder
Jethro Tull
Steely Dan
James Taylor
Frank Sinatra
Stan Getz
Fleetwood Mac
Larry Carlton
Eric Darius
The Doobie Brothers
U2
Gloria Estefan
Diana Krall
Jim Croce
Traffic
Antonio Carlos Jobim
Shakira
Crosby Stills Nash and Young
Wolfgang Amadeus Mozart
Earth Wind and Fire
Luther Vandross

Peter White
Stevie Ray Vaughn
Jimi Hendrix
Seal
Anita Baker
Bonnie Raitt
Led Zeppelin
Allman Brothers
Pearl Jam

She was reading it to me like machine-gun fire. "Okay, Laura, enough already. You know I have most of those recordings, don't you?"

"Yes, but they're not in any kind of order, so you better get going on that project, or have you already started it?"

"No, I haven't done it, but you know what, that's something that you and I and the boys can work on maybe an hour or two every Sunday and it'll eventually get done. It'll help their alphabetization skills and make them learn about great music."

I turned the television on and began watching my beloved Chicago Cubs with the sound all the way down, so as not to interrupt our discussion. I kept watching and checking out the score, and Laura kept skimming my journal.

"Now here's another interesting journal entry. I'm not sure that it's off-topic, but it's amusing. Here's what you wrote:

1. There is no Superman.
2. There is no Batman.
3. There is no Spiderman.
4. There are no other caped or un-caped superheroes. Please attend Comic-Con for the full list.

5. You can't fly at warp speed.

6. There's no such thing as a transporter to beam you down from a spaceship to a planet.

7. There are no wars going on in outer space, here, nor in any galaxy far, far away.

8. There are no vampires.

9. There are no werewolves.

10. There are no zombies, although some of my students in English Lit over the years looked like zombies as I lectured.

11. You can clone human beings, but don't. They have no soul and no ethical or moral center and they will destroy your civilization, just like what happened on Planet 32."

I interrupted her abruptly, saying "Laura, I know what I wrote, just skip down to the last entry."

She replied "Okay, okay." And then she read: "34. But it is terrific fun to write books, make TV shows, and make movies about all of the above because it pushes the creative juices. Just don't get obsessed with it and end up living in your parent's basement until you're 34."

Again, Laura giggled just like Alison.

I couldn't keep quiet about it. "Laura, I see so much of your mom in you and thank you for spending this time with me. It brings me closer to you and keeps me close to her, if even just for a few moments."

"Oh hey, I wanted to share with you that I have finally settled in on my philosophy of life statement that we all have to do as part of our universal education."

"Let's hear it."

"I love everybody, and I understand..."

I interrupted, saying "did you forget the only rule? You can't copy your mom's or anyone else philosophy of life.

Each generation is supposed to help our civilization evolve to the next step. Did you forget?"

"No dad, if you would just let me finish, you'll hear that it is different than moms."

"Sorry. My bad. Go ahead."

"As I was saying, **I love everyone, and I understand that everyone doesn't love me, and that means I don't love them enough.**"

I sat there in my lounge chair completely stunned. It was the most selfless thing I had ever heard, and it came from my daughter. I couldn't have been prouder of her.

All I could muster was "Wow."

Laura knew by the look on my face that I was impressed. No words had to be exchanged.

She said "Dad, come over and sit next to me on the couch, so I can snuggle with you."

Believe me, it was my pleasure to sit and hold my youngest daughter as we watched the game. It was the ninth inning and the Cubs rallied to score three runs and win.

"Laura, you know the Cubs weren't always good like they are now."

"Yes dad, you told us that like a million times and about all of the heartbreak you had watching them in 1969 as a kid."

This question popped into my mind: "Laura, when you and your sisters were kids, did you think I was silly for having such strong emotions about a baseball team?"

Laura said "not really, we were too young to think about it. When we got older, we all grew to love them almost as much as you did. I know mom loved them because it was one of the genuine passions in your life. We all came to the same conclusion, that being a Cub fan was being part of something greater than yourself, and it was always something optimistic and wonderful. To be honest, now that they have won the World Series, I really miss saying, **Wait Until Next Year**."

Laura got serious and said, "I know mom hasn't been gone very long dad, and I'm sure you think of her every day, but I wanted to ask how you think about her. You seem to be okay now. Right?"

"I think you're right, kiddo. I finally succeeded in letting all my sadness go and now I'm able to focus on the wonderful life we had together. At first, when I would hear Alison Krause's song Away Down the River, I would cry. You know that song, right?"

I could see Laura choking up a little. She shook her head yes, because she knew how sad that song could be for someone who just lost their spouse.

She finally gathered herself together and said, "I hope it doesn't make you cry anymore."

That was my Laura, I said to myself. Always thinking more about everyone else than her own needs.

I thought about Alison all the time, but the more I got myself back to being busy, the less I found myself thinking about her being physically gone and wallowing in self-pity. I knew Alison didn't want me to be that way.

Even in my busy life, in the solitary moments, I had time to think of Alison. In the early morning light and in the darkness before sleep overcame me, I would think of Alison and talk to her out loud, as if she were lying in bed right next to me. And every once in a while, I would have a beautiful dream, where Alison and I were staring in each other's eyes in that park at Iowa State.

Acknowledgments

As I said to many people recently, I don't feel like I chose to write this book as much as this book chose me. In that case, it seems logical to give my acknowledgments in the chronological order in which this book was written.

The genesis of this book came from the attempted intellectual discussions with my friend Mat. We covered a number of subjects, and he referred to each as "gold nuggets." He kept a journal of these nuggets which, to this day, brings us a great deal of laughter and joy. Regarding this particular genesis nugget, I was told by Mat that I had lost my mind. At that point, I knew I was on to something.

After my retirement, it was my goal to write a book. As a former basketball coach, I knew that I had to start with layups and work my way up to three-point shots. So, I began writing short stories to ease my way back into the writing craft that I had learned from completing my Bachelor of Arts in English. I was encouraged by my wife, Sandy, and my daughter and editor, Anna, to submit a story in a writing contest at the University of Arizona. My story was published. I told them that now they could put on my gravestone that I was a published writer.

I continued to write short stories, hoping that one day I would find the opening I needed to begin my book. And that's what happened. After a year of writing, I was able to use a small part of my last fictional short story as the opening of this fictional novel.

The one thing I learned about myself as a writer of those short stories was that I could not write unless I had a title. Subsequently, once I started this book, I could not write the next chapter until I came up with a name for it.

But with my first novel, I had to find a genre. Nothing seemed to fit. Apocalyptic, post-apocalyptic, dystopian, pre-apocalyptic... I was getting nowhere. Finally forced to summarize my book in one sentence, I told someone, "It's the Baby Boomer Generation meets *Gulliver's Travels.*" Researching *Gulliver's Travels,* since I hadn't read it in many years, I found the descriptions: allegorical fantasy and satirical fantasy. Neither of them fit. So, I invented a new genre... Counter-Apocalyptic. It's a mixture of the counterculture and the aforementioned genres. It's what happens when you mix science fiction, fantasy, satire, allegory and romance.

Nobody's Coming was written in eight months in 2016. During that time, I became a member of a writer's workshop in Oro Valley, Arizona. Feedback from our meetings was immensely important and educational to me. Moreover, I was invited to form a smaller group where we all edited each other's work. So special thanks to my friends, David, Jerry and Mark for helping me get through three edits of my novel.

I also had many conversations with my friends Matt, Pat, Keith, Jacob and my son in law, Mike, who helped keep me on the path.

When I finished, I still wasn't satisfied. So, I reached out and found a new friend, Phil. He is a professional writer and editor and taught me more about writing over the next three months than I had learned in the last 30 years.

When the book was finished, my final concern hit me right in the face. I speculated at my ability to accurately capture the dialogue of the many female characters in my book. I had no choice but to test drive my novel by reading it to my Writers Workshop and wait for or ask for opinions on that issue. I was happy when many of my female workshop members came up to me and gave me the thumbs up I needed to know that my female characters were genuine.

However, once I had independent corroboration, I realized that my female characters were based on my wife, Sandy, my daughters, Anna, Heidi, and Melissa, my sister, Elizabeth, and my mom, Gisela. All of them are smart, strong, independent, humorous, sarcastic, but most of all... unconditionally loving. For that, I love them and I am immensely grateful for their ongoing encouragement in the writing of this book, but most of all, I am grateful to have them in my life.

Finally, why did I write this book? The greatest lesson my father ever taught me was to speak up for what is right. Here goes...I wrote this book to help save the world. I considered it the most noble of tasks. I hope you agree with that. As with all art, it is up to the reader to decide whether I have accomplished any of that goal. But if I have moved you even in the smallest way to look at our world with hope, then I will have done my job.

Cover photo courtesy of the author himself, accidentally fooling around on his cell phone. "I like myself better as a cartoon character anyway."